KT-561-577

A NEW BEGINNING

Recent Titles by Grace Thompson from Severn House

The Badgers Brook Series

THE HOUSE BY THE BROOK
A GIRL CALLED HOPE
A NEW BEGINNING

The Pendragon Island Series

CORNER OF A SMALL TOWN
THE WESTON WOMAN
UNLOCKING THE PAST
MAISIE'S WAY
A SHOP IN THE HIGH STREET
SOPHIE STREET

The Holidays at Home Series

WAIT TILL SUMMER
SWINGBOATS ON THE SAND
WAITING FOR YESTERDAY
DAY TRIPPERS
UNWISE PROMISES
STREET PARTIES

DAISY'S ARK
MISSING THE MOMENT
THE SANDWICH GIRL
AN ARMY OF SMILES

A NEW BEGINNING

Grace Thompson

This first world edition published in Great Britain 2005 by
SEVERN HOUSE PUBLISHERS LTD of
9–15 High Street, Sutton, Surrey SM1 1DF.
This first world edition published in the USA 2005 by
SEVERN HOUSE PUBLISHERS INC of
595 Madison Avenue, New York, N.Y. 10022.

Copyright © 2005 by Grace Thompson.

All rights reserved.
The moral right of the author has been asserted.

British Library Cataloguing in Publication Data

Thompson, Grace
    A new beginning
    1.   Badgers Brook (England : Imaginary place) - Fiction
    I.   Title
    823.9'14 [F]

    ISBN 0-7278-6228-6

Except where actual historical events and characters are being
described for the storyline of this novel, all situations in this
publication are fictitious and any resemblance to living persons
is purely coincidental.

Typeset by Palimpsest Book Production Ltd.,
Polmont, Stirlingshire, Scotland.
Printed and bound in Great Britain by
MPG Books Ltd., Bodmin, Cornwall.

One

Sophie Daniels shrugged on her WAAF overcoat and reached down for her small case. 'It doesn't seem much to be taking home for the weekend of your wedding,' she said to her friend. Daphne reached for her own bag, which was even smaller.

'I just hope your mother has the dresses ready, or we're going to be in church, smiling at the vicar in our airforce blue.'

'I did think of marrying in uniform, but Geoffrey didn't like the idea. After all, the war is almost over, isn't it?'

'Never over until the last battle is won and we're still fighting, and dying, remember.'

'But we've got the Germans on the run, haven't we, the Siegfried Line is broken and the town of Nancy is freed. And the rumours about a new rocket attack on London might be just that, a rumour.'

'They're calling it a V2, and although the government have tried to hush it up they can no longer pretend it's gas mains exploding.'

'Come on, Daphne, why would they lie?'

'So the enemy won't know where the weapons are going to land and change their direction, of course.'

'I know, of course I know, it's just that my whole family live in the east end of London so I prefer to pretend it isn't happening.' Sophie stared at her friend. 'They've survived this far and I can't bear to think of losing one of them now.'

They had a lift to the station in one of the lorries taking some airmen on leave, and they managed to get seats next to each other on the train to London. Daphne wore her dark hair tucked tightly underneath her cap and was looking forward to allowing it to fall freely when dressing for her friend's wedding. With her large features and being above average in height and strongly built, and with her uniform adding to her imposing stature, she was aware of appearing 'mannish' and longed for the opportunity to remind people that she was truly feminine, despite her impressive measurements.

Thank goodness the strong-willed Sophie wasn't going to have her way about marrying in uniform. There were few chances to dress up in these austere days; even dances were scarce and usually last-minute affairs, forcing them to go in uniform or not at all. Wearing a dress, letting hair escape from the dreaded hat: a wedding was too good an opportunity to waste!

Sophie was much smaller than Daphne and, being extremely fair, seemed fragile beside her friend. They had met on their first posting, at an airfield in Lincolnshire, and had been friends ever since. Their various moves had separated them, but the most recent, to an airfield in the south-east corner of England, had reunited them. Now Daphne was to be Sophie's bridesmaid at a small wedding in the east of London.

Her lilting Welsh seemed incongruous given their destination. Sophie's father had been sent to a factory in London to be the 'chaser', making sure the workers on the benches were kept supplied with the materials they needed. With no sign of the war ending in the near future, the family, including his wife's parents, had moved with him, and had been welcomed into the East London community with warmth and friendship.

When they reached London, they stopped for a cup of tea and a 'wad' – a cake – at the Naafi canteen on the station, then struggled through the crowds to the underground. Reaching daylight from the underground station, Daphne was shocked at the scene that met them. Living in a small town in mid-Wales she was not prepared for the result of the bombing, even though the newsreels at the cinema had shown it many times. Whole streets had vanished, rubble piled up where houses had once contained families.

'I'd no idea it was this bad,' she gasped. 'You see pictures in papers and magazines, but some how it doesn't seem real.'

'Mam and Dad refuse to leave and they wouldn't let my

young brother and sister go into the country as evacuees. We were among the lucky ones – our house hasn't even been damaged.'

Daphne stared around her at the destroyed streets and the people busily picking their way through what was left. The population seemed to be going about their tasks calmly, waving to friends, stopping for a brief chat, carrying on as though life hadn't changed. A partially boarded-up newsagents was open for business according to the sign outside the tunnel-like entrance. She heard someone shout, 'They got some fags in,' and all within hearing ran to get a share, pushing their way in good humouredly, taking out their purses and counting what they had left.

'Aren't you afraid for them?' Daphne whispered.

'Of course, but Hitler isn't going to kill everyone, is he? There'll still be Londoners and houses for them to live in.' She spoke cheerfully, confident that her family would be safe. 'After all, they've survived so far and the flying bombs no longer fly across. Our airforce and gunners put a stop to that threat, and it's only a matter of time now before this new menace is dealt with.' She laughed, encouraging Daphne to laugh with her.

Daphne walked along beside her, a feeling of dread in her heart. Surely it was tempting fate to be so confident?

'Is it much further?' she asked. 'I'm desperate for another cup of tea.' She slowed down, still filled with dread, looking around at the ruined houses, the broken walls piled up, the dangers removed with any remnants of what had once been loved homes. The roads and pavements had been cleared, the rubble pushed back to allow the continuation of everyday life. She was afraid of their arriving to find Sophie's home gone, like so many others. How could anything survive in this?

'Come on, Daph, stop staring at the disasters and come and meet my family,' Sophie said more soberly. 'They'll make us forget the hell of it all, for a few days at least.'

The house in which the Daniels family lived was in a small road miraculously untouched by the bombing. On the corner was a lock-up grocery shop owned by her grandparents, which they had taken over soon after leaving South Wales. They

3

lived on the other side of a small park close by, where trees were wearing their autumn colours and shrubs still displayed a few flowers.

The front door of Sophie's home was open and voices rose and fell from within, punctuated with bursts of laughter. Sophie strode inside with Daphne following, pushing through the chattering neighbours, the women mostly dressed in aprons and wearing ancient slippers, the men in trousers and waistcoats over shirts with sleeves rolled up.

'Whatcha, Soph.'

'She's back'.

'She's here!'

'Here comes the bride.'

'Thank Gawd fer that.' All around them welcoming voices called, until a laughing Sophie reached the kitchen, where her mother and her Auntie Maggie stood near the cooker, pouring teas.

'What's this, a celebration?' she joked.

'Yeh, ain't you heard? 'Itler's dead. Or darn well soon will be.' Surrounded by joking and teasing, being welcomed by the family, friends and neighbours, the shouts were interspersed by a confusion of introductions, including Sophie's younger brother and sister, Carrie and Frank, and the rest of her family.

Daphne sank into a chair. Sophie was in high spirits, returning slick responses to the chorus of saucy innuendo, and Daphne sat nursing her tea, taking in the excitement and everyone's determination to make Sophie's wedding a good time for all.

'When's your bloke arriving?' someone asked.

'Soon.'

'Where's 'e stayin'?'

'I phoned from the station. He's staying with a friend near the place where we're to go on honeymoon. He won't tell me exactly where.'

'Well, it won't be Paris, that's for sure,' Auntie Maggie said, adding lugubriously, 'I've always wanted to go to Paris.'

'He's travelling up tomorrow but we won't meet until we get to the church,' Sophie replied. 'Unlucky to meet before the wedding or something, isn't it?'

'Luck? You've got plenty of that, me duck. A happy life, that's what's ahead of you and that feller of yours,' one of the neighbours called out.

'How many of Geoffrey's family are coming?' her grandmother asked, and Daphne glanced at her friend with some anxiety.

'Oh, none. They're all tied up with war work, you know how it is. Lincolnshire they're from. I'll be meeting them on our next leave.'

'You mean you haven't met them? None of them?'

Daphne jumped up and put an arm across Sophie's shoulders. 'She's marrying Geoffrey, not his family!' She tried to make it into a joke but only a few were amused.

Sophie agreed with her. 'This is wartime, even though we've got Hitler on the run. Nothing is straightforward, is it? Travel difficulties for a start, and you can't just take a holiday from work when you want one.'

'But you ought to see where he's from, dear,' Auntie Maggie said with a frown. 'I though you went there a few weeks ago?'

'No, it was cancelled at the last minute. As I said, everyone is so busy.'

Sophie and Daphne shared a bed in what had been Sophie's room, and when the light went out, Daphne asked, 'You are sure, aren't you? I mean, I know everything's arranged but it isn't too late to, um, delay it for a while.'

'I know what I'm doing, Daph. I didn't force Geoffrey into proposing or arranging for such a quick wedding.'

'But not meeting his family, don't you think it's rather odd? After all, you planned to visit on three weekends, and each time it was cancelled without much of an explanation.'

'Tell the truth, I think he might be a bit embarrassed by them. He's met my family and, although he hasn't exactly said it, I think he comes from a different kind of background and, well, he might be afraid I'd change my mind if I saw where they live. Don't worry, Daph, we love each other and we'll be blissfully happy, I just know we will.'

'As long as you're sure.' Daphne had her doubts. Sophie was enthusiastic about everything she did, pushing her way

5

through objections and doubts, absolutely confident she was right, and she wondered if her enthusiasm really was matched by Geoffrey Roberts. It was odd that she hadn't met his family. Surely he'd have been proud, and would want to show his family his lovely bride-to-be?

'I'm certain, certain, sure,' Sophie breathed, as she relaxed into sleep.

The next day there were errands to do, making sure everything was in place for the ceremony on the following day, but Sophie's mother had organized everything so well, they felt superfluous.

'Let's go for a bike ride,' Sophie suggested, and on the bicycles belonging to her sister and brother, which were really too small, they set off to ride through the streets to call on one or two of Sophie's friends.

Singing at the tops of their voices, they rode past many undamaged houses and Sophie waved an arm imperiously. 'See? Lots of places untouched.' She remained silent as they went through roofless buildings where survivors had defiantly hung union flags on what was left of their homes.

Sophie only sees and hears what she wants to see and hear, Daphne thought. But perhaps that's her way of coping, knowing her family is in great danger, she comforts herself with her over-confidence. She was always so sure about everything, coming up with answers to everyone's problem within seconds and never deviating from what she saw as a simple answer. Heaven help her if she ever made a serious error! Daphne's thoughts had slowed her feet and Sophie was way in front of her.

'Come on, slowcoach,' Sophie called. 'Get cracking, you've got the best bike.' Daphne raced after her, her strong muscles pushing down on the pedals, swiftly leaving her friend behind. Around the next corner she stopped and waited. 'Did someone say something about a slowcoach?' she asked, laughing at her friend's efforts to catch up.

That evening, with the house filled to overflowing with neighbours and friends helping to prepare the food for the following day's celebration, Daphne saw that her friend seemed a little subdued. Sophie was always in the centre of things, her bubbling personality a magnet for anyone wanting fun. Seeing her standing in the hallway alone, staring out into the dark of the September night, she offered, 'A penny for your thoughts.'

'Oh, nothing really, just dreaming of tomorrow when I'll be a married woman.'

'And . . .?' Daphne coaxed.

'And nothing, although I did expect a letter yesterday or today. He promised to write to me and, well, I suppose something came up and he couldn't get out to post it. He'll explain, in –' she glanced at her watch – 'in just over twelve hours.'

'Is there somewhere you can phone? I mean, you must want to talk to him, you haven't seen him for a week.'

'I could ring his friend where he'll be staying, the one who will be his best man, but I won't.'

'Go on, you know you're dying to hear his voice.'

They left the house and, in the telephone box on the corner, both squashed in like excited children, Sophie asked for the number, then waited while the operator connected her. Her greeting was bright but her expression, barely seen in the gloom of the late hour, suddenly changed to a frown. 'But I don't understand. You must know where he is. The wedding is tomorrow and he's supposed to be there with you.' There was a gasp, a wide-eyed stare, and the phone was replaced. She pushed out of the box and waited for Daphne to join her outside.

'I must have got it wrong, he isn't aware of any wedding. I – I misunderstood. Got the name wrong. Geoffrey's best man must be another of his friends. There are so many, with people constantly moving about, coming and going. I must have misunderstood.'

'Of course,' Daphne soothed. 'At least you'll know who he's chosen tomorrow. Just a few hours to go and you'll be able to sort out all the mysteries.' But she was worried. It wasn't natural for them not be in contact so close to their wedding.

* * *

7

The day of the wedding was bright, with a slight crispness that hinted at the approach of autumn. Sophie was awake early and she and Daphne crept down to make a cup of tea, only to find Auntie Maggie and her father and mother already there, teapot at the ready.

'Want a fried egg for breakfast?' Sophie's mum asked, and, surprised at the generosity, they both said yes. Mrs Daniels took a slice of white bread and placed it in a frying pan. She cut a circle from the middle into which she poured reconstituted dried egg mixture and proceeded to fry it. 'A pretend egg is better than none,' she explained airily.

'You don't have a pretend rasher of bacon, do you?' Daphne asked.

'No, but I can draw you one!'

With so many hours to fill before they had to leave for the church, Daphne suggested a walk. They wandered through the streets, where shoppers hurried around with empty baskets that they were hoping to fill. There were queues everywhere, and people joined them and only then asked what was on offer when they reached the end.

The women all looked tired but their laughter rang out as they exchanged stories of their difficult lives. 'Imagine having to feed the two of us on what the ration books provide,' Sophie said as they watched a grocer in Liptons weigh out the tiny allowances of fats and cheese.

'If it were me I'd stay in the WAAFs until food is no longer rationed,' Daphne said. 'There'll be plenty of time for homemaking later. I wouldn't even know how to cook fatless this and eggless that!'

There was no transport for the guests, most of whom were local – they had to walk. There were just two black cars booked, one to take Sophie and her father, and the other for Daphne and Mrs Daniels.

The church was unevenly filled, with no one from the groom's side, so a few of the congregation moved across and filled the front pews. There was no organ music, but the choir of elderly men sang and filled the emptiness while they waited for the bride. Daphne stood in the porch waiting for the first sight of the car, and Mrs Daniels and close family stood with her.

'Where the 'ell's the groom?' Auntie Maggie whispered, and Uncle Albert hushed her urgently.

Ten minutes passed, the bride's car had driven through the battered street three times and there was no sign of Geoffrey. Eyes followed every vehicle that went past and tried to hide their disappointment when he didn't appear.

Finally the car carrying Sophie and her father stopped and Sophie stepped out. In a borrowed white dress and the veil falling charmingly from a pearl-studded head-dress, she looked lovely. 'What's happening?' she demanded. 'Why do we have to keep going round and round like circus ponies?'

'I told you something was up, him not taking you to meet his family,' Maggie said, before being hushed by her embarrassed husband.

'He isn't here yet,' her mother said quietly. 'Something must have held him up. The trains aren't always reliable with all the repairs and everything.'

Sophie seemed unperturbed. She stood in the porch between her parents, hugging her young sister and brother, glancing along the road occasionally for the appearance of her groom. Her laughter filled the air as she made jokes about the delay, and it was another hour before they gave up expecting him and went back home.

No one knew what to do, until someone started on the food, and at once Sophie's mother and Auntie Maggie disappeared into the kitchen to make tea while her father and Uncle Albert began pouring drinks. There was false gaiety as they all filled the embarrassed silences with reminiscences and jokes. Sophie handed out trays of food and Daphne helped serve the drinks, as though there was nothing unusual about the event. Sophie went up at some point to change out of her wedding dress, then she continued to smile and make jokes and pretend to be enjoying the pointless celebration until the last guest had gone. Then she stared at Daphne and said, 'You tried to warn me, didn't you?'

'No, not warn you – I wanted you to be sure you loved each other. I didn't wish this on you, for heaven's sake.

Wartime isn't the best time for making decisions. Especially about something as serious as marriage. That's all I meant.'

They went back to camp even though their leave wasn't over. All of Sophie's family were at the station to see them off. Her tearful parents, grandparents, Auntie Maggie, Uncle Albert, her brother and sister. The noise of the underground train pulling into the station deafened them to the final sympathetic comments, for which Sophie was grateful. They didn't even have time to wave as the doors of the crowded carriage closed behind them.

'At least they're all together,' Sophie said. 'I can imagine them all coping with their days, taking care of each other. I persuaded Gran and Gramps to stay for a few days, just to keep Mam and Dad from grieving. They're all so upset.'

Two weeks later a V2 hit the house, demolishing the whole street. Everyone in the house was killed. Because the house was completely destroyed, the news of the tragedy was a long time reaching her. The funerals had taken place before she was called into the office to be told.

She knew that the reason she had lost the whole family was her insistence that they stay together. If she had persuaded her parents to let Carrie and Frank leave London, allow them to be evacuated to the country, they'd have been safe. If Gran and Gramps had gone home instead of giving in to her pleading to stay with Mam and Dad, they'd be alive.

Numbed by the shock, disbelief gave way to brief moments of relief until the truth re-emerged to shock her anew. She had heard nothing from Geoffrey even though she had written to every address she could think of and asked everyone likely to know. In the midst of this tragedy, she faced the fact that she had been well and truly jilted. Everyone single person she had loved was gone.

When Sophie was given the terrible news about her family, Daphne wasn't there either. She had been moved to another airfield. Later, before Sophie could receive news of her friend, she, too, had been moved. She was among strangers who had their own troubles to cope with, and there was no one to tell about her own. In a world filled with tragedy, there was no one to offer comfort or sympathy.

On her next leave she went to see the ugly sprawling piles of rubble where her home had once stood, but she spoke to no one. She stayed in a small bed and breakfast that had one wall shored up with huge balks of timber to replace the house that had once stood alongside it, and said nothing, asked no questions. She couldn't face any surviving neighbours – they'd be aware of her confident insistence that the family should stay together.

Devastated and feeling she was completely to blame, her know-it-all attitude causing the death of every member of her family, with no one to share her misery, she turned away from the shell of her home and returned to camp. She missed Daphne. With so many changes in personnel she hadn't been close to anyone else. Geoffrey had let her down, and the war had taken away her whole family and the one person who might have helped her. She said nothing to anyone.

She went about her tasks in a dream, refusing any overtures of friendship, gaining a reputation for being standoffish. When she was demobbed, she went from town to town searching for news of Geoffrey and Daphne, but there was no clue to the whereabouts of either.

In the town Geoffrey had told her was his home she tried everywhere, but no one had heard of him. Stupidly, she had lost Daphne's address during the last sudden transfer, and moving herself, so soon after, their letters had failed to reach their destination and contact was lost.

She wrote to the solicitor to ask about the place of burial and he replied to tell her there was a large sum of money waiting for her. She arranged to have it transferred into a building society and swore never to touch it. It was tainted with her guilt. Once the solicitor had finally discovered her whereabouts, he delivered several letters referring to the money she had inherited, and the compensation to which she was entitled. And it was then, realizing how she had gained financially from the loss of those she loved, that she finally cried.

'It was my fault!' she told the solicitor over the phone. 'I told them to stay. My brother and sister would have been safe if I'd encouraged Mam to let them go. My grandparents would have been in their own home if I hadn't persuaded them to stay. And you expect me to be rewarded with money?' she wailed.

She was too distressed to seek company, tears falling when she saw families together, reminding her of the loss of her own. She had nowhere to go; no place to call home.

So she travelled; at first by train and bus, staying in small guest-houses, but once she discovered how many derelict buildings scattered the countryside, she left the towns, surviving on little more than the tramps that wandered the lanes and fields.

It was surprisingly easy to become accustomed to living without a base; with no place to scuttle back to like a wounded animal, she looked no further than the next night's shelter. She covered her trail, contacting no one with the exception of the solicitor. She made a few calls to finalize her business, and left him no way of finding her again. She looked for no company except those wandering like herself, whom she met on the road. She did work occasionally, when she found a place to stay that appealed, but only as a temporary cleaner. People always wanted cleaners, she discovered.

Leaving the comfort of bed and breakfast places, she slept in abandoned houses, sometimes for a night, on occasion staying for a couple of weeks. It was easy to find shelter: there were always barns or ruined cottages, some even boasted a few pieces of furniture. She gathered what clothes she needed from second-hand shops and the occasional jumble sale and she carried very little; she simply wore all the clothing she owned.

Time passed and she began taking an interest in the flowers and hedgerows. She stayed with a group of gypsy travellers for a few months one winter, listening and learning from them how they lived mostly off the countryside. They earned a little here and there, seasonal work for farmers, selling what they made to earn a few shillings. She remembered helping her gran to make jam when she was small, and an interest was revived.

A visit to a local library added to her growing knowledge

and she began to use what nature offered, making meals and preserves and drying herbs for future use. She still had money left in her post office account and she tried not to think about what she would do when it was gone. The other money would not be touched. Her family had given their lives for it, due to her stupid belief that she knew best.

She left the travellers once spring came, when they headed east, planning to work in Kent for hop-picking season. She continued her unplanned wandering, making for the coasts of South Wales, where her parents had been born and where she had lived as a child. Perhaps there she'd find some sense of belonging.

Walking up a quiet lane one March morning she saw a farmhouse and decided to knock and ask for water. As she approached, she saw that the collection of buildings, including a cottage adjoining the farmhouse, was empty. She stepped inside the cottage, which smelled of damp and mice. Then she saw an oven range with a blackened kettle on the long-dead ashes. Outside there was a tap. All around there was a generous supply of firewood, and, against the wall near the staircase, there was an old, mildewed couch. Perfect. What more could she ask of life?

In the long-abandoned garden she found sage and rosemary, mint, fennel, chives and a clump of Welsh onions. Wonderful gifts.

For a few weeks she could live here out of sight, bothering no one. She found a collection of dirty jars and even a couple of battered old saucepans in an outhouse. She could make preserves, dry herbs and perhaps sell them at the market she had passed through at Maes Hir – long field. Work should be easily found in the town just over the hill. It wasn't far away, but having to go up a steep field and through a fairly large wood meant she could stay unnoticed for a while.

At the top of the field a young woman stood watching as Sophie explored the several buildings around the main farmhouse. She observed that Sophie walked crouched over, and wore layer after layer of clothing including shawls. She noticed the bundle of belongings placed beside the door and decided the stranger must be old and perhaps homeless. Well, she was homeless, too, and this place with its sad regrets wasn't going to solve her problems – the dirty old tramp was welcome to it. She turned away, forgetting about the woman as she walked on into the town to try to find a couple of rooms for herself and her son.

Within an hour, Sophie had a fire burning, rather sluggishly as the chimney had been cold for many months, but the sight warmed her and the food she unpacked on to a rickety table rescued from a barn cheered her even more. She piled her clothes on to the couch, pulled it close to the fire and settled down to sleep. This place didn't feel like home any more than any other place she had found, but for the moment it would do.

Two

Betty Connors stopped the van in which she had been to collect some extra supplies for the Ship and Compass, and uttered a mild expletive. Steam coming from the bonnet meant trouble. She felt a momentary guilt, remembering how her brother Ed had warned her that the water tank needed topping up rather too often and the van needed to go to the garage. Irritation quickly followed. Why hadn't he dealt with it? She ran the pub with his help and he shouldn't have left it for her to do.

She sat back in the worn leather seat and wondered why Ed had been less enthusiastic about his work at the Ship and Compass these past weeks. Something was on his mind, and she had a suspicion that it might be Elsie Clements, who ran the bed and breakfast near the post office. Ed had never married and she thought he'd more sense than to consider it at his age, but he did spend a lot of time there, helping Elsie, when he should have been helping her.

The complaints from the overheated metal gradually stopped and she looked at the road ahead. Not far away there was a lane that led to the old cottage and farm buildings where Tommy and Rachel Treweather had lived until their new farmhouse had been built. The cottage, in which old Fred Yates had lived until he retired, might offer help even if it were locked. She seemed to remember it having an outside tap.

Taking a couple of empty flagons from the back of the van, she walked along the quiet lane towards the neglected yard, but stopped before reaching the door. Someone was there and she didn't think it was one of the Treweathers. No dog, for one thing. Neither Tommy nor the boys would be out without at least one of the dogs. Silently she backed away. Best if she

15

didn't confront whoever it was before telling Tommy or Rachel, in case it was someone in whom the police were interested.

She turned away and walked towards the village. Luckily, it was a pleasant spring morning and she wasn't in a hurry. Her brother would open up if she was late getting back. Unless Elsie made him forget the time! What the heck, she couldn't be in two places at once. She walked slowly, enjoying the brief freedom.

Sophie Daniels walked across the fields from the abandoned farm cottage where she had been living for the past couple of weeks. Her beautiful gold-flecked hazel eyes were filled with sadness, and she walked with her shoulders drooped as though trying to hide. The uniformed, outgoing young woman was lost in memory. She moved slowly, glancing right and then left, then retraced her steps, searching the ground. But what she was seeking eluded her.

She wasn't tall, and her slim figure, lost in the layers of soft cotton dresses she habitually wore, made her appear waif-like. Her hair flowed around her shoulders, fair, flyaway, framing her pale face in which the dark-hazel eyes were an almost harsh contrast.

She wore a shawl about her shoulders, and another, small and fringed, draped loosely over her head, not to hide her hair or protect her from the chill of the morning, but more as an ornament. From even a short distance she seemed ageless. A dozen guesses would have given a dozen answers. The habit of wearing all those layers had remained with her even though she no longer travelled. She needed the assurance of knowing that if she were moved on she would have most of what was important with her.

After an hour of walking over the field, stopping occasionally to admire the celandines that glowed like golden coins in the morning sun amid their heart-shaped rich green leaves, she gave up her patient search and returned to the cottage. A fire burned in the oven range against one wall, an oven issued tantalizing smells of a vegetable casserole cooking. There was a loaf of bread on the table, which was rickety and dependant on books to keep it level.

The building was small and triangular in shape, having been built against the main farmhouse for one of the workers. In spite of being unoccupied for some time it was still reasonably sound. There were only two rooms up and two down, but behind it was an outbuilding that had once housed a couple of horses.

Besides making the cottage comfortable, Sophie had cleaned the outhouse and whitewashed the walls, and now it had shelves, amateurishly arranged by supporting the ends of wooden planks with old scrubbed and painted bricks. The shelves were filled with jars containing jams and marmalades, chutneys and pickles as well as an assortment of dried foods – tomatoes, mushrooms, onions, herbs and spices. The time of the year limited what she could make, but when summer came she would fill the shelves with fruits and pickles and earn enough to survive the winter.

Tomorrow was market day in Maes Hir. She gathered the items she hoped to sell and put them into willow baskets, which she would carry on her arms. She had lost her purse, so she would have to walk the three miles. At least if she sold her goods she would be able to take the bus home, she thought with a shrug.

Before settling herself to sleep, she stepped outside and looked up at the late-evening sky. Too early for stars – she slept early and wakened with the first light. As she turned to go back inside she saw a movement, and by concentrating her eyes and staring, unmoving, she saw that up at the top of the sloping field, almost hidden in the hedgerow, someone stood watching her. The cottage was in darkness and even the fire had been allowed to die so she slipped cautiously around the door and closed it. Perhaps she hadn't been seen.

It was a long time before she could relax, listening for the sound of footsteps, afraid of someone banging on the door demanding she left. It had happened before, when a farmer had resented her presence, although never at night. But an hour passed and nothing moved, and she slept.

In the post office of Cwm Derw, Stella Jones sighed as she looked at the queue. It would be difficult to manage a cup of tea during the next half-hour and she was gasping. It was with relief that she recognized Connie Tanner entering, squeezing into the tiny shop and giving a wave.

'Connie, love, go into the back room and make a cuppa, will you? Sinking I am, and I'll soon be nothing more than a pile of bones on the floor if I don't have a drink soon.'

Connie ignored the complaints as she pushed a path through the customers and worked her way to the door leading to Stella's living room. It was cluttered and untidy but the tray was set neatly and a tin of biscuits was at hand. At the side of the roaring fire the kettle hummed softly and the teapot had been placed close by to keep warm. Knowing how fussy Stella could be about her famous brew, Connie warmed the pot with hot water and dried it before making the tea. Then she sat and cuddled Scamp, the little terrier, for a minute or two before pouring the teas.

When she went back into the shop Stella was serving the last customer.

'Phew, Connie, I don't know what's got into everyone today! They all came at the same time, and the moaning because they had to wait, you'd never believe. Half-day closing and you'd think they were preparing for a siege!' She took the cup of tea then groaned as the door opened again. This time it was old Mr Francis, and he held out a red leather purse.

'I found this,' he said. 'You must know whose it is if anyone does, you seeing every purse in the town.'

Stella shook her head and offered it to Connie, who did the same. 'Sorry, but we don't recognize it, Mr Francis, but leave it with me, someone will claim it, sure to.'

'There's a name inside but not one I know,' the old man added.

'The post office is the place, then,' Stella said. 'Fount of all knowledge this place is, for sure.' But she frowned as she read the name inside. 'Sophie Daniels? That isn't a name I know.'

'That's the crazy woman hiding out in Fred Yates's old cottage,' a voice from the door called. 'Him who used to work for Farmer Treweather.' A boy of about eight or nine stood half in and half out of the door, feet apart as though preparing to run.

'Bertie Grange, why aren't you in school?' Stella demanded. When the boy ran off, she added, 'Wild he is, that one. Never where he should be.'

'His mother doesn't care. Earns plenty of money in the factory but spends it having fun with her friends. Did you see his shoes? The woman's a disgrace.'

'Yes, the poor boy deserves better than Sarah Grange gives him. Look, there she is now.'

A row of women turned and stared as Bertie's mother walked by with a group of young women. She still wore the overalls she used in the factory and her hair was carelessly pulled back and fixed with a scarf. The disapproving faces swivelled until Sarah was out of sight.

'Bertie could be right about Fred Yates's cottage, mind,' Connie said. 'People have seen lights there at night, courting couples and poachers mainly, and there are rumours about a woman living there. Someone who keeps to herself. The farmer hasn't let the place. It needs too much work before he could do that. But a woman is definitely living there, although no one knows who she is.'

Stella looked at the purse, which contained seventeen and sixpence ha'penny. 'I'd return it myself, but I have to do some work on the allotment this afternoon. I promised Colin I'd sieve a patch of ground for some seeds.'

'I'll walk across there this afternoon with Geoff, if you like,' Connie offered. 'Half-day closing for us as well as the post office, remember. Geoff and I usually go for a walk after the deliveries.'

Connie and her husband, Geoff Tanner, owned the local hardware store. They had only been married a few weeks, but although Connie had been a newcomer to Cwm Derw, she had settled into the small South Wales town and had become an accepted part of it. They lived in the rooms above the double-sized shop premises on the corner of Steeple Street and, not having a garden, they usually walked through the fields or on the local beaches whenever they were free.

Every Wednesday, after the shop closed at one o'clock, they

went out in the van to deliver paraffin and any other goods that had been ordered. Once the round was finished they set off either by van to the nearest beach or on foot through the fields. That day they went by direct route to the lane leading to the farm cottage. The day was clear and mild, with the excitement of spring in the air. Birdsong filled the woods and hedgerows, new growth startled the eye with its bold greenness and everywhere was the promise of wonderful days to come.

When they reached the poor, shabby cottage they knocked but there was no reply, and Geoff tried the door, which opened easily. He called but no one answered.

'Should we just leave the purse?' Connie asked, but Geoff shook his head.

'It's a pity to waste an opportunity to talk to her, find out a little about her in case she's in trouble.' He took a page from his order book and wrote a short note, explaining that the purse had been found, and, if it belonged to her, she would find it either at the post office or Tanner's hardware store.

Unable to resist giving in to their curiosity, they stood for a while looking into the neat but sparsely furnished room. The fire burned low in the oven range, a red glow almost invisible amid grey wood ash. The curtains across the windows made the room dark and it didn't seem a very inviting place in which to live. Derelict farm buildings were the only neighbours, empty fields and silent woodland beyond, and beside it the lane, which went no further that the muddy yard.

The fire settled in the grate with a display of sparks, startling them, and they knew it would soon be dead. Wood didn't last long without coal to bank it up and when the woman returned she would probably have to relight it before she could make herself a hot drink.

The room smelled of fruit and spices, edged with the sharpness of vinegar.

'She's been making pickles, or has spilled some,' Connie whispered.

In the distance they heard singing on the calm, still air. Someone was approaching and at once they darted out of the doorway and closed the door, giggling like guilty children.

Then they turned to greet the person they presumed would be the tenant for whom they were looking.

In the lane, Sophie Daniels stopped singing as she saw a movement near the door of the cottage. She threw down the now empty baskets, and hid behind the thick trunk of an oak.

Geoff had seen her but, not wanting to frighten her, he said loudly, 'Come on, then, let's go home, love. She isn't here. We'll leave the note and she'll know where to find us.' Holding hands, he and Connie walked away, watched by a nervous Sophie.

Allowing time for them to get well away, even following them for a while to make sure they were really leaving, Sophie went back to the cottage and slipped inside. She didn't pick up the note: it might tell her she had no right to be there, and demand that she leave. She shivered and began to add screwed-up paper and kindling to the still warm ashes of the fire.

Kneeling on the rag mat she slowly added more wood until the blaze lit the room. How she would hate to leave this place. It was the first place that had even remotely felt like a home since her family had died. There had been many other places but this was the only one she could honestly call home. Her thoughts drifted, remembering places she had used as she had wandered without any purpose, begging at times, selling her produce when she settled for long enough to make any, and working occasionally – when she felt able to cope with other people for a time. She earned enough to feed herself, but there wasn't a lot of money left in the post office – not enough to pay rent unless she touched the bank account and she didn't want to do that, the money was tainted.

It was much later, after she had gone outside out for a last look at the sky before trying to sleep, that she read the note. It made her sad. They had been so kind, bringing it and trying to find her. But how could she go and collect her purse from strangers? They would ask questions and news would spread and she would be told to leave. Better to lose the few shillings the purse contained than risk that.

A week passed and Geoff and Connie still had the purse. It was the fickle month of April and the weather had become cold, the promise of spring forgotten. There was even a thin

21

covering of snow one morning, and Connie wondered how the lonely woman was coping. She imagined her getting out of bed and coaxing the fire into life before being able to boil water for a cup of tea. She shivered at her sad imaginings.

'Not worth going to the beach today,' Geoff said. 'But we could—'

'Visit Sophie Daniels again,' Connie finished for him. They laughed at the confirmation of their togetherness.

This time they took the van, and in the back Geoff placed a couple of half-full sacks of coal, mostly dust and small pieces, which, together with wood, could be used to bank up the fire and keep it alight for a few hours. It began to rain and the rarely used lane was quickly reduced to mud, the ridges previously left by vehicles collapsing and making the wheels sink until Geoff was afraid they might become stuck. He parked on a high area where a cobbled surface was still visible and, while Connie waited at the door, behind which she could hear the woman singing, he carried the sacks and placed them in a sheltered spot and covered them with several empty sacks to keep them dry.

The singing stopped and the door remained firmly closed. They knocked and called softly, assuring her they had only called to return her purse.

'There's a mistake, it isn't mine,' she replied after a few minutes had passed, her voice high pitched and light.

'It's all right, we haven't come to pry,' Connie said. She pushed the red purse under the door, where the earthen floor had been worn down by hundreds of feet passing through. 'Nor to ask questions,' she added. 'We'll help if you need it but won't call again, unless you invite us.'

The rain was persistent, drumming on the ground and playing a tattoo on the black umbrella Connie held. They moved away and began to walk towards the van. The door scraped harshly against the floor and they stopped and turned. Sophie opened the door wide and invited them in. They were both shocked to see a young and rather beautiful girl, not the frail old woman they had expected.

Somehow the room looked different with her there. The fire sent its cheerful glow on to the walls. Brightly patterned curtains and cushions were spread across the shabby furniture, which had presumably been left by previous tenants. On closer examination, Connie saw that the fabrics were worn and old, and the curtains were ill fitting, obviously intended for other windows, but the effect was of a cosy, comfortable room.

Connie held out the purse. 'Mr Francis found it and it was Bertie Grange, a young boy who wanders the fields when he should be in school, who told us it might belong to you.'

'Thank you. You're very kind.'

They turned to go and Geoff said, 'I hope you don't mind but we have rather a lot of small coal and we brought it in the hope you might use it. We'll take it away if you prefer.'

'We really don't want to intrude,' Connie assured her. 'But you might find it useful for keeping the fire alight while you're out.'

'I go to the markets and sell what I make – it's a long journey but I can only carry a little each time.' She spoke vaguely, almost as though she wasn't interested in them, so they were both surprised when she invited them to see her store.

The day was gloomy, and, carrying a torch and wrapped in an oversized mackintosh, she led them behind the cottage to the storeroom that had once been a stable, the hay containers still fixed to the wall. The bright beam of the torch shone around and they saw two well-scrubbed tables, large preserving pans, ladles, wooden spoons of many sizes, empty jars and row upon row of jams and preserves.

Sophie watched them but said nothing, and, feeling ashamed, as though their kindness had been a front for nosiness, Connie and Geoff made their excuses and left.

As they were getting into the van, a small figure appeared and a voice called, 'It's called Threeways. Daft name, innit?'

'What are you doing out here in this weather, Bertie?' Connie demanded. 'You'd better get in and we'll take you home.'

'The house where the crazy woman lives, it's called Threeways,' he repeated.

'Why do you call her a crazy woman?'

'Always singing, that's why.'

'And that means she's crazy?' Connie laughed, and she and Geoff at once began to sing, 'It ain't gonna rain no more no more, it ain't gonna rain no more.'

'You're crazy, too,' was Bertie's bored response.

They stopped outside the house in which he told them he lived, but when he got out he ran off and disappeared in the gloom of the late afternoon.

'I wonder where he really lives,' Geoff mused. 'He certainly didn't want us to know, yet it can hardly be a secret. Not in a small town like Cwm Derw.'

'Some mother he's got, letting him wander the way he does, and in this weather, too. I think I'll ask Stella where he lives. She's bound to know.'

In the shadows, Bertie stared wistfully after the van, wishing he could have gone home with them, just for a while, instead of going to his own home, where his mother would be sleeping, unless she was out with friends. He fingered the sixpence Geoff had slipped into his cold hand and turned towards Gwennie Flint's. Chips for his solitary supper again.

A hundred miles away, Daphne Boyd was packing clothes and toilet items into two RAF pannier bags, which were fixed to the back of her bicycle. With three friends, she was planning a cycling holiday, staying at youth hostels and heading for South Wales. The choice had not been hers, but she was pleased to agree. However slight, there was a chance of finding Sophie Daniels. She had tried every lead but without success, and the only hope was to travel through the area where her friend had once lived and ask at every town and village they passed.

Before she left, she sat and wrote down everything she could remember Sophie telling her about her old home. Barry Island had been a regular place for summer visits, and Cardiff, with its castle and fine shops. She studied her map and saw with growing dismay just how many villages were contained between those two centres. Packing the map into one of the panniers, she shrugged. At least she'd have a good holiday, and finding Sophie would be a bonus.

*　　*　　*

Tommy Treweather, the farmer who owned the farmhouse and cottage, knew about their uninvited tenant but decided not to complain. The house was no use to him; in fact, it would be demolished when he got around to it. A builder had told him it was past repair. The cost would be more than the value of it once the work was done. And who would want to live in an isolated cottage propped against a farmhouse at the end of a lane leading nowhere?

From what he had seen by peering through windows, the woman was living on the ground floor, so there was no real danger to her. The ground floor was sound enough. It was just the roof that seriously needed attention, and that, together with the other work needed, made it too expensive to bother.

March and April were very busy months on the farm and he really didn't want to get involved. He thought he might go and see her or send one of the boys, to explain about the roof in case she went upstairs, but winter was behind them and it was unlikely she would stay much longer. He hadn't seen her but presumed she was a woman wandering the roads, some lonely old tramp. Always plenty of those about. Perhaps, if she stayed more than a few more weeks, he would report her to the authorities and maybe get her placed in a home for vagrants. He discussed it with his sons, Ryan and Gareth, and they decided that for the meantime, while they were busy with lambing and the many other seasonal jobs on the land, they would ignore her presence.

He stood shielded by the overgrown hedge, his eyes moist as he looked down at the house where he and Rachel had lived and brought up the boys. It looked so derelict it was hard to remember it as it had been then. Gareth and Ryan had persuaded him to build a new farmhouse and move out, but after what they had told him this morning he wished he hadn't bothered.

He'd been so thrilled when Rachel had given birth to boys, imagining the land being passed on to another generation and perhaps surviving to see grandchildren taking the same interest as he had as a boy. Continuity was his dream, to retire some day soon so he and Rachel could enjoy themselves, be free of the long days and worrying times and watch their sons take over. Instead, a few words, and everything was ruined.

As they had sat down to breakfast after two hours of routine work, like they did every morning of the year, they had told him neither of them wanted to stay. There would only be his nephew, his brother's son, Owen, which meant he and Rachel would have to continue well into old age – or sell.

It was 1949 but still the war was blamed for everything that was wrong with the country. Perhaps the six years of the conflict *were* responsible for unsettling Ryan and Gareth. Making the stay-at-home life of a farmer unacceptable. Perhaps if they hadn't taken the opportunity to leave and see a wider horizon they might have remained. Foolishly the words of a popular song came into his mind: "How you gonna keep 'em down on the farm, now that they've seen Paree?" Yet they hadn't left the country, just moved far enough away from Treweather Farm to glimpse the possibilities of another kind of life.

'You're in a reserved occupation, you don't have to join the army,' Rachel had pleaded with them.

'But we do,' Ryan had insisted.

'Cowards we'll be if we stay,' Gareth had added.

Two years away and never leaving the country, yet it had been enough for them to decide that farming the land owned by their forbears was not what they wanted.

He turned away from the quiet scene with its memories of a time when everything had been certain, and headed back to the new farmhouse, where he had never felt at home.

There was no sign of the boys when he reached the yard. He heard the sound of laughter and turning the corner saw Rachel trying to fasten clothes to the washing line, Owen helping.

'Where are the boys?' he asked.

'Gone into town,' Rachel replied. 'They said something about an appointment but they were vague about what it was.'

'Ryan wants to teach,' Owen told them. 'They've gone to see about going back to college.'

Without another word, Tommy stomped into the porch and threw off his wellingtons, as if they were to blame for his sons' disloyalty. Standing at the door he said irritably, 'You can go and see that old woman living in our cottage and tell her to leave. Right?'

26

Owen nodded, but didn't look too pleased.

'She isn't doing any harm,' Rachel whispered. 'Best do as he says, though. Upset he is, with both Gareth and Ryan telling him they aren't going to stay.'

'Don't worry, Auntie Rachel, they might change their minds, and I'll be here. I'm not going anywhere,' he assured her. 'At least you can rely on me.'

On Sundays Geoff Tanner brought his books up to date and then he and Connie were free. This Sunday rain fell unceasingly and the air was chill, so instead of going for a walk and getting soaked they decided to check on the house Geoff owned, Badgers Brook. It had been empty for a while, and although Geoff appeared to be looking for new tenants Connie knew he was not. He was waiting until someone turned up who was in need of it.

Badgers Brook was a strange house, always attracting people in trouble, and giving them a place to stay while they solved their difficulties. She knew that Geoff superstitiously believed that the house found its own occupants, and in this she indulged him, even though she doubted the truth of it.

It was a fact, however, that she had experienced its soothing atmosphere herself, when she had come to Cwm Derw after the break-up of a love affair. It was while she was living there that she had met and married Geoff. She knew how calm, soothing and relaxing the house was, how it seemed to ease away pain and allow time for meditation and healing. She remembered the luxury of sleeping soundly and waking refreshed, with a clear vision of what was needed to solve problems that had once seemed overwhelming. But surely it was to do with who lived there, not the stones of its walls?

They drove down the lane with the woods on their left and, on their right, through trees that were not yet fully in leaf, they saw it. Connie was aware of a lifting of her spirits even though she was far from unhappy. There *was* something strange, even enchanting, about the place, however hard she tried to deny it.

They went into the house, which still smelled fresh, the windows regularly opened by Kitty Jennings, who lived on

27

the lane. Through the living-room window that overlooked the back garden, they saw someone digging. 'Bob Jennings,' Geoff said with a smile. 'He loves working on this garden. He can't keep away, even though there isn't a tenant.'

'Lucky I brought extra cups,' Connie replied. While she unpacked the thermos and the food she had brought, Geoff went to see Bob.

'A bit soggy for digging, isn't it, Bob?' Geoff said as the man looked up and waved.

'A bit of sun will soon dry it. I want to get the onion sets in this week if I can. All right,' he said with a groan, 'I know there isn't anyone living here, but there's no point in waiting till there is. It'll be too late for many crops if it isn't started now. Got anyone in mind?'

Geoff hesitated, then shook his head. 'No hurry, I'll find someone soon.'

They worked together for a while, Bob explaining what they needed to buy if they were to keep the gardens in order. He pointed out the rows marked with paper flags, where carrots and salad crops were already in the ground.

'I really should pay you for all the hours you work, Bob.'

'No need. I take what Kitty and I need, and I enjoy it. Besides, it would be a pity to let it all go back to how it once was.'

As they drank the tea and ate the cakes Connie had brought, Bob said, 'You know you might get some cabbage plants at the market in Maes Hir. Cheaper there than the shops.'

At once Connie offered to go. There was a chance she might see Sophie Daniels there.

On the morning of market day, Sophie was up early. She opened the door and stood outside, relishing the calm, fresh beauty of the early hour. It was not yet six o'clock and the birds were filling the air with song, adding to the joy of the morning. Behind her the fire crackled as the sticks blazed. The kettle, left overnight on the dying fire to retain some precious heat, wouldn't take long to boil.

She was about to go back inside when a movement caught her eye. She stood still, expecting to see a cat, or the rich red of a fox, but the movement was something larger. A man stood in the top corner of the field, half hidden in the trees, a dog sitting at his heels, a broken gun over his arm.

He was tall and strongly built, she couldn't guess his age, as the clothes he wore were those worn by most who worked on the land, whatever their age, although she had the impression he was dressed more smartly than most. It might be the farmer who owned the cottage. Hoping he hadn't seen her, she sidled back around the doorpost and slowly closed the door. Heart racing, she watched through the window, expecting him to walk towards her, tell her she must leave.

Tommy Treweather's son Ryan had been standing there for a while, perfectly still, looking down at the cottage. There were few discernable changes, yet it was different. It was no longer wearing the shroud of abandonment. There was an orderliness about the way brushes were lined up against the wall, a bucket precisely placed beside them. Curtains hung at the window, too, through which he could see an occasional flicker of flame from the fire, and a thin column of smoke issued from the chimney,

As he watched, the door opened and the woman came out draped in a blanket of some sort over long skirts. She appeared stooped as though bent with age, but from that distance she looked ageless. Fifties? Seventies? Certainly too old to be living in such an isolated place alone. He vaguely wondered whether something should be done. Then he moved away, unable to hear the sigh of pent-up breath that made Sophie's shoulders droop even lower with relief.

An hour later she was ready to leave. She had filled her two willow baskets with jars of her home-made jams and pickles, and beside them were small paper bags labelled with the herbs she had gathered and dried. As she was about to close the door behind her she again saw a movement at the top of the field and darted back inside.

Through the window she saw a man approach, different from the first, impatient, walking purposefully towards the cottage. It wasn't the man she had seen previously. This man was in his late thirties, smaller, slimmer, and he was dressed almost shabbily. A farm worker perhaps?

She quickly put the laden baskets back in the kitchen beside the sink and stood, anxiously waiting for the man to knock. Should she answer? Or just stay silent and hope he would go away? The decision was made for her as he walked straight in.

'Who are you, and what are you doing in my uncle's house?' he demanded.

'Sheltering for a while. Doing no harm,' she replied in her high-pitched voice.

'Then I have to tell you to leave.' he said, looking around, taking in the attempts at furnishing the room. Trying not to look at the pale face of the young woman. Why had they presumed she was old? 'Now. Today.'

'Why?' she dared to ask. 'No one needs it and I haven't done any damage. I'll leave as soon as I find somewhere else but please, not today, there's no need to be so unkind.'

He went through the room and looked into the kitchen. 'What's this?' he asked, pointing to the baskets.

'I make preserves when I can, and sell them at Maes Hir market.'

'So you run a business and pay my uncle no rent?'

'Hardly a business. Just enough to buy food.'

He looked at her then, and saw the anxiety in her eyes. She was no tramp, she was beautiful, and so young. Questions teamed through his mind, and he wondered why she was here all alone. She continued to stare at him and he started to feel uncomfortable. Uncle Tommy should have told her himself, not left the dirty work to him, as usual. 'A week,' he said more gently, 'then I really will have to tell you to leave.'

'Thank you.'

When Owen returned to the farm he turned on his aunt and uncle, telling them he wasn't a dogsbody, to be given jobs no one else would do. 'If you want her to leave then tell her yourselves,' he said as he left the house minutes after walking in.

Ryan and Tommy stared after his retreating figure with surprise. It was not like Owen to be so outspoken, almost rude. He never complained, whatever he was asked to do; subservient would be how Ryan would have described him: aware of his lowly position in the family, so polite that the

30

boys teased him. He wondered what the old vagrant woman had said to upset him so.

The small market town was bustling with its extra visitors. Connie Tanner walked among the stalls, taking in what was on offer but at the same time searching the crowds in the hope of seeing Sophie. She had been there for an hour and was about to give up when she saw her alighting from the bus.

'Hello,' she said, stepping forward to help with the heavy baskets. 'I thought you weren't coming.'

'I was delayed and almost didn't come at all.'

Connie didn't dare ask a question, instead she dropped the basket when Sophie had chosen a place just outside the area of stalls, where she hoped not to be charged rent, and with a friendly smile she wandered off to meet Stella as arranged.

They watched for a while as the girl sold her stock, smiling at people she had seen before, dropping the coins into a bag strung round her tiny waist. They bought cups of tea from the café and took one to Sophie, ignoring her refusal, leaving it on the wall behind her. She drank it gratefully. With the visits from the farmer and his nephew, she hadn't managed to have more than a glass of water that morning.

When they saw that her baskets were almost empty Stella went up to Sophie and offered her some early rhubarb. 'My Colin grows it on our allotment, see,' she explained, 'and there's more than we'll ever use. A bit of ginger and you'll make a delicious jam.'

Somewhat doubtfully, Sophie thanked her and wondered with dread if the woman would call to deliver it.

'I've got some spare jars, too, and if you'd like to swap for some tea, I can let you have some sugar,' Stella went on.

More subdued thanks and Connie added, 'We won't call, though, it's a long way, but if you come to the post office they'll be there on the counter for you to pick up. Right?'

A woman in the familiar uniform of the WAAF walked past and Sophie followed her with her eyes, a longing to see Daphne filling her with an ache. A friend to share some of the lonely hours was a luxury she would never find. When she had lost her family she abandoned everyone else, too.

31

At the bus stop Sophie stood in the queue for the bus to Cwm Derw, but when she saw Stella and the others at the end of it she changed her mind and hurried off. Better to wait for the next one rather than have to talk all the way back. Kind as they were, she couldn't cope with that. People exhausted her, and there was always the fear of someone trying to get too close, and asking questions she didn't want to answer, reopening old wounds.

To her dismay, a small figure was sitting leaning against her door when she reached the cottage. The small boy waved and ran to meet her. 'I brought you some jars and things,' he said proudly. 'I heard Stella Jones, her at the post office, talking to her old man about you and your jams and things, so I brought what I could find. They'll need a wash mind,' he warned.

She smiled. It was such a kind thought even though he was probably hoping for a few pennies. She put down the baskets and offered him a sixpenny piece.

'Ta, miss. A bag of chips for supper. Smashing.'

She stood waiting for him to leave but he seemed in no hurry.

'Like chips, do you?' he asked.

'I don't buy them very often.'

'What d'you have for supper then?'

'Toast in front of the fire once I get it glowing sufficiently.'

'That sounds good. I get fed up with chips. Mam doesn't like cooking, see,' he explained.

'And what about your father, does he like chips?'

'Oh him, he hopped it years ago.'

She invited him in.

They ate salad, which included dandelion leaves and the first pickings of watercress from the brook a couple of miles away, and home-made bread with a bowl of soup made from onions, carrots and the tops of nettles that were just beginning to grow at the edge of the field. Bertie pulled faces but accepted a second helping. He walked home feeling bloated after the unusual and delicious meal, and it felt good.

The following morning when Sophie stepped outside and looked up at the sky she saw clouds, fast moving, driven by a strong wind. They darkened and dropped lower as she walked around, the scent of garlic strong as she crushed the new leaves. She admired the new growth all around her: the hint of purple on distant birch trees and the spears of blue-bells already piercing the soil. A few wild daffodils had survived the children's gathering and the fields were edged with blackthorn, delicate white flowers against the dark branches. She felt the chill of the rising wind and stood for a while enjoying the freshness of the disturbed air as she waited for the kettle to boil on the fire.

After she had made a loaf of soda bread and prepared a vegetable casserole for later, she threw on a cloak and picked up a basket to search for whatever she could find in the fields and woods.

The wind continued to pick up and there was a restlessness about the trees. The birds were now silent and in spite of the movement there was a kind of hush, an expectancy: a storm was brewing. Tightening her belt and fastening the shawls around her head more securely, she walked on. She wandered further than usual and found herself in the wood near Badgers Brook.

She came at the house from the back, where the garden faced south and was bounded by a beech hedge. There was a gap through which she could see the house, and she was curious. The place had an abandoned unlived-in look. Leaves and branches and a few newspapers had blown against the walls and doorway. Abandoned toys and a broken chair had been piled as though ready for a bonfire, and there were no curtains at the wide, rain-splattered windows. Looking up she saw that at one window a curtain had been caught as the window had been closed, the tattered material waving sadly, like a flag when the carnival has moved on.

Pushing her way through the hedge at the weak point, she went closer. She stared into the ground-floor rooms; in one a couch stood near an empty grate and in another, the kitchen facing the lane, there was a long, scrubbed table and two chairs. The place was hardly enticing, but something about its strong walls and its isolated situation appealed to her. 'If only I could live in a place like this,' she whispered, 'I just know I'd be happy.'

33

She heard voices then and looked around for a place to hide. As she turned to run back to the gap in the hedge, she saw Connie and Geoff watching her, smiling in a friendly manner, Connie holding out her hand.

Geoff said, 'See? I told you she'd find her way here.'

'I'm sorry, I know I'm trespassing, but I was curious and—'

'It's all right,' Geoff said. 'You're welcome. Would you like to see inside? Come on, let's get out of the rain for a while.'

While Connie unpacked the usual picnic in the kitchen, Sophie happily wandered from room to room, imagining herself living there, alone but content, and perhaps gaining strength and gradually making friends.

'I love it here,' she said when they had eaten Connie's picnic. 'I can't imagine anyone being unhappy here for long.'

'And are you unhappy?' Connie asked.

'I need solitude, but that isn't being unhappy, is it?'

'The place is for rent,' Geoff said.

'I don't think I could afford it, I don't make much with my preserves.' She began to move towards the door.

'Get a job and earn a little, the rent isn't high.'

'I'm not ready for that, not yet.'

Connie packed the remnants of the food back into the bag and they stood to leave. 'You know where to find us if you change your mind,' she said with an encouraging smile.

When Sophie went outside the wind was bending the slenderest trees this way and that, in a wild dance. She walked through the wood to where the stream passed through the trees like a silver ribbon, glinting and darkening as the trees moved to allow the light to reach its ruffled surface. The sounds of creaking, and the weird, unworldly, discordant shrieks as branches rubbed together, began to seem like threats, a reminder that she ought to be away from falling branches. She protected her half-filled basket under her coat and hurried home.

On the step, his coat pulled up to cover his head, looking a picture of misery, was Bertie.

'Any chance of something to eat?' he asked, following her

34

inside. He revived the fire, and pushed the kettle over its flames. Smiling, she put two plates on the hearth to warm and tested the heat of the casserole. 'You shouldn't be out in weather like this,' she scolded mildly.

'Neither should you, miss,' he retorted.

'Stay for supper but then I'll walk you back home,' she told him.

'No need, eyes like a cat I have, be home in no time.'

'Don't go through the woods, the trees are waving dangerously. Some branches will fall.'

'All right, miss.'

For a while the stout old walls gave a comfortable sense of security as the storm howled around them. Smoke failed to go up the chimney; instead the wind sent it puffing into the room and the fire burned sluggishly.

They ate a meal and hung the herbs she had gathered in the chimney corner to dry, wondering if they would taste of anything other than smoke and soot. She felt the draught as the door opened and with a 'Ta, miss,' Bertie was gone before she could do as she intended and walk him home. She opened the door and called for him to wait, but he'd been swallowed up by the darkness.

It was too early to sleep but there was little she could do. The room was cold, as though the wind was sucking out all the warmth; better to save the candles and go to bed.

She lay on her makeshift bed on the couch against the wall opposite the fire and for a while she thought about living in Badgers Brook. She had enough money to rent it, if she succumbed to her weakening reluctance and spent some of the money in her bank account. But wouldn't it would be a mistake to spend money on renting a property that was too large, and with all that garden? It was much more than she needed, or could manage.

What would she do if she did move in? Was the house worth making the necessary effort needed to force herself to face the world and find a job? She couldn't. She wasn't ready. She closed her eyes but knew she wouldn't sleep. The storm was worsening and the wildness was exciting and would keep her awake. Ten minutes later she was asleep.

The storm invaded her sleep and brought a return of the nightmares she had suffered at the time her family had been taken from her. She saw falling masonry and heard the sound of smashing glass, the screams of those trapped and injured, and the faces of those she had lost came to her one by one. She felt them close to her: Mam, Dad, Carrie and Frank, Auntie Maggie, Uncle Albert, Gran and Gramps.

At one a.m. she was woken by the realization that the shattering of glass wasn't a dream. All around her were warnings of danger, tapping and banging, louder and louder. Something was happening to the house itself. She reached for her coat and slid from under the covers.

The cacophony was alarming. Things were being blown around in the yard, windows rattled and the whole house was shaking as though being pulled apart by a giant hand. The loud banging came from above and she was relieved when it stopped. Yet she still held her breath and waited. Would it return and destroy the place and bury her? She couldn't escape, there was nowhere safer than the building where she stood. But she was very afraid.

She couldn't see anything through the windows and the sounds were impossible to identify. She crouched near the door and waited for the storm to blow itself out, but it wasn't finished yet.

The loud banging began again, and this time the walls seemed to shake with the force of it. Then she heard tinkling glass, almost musical but swiftly followed by fierce cracking sounds and a kind of roar. Then something cumbersome and heavy, sliding, shrieking as though in agony, and falling. It went on and on. Surely it couldn't be the roof? A draught filled the room and lifted ashes in the grate, snatching at the bedding and swinging the curtains like the skirts of a dancer.

She went to the stairs and took a few hesitant steps. She looked up. Rain was falling on to her face and the sounds had changed to a high-pitched wailing. The banging had changed to a constant rattling. The roof was gone.

She had to get out, but to where? She couldn't go into the farmhouse, which was always locked. There was the outbuilding, but that was more dilapidated than the house, although it did have a roof. She wrapped herself in as many clothes and blankets as she could, and, in a brief lull in the weather, she ran to the other building. The door was swinging and she closed it behind her with difficulty, then stood panting, as though she had run for miles, before slowly sinking to the floor.

She had to find a safe place. This was a reminder that she couldn't go on running away. The offer of Badgers Brook followed by the storm that had destroyed her temporary home must be a sign. Tomorrow she would go and find Connie and Geoff Tanner and, somehow, she would find a way of staying in Badgers Brook. She was frightened at the prospect, facing people and answering their questions would be hard. But once it was done she might find peace again. Peering through the hedge and finding the house, and within hours losing the cottage in the storm; surely it meant something was telling her it was time to end her isolation? She was frightened but she knew the time was right.

Three

People awoke the morning after the violent storm, with memories of air raids during the recent war painfully revived. The aftermath of that wild night, the anxious moments as daylight dawned and they checked their properties, and ran to make sure families, neighbours and friends were safe, were strong reminders of those terrible years.

Bob checked their house on the lane near Badgers Brook while Kitty brushed away the rubbish gathered outside the house. Stella and Colin checked and found to their relief that no serious damage was apparent at the post office. Both wondered how their allotment had fared, but neither had time to go and look. Geoff checked on his stocks of wood, including plywood for boarding up the inevitable broken windows, and nails and screws, which he knew would be needed in large quantities as problems were revealed.

On Treweather Farm the men went out and found the animals nervous but safe. A door had been blown off its hinges and the chickens were chortling happily as they wandered around the yard, freed from their night-time shelter earlier than usual but unharmed.

Betty Connors spotted a slipped slate on the roof of the Ship and Compass and called to her brother to get in touch with the builder to get it fixed.

'Later,' he said, to her surprise and irritation. 'First I'm going to see if Elsie needs help.'

'Ed, I need you here. If that slate isn't fixed others will follow it and—' She was wasting her breath, Her brother had grabbed a coat and was heading for the door. She ran after him and called, 'Ed, it's here you work, not Elsie's B&B!'

'Then as an employee,' he said sarcastically, 'I'm letting you know I won't be in today.'

'Don't be ridiculous.' She was shocked by his attitude. What was the matter with him? He worked here, lived here and she should be able to depend on him. She reached for the telephone and irritably asked the builder to call and deal with the roof. Then she thought maybe she was being selfish – it was only a slipped slate and there would be plenty of others in more urgent need of help this morning. Then she remembered Sophie.

Sophie stayed curled up in a tight ball, wrapped in the bedding she had brought, close to the door of the building she used as a storeroom. She had ventured no further in as she was afraid of being trapped, with the wind lashing against the walls and the alarming sounds of large objects being thrown about outside.

She must have dozed eventually, as she became aware of light defining the edges of the door and the silence beyond. She didn't move for a moment or two, afraid of a revival of the storm, but it had blown itself out, and outside, where dawn was breaking, birdsong was a gentle chorus to greet the new day.

She stretched and stood up. Then, still wrapped in the bedding, she opened the door and looked out. The yard was strewn with branches and several items she hadn't seen before: boxes, empty paint tins, a bucket, a broken chair. A door stood propped at an angle against a wall, and she vaguely recognized it as being from one of the half-demolished outhouses. Then she looked up at the cottage and saw to her disbelief that it was a different shape. A large section of the roof had been lifted and tilted and was now leaning lazily against a wall of the house it had once protected. She went cautiously outside and looked around her. Nothing was where it should be; buckets and brooms and the small ramshackle shed housing her woodpile had all vanished.

She was chilled and thirsty and went into what remained of the cottage, to the hearth where the previous day's ashes were covered in a thick layer of soot. It would take ages to clean and it would have to be done before lighting a fire. There was no alternative as she desperately needed a hot drink. She put aside the bedding, rolled up her sleeves and began. Without a shovel or a bucket it was difficult, but she used cardboard to lift the soot, which she placed on to spread newspapers. An hour later she had a fire burning and the kettle was beginning to hum.

She had cleaned the living room as well as she could and was sitting beside the now blazing fire hugging a cup of tea when she heard voices.

'Sophie? Are you all right?' Geoff called.

Sophie went outside and waved her cup. She didn't want visitors but knew that the previous night's plan must hold. The time had come when she had to accept the hand of friendship when it was offered, before loneliness became an unalterable way of life.

'Would you like some tea?' she invited, and went inside to wipe clean another cup and saucer.

'Are you all right?' Geoff repeated. 'We were a bit worried, the storm was so fierce.'

'I went into the outhouse as it seemed safer, but this room isn't damaged, except that the fireplace was a mess of soot and it took an age before I could make myself a cup of tea.'

'You obviously can't stay here now,' Geoff warned, putting the bread and milk Connie had sent on the dust-laden table.

Suddenly in a panic Sophie revoked her decision to move. She needed the solitude and security for a while longer. She wasn't ready. 'I'll be all right. Once I block off the stairs to cut out the draughts it'll be cosy,' she insisted.

'Badgers Brook is empty.'

'I don't want to pay rent until I can earn some money. Savings soon disappear once the first few pounds are used.' The main fear was not of her savings, which she had sworn not to touch, but the thought of becoming a part of a community; she still wasn't prepared to cope with that. But, a voice inside her warned, how much longer can you wait to be ready? Time is passing and every day is making it more difficult, not easier. She knew she was running away from a problem that couldn't be outpaced.

Geoff helped her to clear away the worst of the outside rubbish, dragging branches away from the cottage, heaving against the roof to make sure it wouldn't fall any further.

'Are you able to work? Do you have any qualifications? Experience?' he asked, and when there was no reply he apologized. 'Sorry, I don't mean to pry.'

Perhaps now *was* the time to make the break from her isolation. Perhaps these patient and kindly people were the sign for which she had been waiting.

'I'm sorry if we're interfering. Perhaps I should go.' He looked out through the doorway and added, 'I'll just move the last of the branches away from your path then I'll get back to the shop. Connie is bound to be busy and she's only got young Joyce to help her.'

Almost startled into the present, pulled away from her thoughts, Sophie hurriedly apologized. 'Sorry, my mind was drifting. I know you don't mean to pry. It's just that I'm not ready yet, to work or to answer questions. Making a decision can be frightening.'

'Or exciting. And sometimes the decision is made for us.'

Sophie agreed. His words were echoing her own thoughts.

'We can give you a month before you start paying rent, but we'll understand if you think we're interfering,' Geoff said after dragging away the final barrier to her path. 'But think about it. We just feel that the house is the right one for you.' He looked at her and saw that her face was troubled. He picked up his coat and stepped through the door. 'You'll find us at the hardware store on Steeple Street,' he reminded her. 'Just come when you're ready.'

She thanked him for his help and promised she would give consideration to the idea of living in Badgers Brook.

She sat for a long time after Geoff had gone and she was so wrapped in her thoughts that she was startled to see a man standing in the doorway. She hadn't heard him coming. He wore a well-fitting countryman's jacket, and leather leggings confined his corduroy trousers. A gun hung over his arm, which he put down to rest against the door. Sophie didn't recognize him; it wasn't the farmer who had told her to leave. This man was larger, younger – and he was smiling.

'You survived the storm, then?'

'If you've come to remind me I have to leave, please give me a few more days. I have to find a new home and move all my possessions, you see.'

His smile widened as he looked around the shabby room with its makeshift furnishings. 'No van needed, then. A couple of wheelbarrow loads will suffice! But no, I haven't come to ask you to move. I wanted to make sure you were unhurt. You aren't doing any harm and there's no one else wanting to live here in the back of beyond. But I do think you ought to find a better home. This one is no longer safe.'

'But the other man told me to get out within the week,' she said with a frown.

It was his turn to frown. 'That was probably my cousin, Owen. I'm Ryan Treweather, by the way, my parents and my brother and I own the farm, and the big house next door was our home when we were small. Owen works for us. So I'm your landlord, I suppose. If you want anything, I'll try to help – short of replacing the roof. It's a miracle it's lasted so long. It was an odd shape with the cottage tacked carelessly on to the farmhouse and the walls being only mud, and it wasn't property secured.'

'How long has this place been here?' she asked.

He looked at her, wanting to share the joke, head back, filling the room with his laughter. 'Only a mere two hundred years!' He looked at her more seriously and said, 'But the place has really gone now. I can't help you stay here, but anything else I can do, please ask.'

'Thank you.'

'Any tea in that pot?'

Ryan stayed for a couple of hours, helping to clean the room and making it safe by fixing a door at the bottom of the stairs where there had been one long ago. Together they gathered wood suitable for the fire, which they put into a rickety shed, now lacking a door. He talked about his child-hood, and Fred Yates, who had once lived in the cottage, seeming to enjoy the journey into his past. Sophie said little, just enough to start him off again when he fell silent. When he left he promised to call again. 'And I'll bring a wheelbarrow when you're ready to move out,' he said as he walked away laughing.

First Geoff Tanner and now this smiling, kind-hearted farmer's son. Life was certainly telling her something!

She knew the laughter drifting back to her was friendly, and stood waving until he was lost to sight among the trees at the top of the field. The room seemed empty without him, the loneliness no longer appealing.

Everywhere she walked that afternoon she saw evidence of the storm. As she approached the town she heard the sound of hammers and saws and imagined the activity as repairs were hastily carried out for fear of a return of the winds as night approached.

Badgers Brook appeared to have survived unharmed. Some twigs had fallen from the ash trees near by. Late to leaf, early to fall, and always quick to shed small branches, they were never chosen by nesting birds. Beautiful but barren, she mused. Everything else about the solid-looking house seemed unharmed. The windows shone in the afternoon sun and she smiled as she looked up at the roof, sound and secure without even a slipped slate.

She knew then that she would live there. From the first glimpse through the hedge she had dreamed of it being her home, yet at that moment it had been a ridiculous thought. Even now the idea was completely without logic. She could manage perfectly well in one room, so why was she even considering this large house? Yet she peered through the windows, imagining herself there. The rooms were large and quite a few pounds would be needed to furnish them. It would mean invading her bank account – money she didn't want to use.

She took a bus into town and stepped off near the hardware store. Through the window she saw Geoff serving a customer, and beside him Connie, writing something in a ledger. When she opened the door they smiled and waved a welcome, but neither seemed very surprised to see her.

News travels, and the following morning Ryan Treweather arrived pushing a large, seriously rusted wheelbarrow.

'I hear you're moving,' he said, laughing at her expression

as she stared at the dilapidated barrow. 'I've come to help.' She smiled, enjoying the joke as he pushed it into the hedge from where he had taken it.

He went inside and listened as she began to tell him of her decision to rent the house owned by Geoff and Connie Tanner, but he knew all about it.

'Stella Jones at the post office filters all the news, and she heard it from Connie and spread it wide. It doesn't worry you, does it? I'm afraid Cwm Derw is the sort of town that thrives on gossip.' She looked serious and he wanted to make her smile. 'There was the time the postman met my mother and told her I was coming home the following day. "Just delivered the card, so you'd better get some extra food to save you coming down again," he told her. There isn't much that goes on here that isn't passed on, but in a caring way,' he said. 'A postcard came once for Elsie Clements confirming a booking for a group of cyclists arriving the following day and the baker and the milkman knew before she did.'

'There are a lot of cyclists passing through, usually in groups. Heading for the youth hostel, I suppose. It must be a pleasant way to travel.'

'Have you ever tried it?'

'I had a cycle once.' She thought of the happy holidaymakers and of the last time she had ridden. She and Daphne riding through ruined streets, so sure that her family were safe, protected by her confidence. She remembered them laughing, excited, on the morning of what should have been her wedding day.

'Why the sad face?' Ryan asked. 'Sad memories?'

'Just people I've lost.' Hurriedly, anxious to change the subject before Ryan asked more questions, she smiled and said, 'I think this is the right place for me to settle. I've been wandering around for years looking for a community to which I can belong. If I can be healed, it will be here.' She moved abruptly then, as though regretting having said so much, revealing something she wanted to remain hidden.

'Let me know when you're ready and I'll bring a van,' he promised, touching her shoulder in a way that promised friendship, before leaving.

Once again she felt a loss as he disappeared through the trees.

'Telling you to go, was he? Miserable man.'

She turned to see the boy watching from the corner. 'No, Bertie, he was offering to help me. Now, why aren't you in school?'

'Headache all over, miss, right down to me big toe,' he replied before running off.

On market day Sophie went with two heavy baskets and sold most of her produce, and the following day she went looking for furniture. Having seen that there was already a couch and a kitchen table at Badgers Brook, she listed the larger items she would need: bed, cupboards, chests of drawers, a few chairs. Besides these, her greatest need was for bed linen and soft furnishings, and all these she managed to buy second hand with a promise of delivery the following weekend.

On the day she had arranged to move into Badgers Brook she woke early and began to put her possessions and the last of her stock of preserves outside ready to go on to the promised van. A car stopped in the lane and she glanced at her watch. If it was Ryan he was much earlier than planned. But it wasn't the friendly Ryan, it was the older man, Owen. And he was not friendly.

'I thought I told you to leave! Get off this land, you're trespassing. And take all this junk with you.'

'But I am moving. Today. You can see that. I'm waiting for the van to arrive.' She almost said, 'Waiting for Ryan, your cousin,' but did not. She simply wasn't any good at confrontations. 'I'll be as quick as I can.'

'Be out of here in an hour or I'll bring the tractor and run over this mess, and that's a promise.'

A stone hit him on the shoulder, and although it obviously had not come from her direction he turned and glared at her. 'Who threw that?' he demanded. A second stone caught him on the ear and he put his hand up and held it, twisting round in pain. Sophie had her suspicions but said nothing.

She heard a van pull up and was relieved to see Ryan appear.

45

'Owen?' he said at once. 'What are you doing here? Is everything all right?'

'Just telling this trespasser to leave. She was told to be gone days ago.'

'You won't have to wait any longer,' Ryan said grimly. 'In fact, now you're here you can help me load up the van, and be careful not to damage anything.'

Sophie went back inside leaving the two men arguing. She walked around the room that had been her home, touching the walls, opening and closing the oven door beside the now cold fire. It was exciting to be leaving but there was a foolish part of her that felt she was letting the house down by abandoning it to its fate.

She unnecessarily checked to make sure the fire was completely out, piled into a cardboard box the small amount of firewood she and Ryan had gathered ready to be transported to her new home, and when she went outside again the van was packed and Ryan was waiting for her.

Ryan helped her into the passenger seat and drove down the lane, but although she wanted to look back for a final glimpse of her temporary home, she couldn't. In the van close behind them she'd have met the angry gaze of Owen Treweather.

Ryan didn't stay. He carried her belongings inside and after seeing that a fire was burning in the living room and there was a kettle ready filled on the gas cooker he left her to sort herself out.

Owen was furious. Being made to look foolish in front of that woman was the very end. For years he had suffered the constant reminders of his lowly position in the family. He and the twins had the same grandfather; he belonged on Treweather land as much as they did.

Something twisted within him as he stood on the field amid the sheep, looking around him at the land owned by Tommy. He was a Treweather, and therefore entitled to his share of the family money, and if he wasn't going to be given it then he would take it. Right was on his side even though the law was not.

As he walked back to where he had parked the van he saw Sarah. In his present mood his anger and frustration at the way his life was going simply overflowed. 'What are you doing here? You don't have the right to walk these fields.'

'A few branches of catkins? If you can't spare them you can have them back!' She thrust the branches at him and turned away.

She was trying not to cry when she met Bertie from school. She thought a couple of branches with the catkins might have cheered her a little. He even had to spoil that for them.

The accommodation she had found for them was even sadder than before. A rather dark room at the back of a house with a shared kitchen and an outside lavatory. What a mess she had made of her life. 'Hurry up,' she said to Bertie as he scuttled along in shoes that were a couple of sizes too large. 'I've got things to do if we're going to get settled before bed time.'

'I'm hungry, Mam.'

'We'll have some toast later if I can get the fire to draw properly.'

'Can't I go and see Miss? She always has something nice to eat.'

'No, and you must stop bothering her, d'you hear me?'

Bertie kicked out at a dandelion and his shoe sailed through the air. He laughed but Sarah didn't.

At Badgers Brook the furniture Sophie had bought had arrived and she busied herself setting it out and making up the bed in the room she had chosen: one that overlooked the garden. Then she checked inside and out and was pleased to find a store of wood and some coal. A note on the kitchen table had welcomed her to her new home and contained an explanation of the workings of the geyser in the bathroom and a few other pieces of information.

She was anxious when a knock at the door heralded a visitor; she wasn't ready to face new people. But she looked around the house as though seeking encouragement then pulled back her shoulders and went to face the beginning of her new life.

The caller was the first of several, neighbours mostly, as

47

well as Betty Connors, who left the Ship and Compass in her brother's reluctant care to bring Welsh cakes – the flat spicy cakes cooked on a griddle – plus coal and salt for luck. Gradually Sophie relaxed and accepted the welcoming visits, which were friendly and mercifully short. None stayed to ask questions, the thing she had most dreaded.

A few days later Badgers Brook had woven its spell and she couldn't imagine living anywhere else. Her reticence was simply ignored, and a stream of visitors continued to pass through, bringing small gifts, offering help if needed, and wishing her well. The town of Cwm Derw had taken her to its heart.

Stella's shop had a queue down to the corner and around into the next street. Sweets were off ration from the 24th April and the children were not alone in wanting to give themselves a treat. Colin worked on the railway and as he was on a late shift he was free to go to the wholesalers for replenishments as the stocks ran low.

'Damn me,' he said when he had to go a second time. 'At this rate they'll be back on ration again soon!' He was unaware of how prophetic his words would be.

When the doors finally closed on the post office, and with the last of the customers' complaints at having to wait ten minutes to buy a stamp ringing in her ears, Stella called at Badgers Brook with Colin, bringing a box of plants. 'Herbs they are, a bit small, mind, but well rooted. Marvellous gardener, my Colin, we've got an allotment – you must come and have a cup of tea in our country cottage.'

Sophie was curious as she had presumed they lived behind the post office, but, typically, she refrained from asking where the country cottage might be. She didn't want to answer questions so tried not to ask any.

Kitty and Bob Jennings came with cakes and a precious packet of tea, spared from their small ration, explaining, 'You'll never keep up with us all popping in to say hello, otherwise.' She laughed then. 'Don't worry, it won't be as bad as you fear. Once you settle in and people have all had a good nose they'll leave you alone.'

48

The one visitor she had expected didn't come. Ryan Treweather seemed to have forgotten all about her. She wasn't sure whether she was disappointed or relieved. Close friendship was not what she was looking for. She was all alone in the world and, being alone, she needed to *be* alone to sort out her feelings.

Three cyclists had travelled fifty miles in the rain and decided not to continue for another ten as planned, but stay in the next town they reached. They found a bed and breakfast where the landlady kindly dried their wet clothes and fed them generously before showing them a room with three single beds. Their next destination was only ten miles away, so, accepting that they were a day behind their schedule, tomorrow would be an easy day. Time to explore. Before they set off the following morning, Daphne asked at the post office if there was a Sophie Daniels living in the area but, as so many times before, the answer was no.

Sophie had allowed herself a week to settle in and then she had to face up to her fears and find a job. While her mind spun with the number of ways in which she could earn a little money she explored the garden. It seemed well stocked and she wondered who had looked after it since the previous tenants had left. In a sheltered corner rhubarb was still protected by broken upside-down buckets filled with straw, and the pale pink stems were already tall and strong. They would make some attractively coloured jams. Fruit bushes and trees were an exciting find, and there were a few spindly leeks and some winter cabbages left. Vegetable seeds were planted in neatly sieved ground with labels showing what each row held. Carrots, radishes, parsnips, peas. Some were already breaking through the earth. The rest of the vegetable garden was dug ready for the new planting and she lifted handfuls of the rich loam to her face, its smell filling her with indefinable excitement.

Brambles were growing in a sunny corner and she picked some of the freshly sprouted leaves for drying to make a substitute tea. Kitty Jennings had been right about the need for tea to supply her many visitors. She would drink the substitute tea, and the coffee-flavour drink she made from the roots of dandelion, and save the ration for them.

There were a few things she still needed, and, carrying one of her large baskets, she walked to the end of the lane and caught the bus into the town. The post office was empty and Stella persuaded her to stay for a cup of tea, telling her to go in and make it. Three cats ran off, deeply offended at being disturbed, and the little dog wagged his tail then settled back to sleep. She carried the tray into the shop and, sitting on a chair beside the counter, answered Stella's questions while managing not to tell her all she wanted to know.

When she left, grasping a hastily drawn map that she was told would lead her to Stella and Colin's allotment and country cottage, she headed for the second-hand shop in the hope of some plates and dishes. On the corner, not far from where the bus stopped, she saw a small figure bending over and selecting things from the gutter. She didn't call but walked towards him. He hid what he had in his hand and looked guilty.

'Hello, miss. Where've you got to? I've been to the cottage but it's empty.'

'What are you doing, Bertie?' she asked, making a grab for his hand, which was making a tight fist. 'Let me see, please. I'm not going to harm you.' Slowly a grubby hand uncurled to reveal three cigarette ends.

'Bertie! Surely you don't smoke these filthy things?'

'Not me, miss, but there's an old man who lives under the railway arch who does. I get him some when no one's looking so he don't have to go out in the rain, see.'

'Doesn't have to go out in the rain,' she corrected automatically.

'Doesn't have to go out. He sleeps in his clothes and it can't be no – any good for him, can it, miss?'

She smiled her slow, gentle smile and held out her hand. 'I think it's best not to collect them for him. They aren't clean, you see, and they could harm him. Besides, I think your mother would be upset if she saw you, don't you?'

'She does fuss a bit, miss.'

'Will you let me walk home with you?'

'No need, I've got a brand new bike over there.' He pointed vaguely towards the row of houses adjoining the post office and ran off. She went around the other end of the row and watched as he walked disconsolately away. The new bike was a dream, and she knew all about dreams.

A few days later he called at Badgers Brook and offered to show her where the badgers lived. She invited him in and after they had shared a meal of sour milk cheese and soda bread she again asked why he wasn't at school. He coughed loudly and theatrically and explained he was too ill to go. She encouraged him to talk about his favourite lessons and those he disliked, trying to pick up a clue to tell her the real reason he avoided school.

The following morning there was a loud knocking at the door and Sophie left the salad she was making and went to open it, smiling in expectation of seeing one of her new friends. A woman stood there, someone she hadn't seen before.

'I've called to ask you to please stop encouraging my Bertie to stay away from school,' she said. She was fair, her face pale, the blue eyes gentle. She stared as she waited for Sophie's response. Her voice was soft, without anger, even breathless with anxiety.

Sophie stared at her in surprise. 'Are you Bertie's mother?'

'I am, and I've had the school board man round again this morning.' She gave a deep sigh. 'I send him off every morning but he never gets to the school gates. I want you to stop inviting him here.'

'I'm sorry, Mrs – er – but I have no control over your son. Do you have any idea why he isn't attending?'

The woman shrugged. 'He says he gets muddled with arithmetic, but he won't let me help.'

'Perhaps, if we put our heads together, we might work out a way to help him.' Sophie opened the door wider and invited the woman inside.

'He hasn't got a father, see, but that applies to many of his friends and they don't cause their mothers such trouble.'

'Mitching from school isn't such a terrible crime, and it's usually sorted fairly easily. Don't let the school board man

51

frighten you, Mrs . . .' Again she allowed a pause, inviting the woman to give her name, but it was ignored.

Sophie made tea and brought out some small cakes flavoured with honey and cinnamon. They discussed the various reasons for Bertie avoiding school and his mother admitted to letting him wander as and where he wanted, without much attempt at controlling him.

'I have to work, you see, having no husband, and my parents aren't much help, so when I'm late home or I have to leave before he gets up in the mornings I really can't be sure he does as I tell him.'

'And you can't change your job? Find something that will enable you to be home when he needs you?'

'I'm not trained for anything. I worked in a factory during the war and when the war ended, being on my own, I stayed on there, making different things, of course, but still with the awkward shifts. I don't have much choice, do I?'

'Your husband?' Sophie asked softly. 'He was a victim of the war?'

'Not him. He lives not two miles away and ignores us completely.'

'How can that be?'

'I had a baby, Bertie. It happened while he was away in the army, and he'll never forgive me.'

The woman left soon after and Sophie sat for a long time thinking about what she had learned, and about Bertie. She'd been surprised to learn that Bertie was only eight, younger than she had imagined. Being allowed to run wild had given him a spurious adulthood and encouraged him to think he was too old to listen to the childish chatter of his classroom friends. After all, he was the man of the house, wasn't he? Poor little love.

It wasn't until later that day that she realized how easily she had got into conversation with the stranger at her door. A few short weeks ago she had been too afraid to say more than the few words necessary to sell her produce. She had changed so much, although the underlying fear of friendships and sharing her tragic history was still there. Would that ever leave her? She looked around her, at the walls of the house and through the windows at the garden and woods beyond, and knew that this was a haven, a place where she could lick her wounds and where, one day, she would recover.

She wondered about the absence of Ryan Treweather and decided that he, too, had simply wanted her to leave but had dealt with her removal in a more kindly manner. Whenever she thought of him she imagined him laughing.

One sunny afternoon she set off to explore the woods across the lane. The ground was muddy and she gathered a stick to use as support when she crossed particularly slippery places. She found the route used by animals crossing the stream, a well-worn path clearly seen. On the branches nearby and on wire fences she found coarse grey hairs and knew she was in the area used by badgers.

The sett was not far inside the trees, and she stood marvelling at its size and wondering if she could find a place to stand and wait for them to emerge one evening. She'd never seen one of the shy creatures and determined to try.

'Don't talk about it, or tell anyone where to find it,' a voice warned, and she turned to see Ryan watching her from the shadows of the trees.

'Hello, I didn't see you there. I'm just exploring my new neighbourhood.'

'You live near here?'

'Of course I do!' She laughed, presuming he was teasing.

'I haven't seen you around before. If we'd met I'd certainly have remembered.' He was frowning and she became alarmed. From his expression he wasn't joking. So why was he pretending not to know her?

'Come on, you helped me to move,' she said, edging away from him. 'You remember that, surely? From Threeways cottage?'

His expression changed, his eyes softening from curiosity into amusement. 'You're the woman who lived in Threeways cottage?'

Still alarmed, she said, 'I am the woman who lived in the cottage, you know that full well, so why the pretence?'

He stepped forward and held out a hand, the smile widening. 'I'm Gareth Treweather, Ryan's twin.' He watched her as realization dawned. Then she tentatively held out her small slim hand. He held it and said, 'I've only seen you from a distance and I thought you were about eighty!'

'Really? Why?'

'You were wrapped in layers of shawls and blankets and you stooped, as though afraid to stare life in the face.'

She was startled by his observation. 'I don't bother much about clothes. And when you travel it's the easiest way to carry them'

'Look, the farmhouse is only five minutes away, come and meet the rest of the family.' Without giving her a chance to refuse he took her arm and guided her through a gate and across a field, beyond which the roof and smoking chimney were just visible over the hill.

Before they reached it, a man appeared, carrying two sticks across his shoulder, to which were tied a dozen rabbits. Sophie shuddered and looked away. The man at once noticed her distress and dropped them to the ground and covered them with his coat.

'Who's this?' he asked, offering a hand.

'I don't know her name but she was living in old Fred Yates's cottage until recently.' Introductions made, Peter Bevan went on his way, to tell his wife he'd met the newcomer to Cwm Derw.

'Peter used to sell from a horse and cart but he's recently opened a fruit and veg shop,' she was told. 'He sells off-ration rabbits and pigeons that he takes from our fields. Rooks, too, when food is short – it helps to feed families.' There was a hint of disapproval in his voice, aware that she hadn't liked the sight of dead animals, and presuming that, like most, she hated the evidence but never refused the food. Death of an animal was treated like murder but most willingly accepted the meat when it was cooked and offered on a plate.

'I never eat meat,' she said. 'I can't bear to look at a beautiful animal and imagine its end.'

'Don't tell my parents. It's how we earn our living.' The criticism was still there.

'There has been so much killing,' she murmured. 'Too much. I can't accept it, not even to help feed families.'

His disapproval was like a cloud settling around them. They walked in silence and she studied him and noted the ever so slight variations. Identical they might be, but to her there was a difference between the easy smile of Ryan and the more serious expression of Gareth. And there was a slight fullness around his face that Ryan lacked.

Ryan and Gareth's parents were in the milking parlour, washing down from the evening milking. Without stopping their work they called a welcome and promised tea if she would give them five minutes – which turned out to be twenty.

Tea was set out on the huge kitchen table, which was dressed with a spotless white cloth and fine china. Sandwiches, cakes and home-made pickles were offered. Sophie admired it all but guessed this was their usual standard and not a show to impress a visitor. She asked about the pickles and explained about her own, sharing a few ideas with the twins' rather serious-looking mother, Rachel. It all sounded friendly, but there was an edge, and she had the idea she was being judged and found wanting. Gareth must have told them about her distaste for meat. Like chalk and cheese, moral vegetarians and farmers could hardly be expected to mix.

'How d'you know our Gareth?' Tommy Treweather asked. 'Not much of a social man, neither is Ryan.'

'Ryan helped me to move my things when I left the cottage called Threeways.'

'We met in the wood and she mistook me for Ryan,' Gareth explained, with a smile similar to that of his twin.

'You lived there? In Fred Yates's cottage?' Tommy glanced at his son, a puzzled expression on his weather-beaten face.

Sophie smiled. 'Yes, I was the person the other farmer told to leave.'

'Good heavens, I thought you were—'

'At least eighty?' she finished for him.

'What's she doing here?' Owen stood in the doorway. 'I thought we'd seen the last of her.'

Sophie stood, pushing back her chair. 'I was invited,' she began anxiously.

'Stop fussing, Owen, and pour yourself a cup of tea,' Tommy said, gesturing for her to sit.

'But what's she doing here? Living like a tramp she was, trespassing, making a mess of the place.'

Rachel lifted the large teapot and thrust it at him. 'More hot water, please Owen,' she said firmly. Turning to Sophie she said, 'Take no notice of him, bad tempered he is, our Owen, but no real harm in him.'

'Where is Ryan?' Sophie asked and when Rachel explained Tommy snorted with obvious disapproval.

'Gone for an interview. He's restless. They both are. The war's been over almost four years and he's still finding it hard to settle.'

'Ryan wants to teach,' Gareth explained, 'and Mam and Dad don't want him to leave the farm.'

'It's been in the family for about six generations,' Tommy added gruffly.

'Long enough,' Gareth muttered, glaring at his father.

Aware of an unfinished argument, Sophie concentrated on finishing her slice of seed-cake. Owen returned with the replenished teapot and Sophie was left with the idea that there was much more to be said. She was aware of a serious disagreement within the family, with Ryan and Gareth on one side, Rachel and Tommy on the other, she thought curiously, and with Owen watching both sides to see where his best interests lay.

When Sophie left, Gareth walking with her to the lane, Owen turned to his aunt and uncle. 'Don't encourage that one,' he warned. 'She'd be no use as a farmer's wife. Soft and frail and I doubt there'll be a good day's work in her.'

'I agree,' Tommy said, pushing the plates away for Rachel to clear and opening the evening newspaper. 'But our Gareth isn't daft. He'll see she isn't the one to marry if he stays on the farm.'

'If he stays,' Rachel said sadly.

'Oh he'll stay, and so will Ryan,' Tommy assured her with false conviction. 'They're just a bit restless, it'll pass.'

'They seem determined to go.'

'Hush your worrying,' Tommy warned.

Owen listened and said nothing.

* * *

56

Peter Bevan went to the shop, where his wife, Hope, was sorting out apples, discarding some and polishing others to replenish the window display. The box containing damaged fruit was full.

'Not enough fat to make pastry,' she told him after a kiss. 'It will have to be stewed apples.' She looked at the large boxful of damaged fruit. 'Stewed apples for ever, by the look of this pile! I'll be glad when we get into the season and the fresh British apples come on sale.'

'If we can find some containers we can give these away. Plenty will be glad of a free treat, even without sugar.'

She carried the worst of the fruit through the shop to the kitchen wastebin while Peter tied the rabbits on a hook beside the shop doorway. 'Did you know there's a new tenant in Badgers Brook?' he asked when she returned with a knife and a pan of water, to which she'd added salt to keep the cut apples from going brown.

'Stella told me. A young woman on her own, I believe.'

'I met her as I walked across the fields.' He laughed. 'Upset about the rabbits, she was, probably one of those vegetarians. She was going to the farm with Gareth – or Ryan. Never could tell which is which of those two.'

Hope had been the most recent tenant of Badgers Brook and she was curious. 'D'you think she might like a few apples? According to Stella, this Sophie Daniels makes chutneys and jams.'

'Be honest, love, it isn't chutneys you're thinking about, it's curiosity. You want to go for a good nose, find out all you can about her.'

'All right,' she said with a laugh, 'I want to go because I'm "nosy", will you come?'

'Of course. I'm nosy too.'

Jason, the horse who was no longer needed to pull the cart, lived in a nearby field. On Wednesday they fitted his head harness and rein and, sitting three-year-old Davy astride him, they walked down the lane then tethered him to the gate where he could crop the sweet grass on the wide verge. Lifting the little boy down, and carrying the best of the damaged fruit, they knocked on the door of Badgers Brook with a strange

57

feeling, having been able to walk straight in only a short while ago. Hope had lived there with her first husband, Ralph, and Davy, and built up a dressmaking business after she was widowed.

Knocking on the door of her one-time home brought her no sensation of regret; she and Peter were very happy together, and Ralph a distant and sad memory.

The door opened at once, the welcoming smile widening as Sophie recognized Peter. 'The man with the rabbits,' she said, inviting them inside.

'You'll no doubt be better pleased with what Hope has brought,' he said, after introducing his wife.

Sophie was delighted with the fruit, offering to pay, telling them she would make some apple and mint jelly. 'I'll save a jar for you,' she promised. She showed them the jars of produce she had made and remarked on the difficulty of finding enough sugar and empty jars. The jars each had a neat label and a covering of gingham. Peter looked thoughtful.

They didn't stay long but later Peter delivered a box filled with empty jars of varying sizes. 'Fill them and I'll sell them,' he said.

She laughed. 'I'd never make enough to supply a shop, but I'll bear the idea in mind.'

'A few will do, to start. Come and talk to us when you're ready.'

Starting a new business was still far from easy, especially when rationed goods were involved. But with perseverance and a polite manner Sophie thought she could persuade people to save their jars for her and even exchange other rationed goods for sugar. She had never used her meat or bacon ration but found it difficult to offer those; it would be condoning the slaughter of animals even though she didn't eat the meat herself.

It wouldn't be a proper business but selling to Hope and Peter would be less time consuming than travelling to the market at Maes Hir, and would perhaps prolong the time before she needed to use the money in the bank. Then she admitted she was pretending. There was hardly any money left in the post office account now she had paid rent and bought her few pieces of furniture.

The jars she took to the shop were each capped with a circle of gingham, some red, some blue and a few green. The shop was busy but only Peter was serving.

'Where's your wife?' she asked in a brief lull.

'Hope has her own business,' he explained. 'A dressmaker she is. Go through if you want a word.' He stared at the jars and added, 'See what Hope thinks of the idea of using the tops as a sort of trademark. Some material that's different from the rest. You never know, a real business could develop and you'll be glad of a recognizable style.'

'I'd like to talk to both of you,' she replied.

'Then if you can wait until one o'clock? I close the shop for lunch then.'

The idea of using her natural skills to try new combinations and sell her own unique recipes was exciting, and perhaps one day she might develop it into a proper business, once rationing finally ended. Meanwhile, she had to find some hours each day to earn money. The rent, the heating and lighting, her daily food, as well as the finances needed to build the business, could never be found out of the small quantities she could make. She had to find work.

Later she went to where the badgers roamed, and sat relaxing with the gentle sounds of the wood surrounding her, going through the possibilities. She had begun to train as a teacher before she had volunteered for the WAAFs. Opening a nursery was a possibility, with more women wanting, and, in many cases, needing, to work, but that didn't marry very easily with her cooking plans. So much preparation was needed to run a nursery successfully that there would be little time for anything else. And Geoff and Connie might not allow it anyway.

She heard someone moving noisily through the trees and waited until Bertie appeared, dusty, covered with dead leaves and dragging a large branch. 'Here, miss, look at this, make a few good logs won't it?'

'Oi, you!' Suddenly Owen appeared and chased the boy off, threatening him with the police if he trespassed there again. Sophie went to run after him but Owen stood in her way.

'Going somewhere?' Owen Treweather stared at her, a deep, disapproving frown on his brow.

She tried to push past him. 'How could you speak to a child like that? Frightening him for simply walking through the trees.'

'He isn't welcome here and neither are you.'

'Am I trespassing too?' she asked. 'I thought the woods allowed public access.'

'I don't like people wandering around. The farm is a dangerous place and too many people wandering about can upset the animals,' he replied.

'It's a pleasant place to sit and daydream,' she said, hoping to ease him out of his aggression.

'Better on your own property I think, don't you?' He took a step towards her, ushering her towards the edge of the trees.

She rose and without another word walked away, aware of him watching her until she went through the gated fence out on to the field. Below her was the three-cornered cottage that had so recently been her home. If she went this way she had a long walk to get home. Perhaps, if she sat a while, he might leave and allow her to slip back through the wood the way she had come.

As she studied the cottage below her, with its damaged roof and sad, forlorn air, she saw the movement of a ragged curtain and realized there was someone inside. She squeezed her eyes almost closed to try to see if there was a vehicle of some kind in the lane, and spotted, almost hidden by the newly clothed hedgerow, an open-topped van. Although she couldn't see anyone, she waved her arms.

Footsteps and a rustling of leaves behind her. Owen was not going to leave until she did, so, taking a chance on seeing someone more friendly, she walked down the steep field towards the cottage. The door opened and a man stepped out.

'Hello, Ryan, are you repairing the place after all?'

'How d'you know I'm Ryan and not Gareth?' he asked curiously. 'Very few people can tell.'

'A difference about the eyes. Gareth's eyes are restless. A more relaxed jaw. Little enough, but you are two separate personalities, aren't you? Identical doesn't mean everything

60

about you is the same. I don't know either of you well, but I think you are happier, more content than your brother. And both of you are far happier than Owen!'

'Would you like a lift back or are you out for a walk?' he asked, obviously pleased with her comments.

'I was out for a walk, intending to sit and think about what I'm to do with my life, but your cousin reminded me that once again I was trespassing.'

'We have to make allowances for Owen. He was hurt and I don't think he'll get over it,' Ryan said. 'It makes him bad tempered and a bit unreasonable.'

'Even so there was no need for him to be harsh with a little boy, was there? He sent Bertie running off with threats of police and prison, would you believe?'

'Sarah is Owen's wife, but Bertie is not his son.'

Sophie digested this, surprised at the relationship between the sour Owen and Bertie's sad mother. 'Poor little boy. Forever in the wrong through no fault of his own.' She wanted to ask what he felt about a little boy being brought up with no one to care for him except a young mother who had to work. But she didn't. Instead, she said, 'About this trespassing: I need to walk through the fields and gather herbs and wild fruits, and mushrooms and flowers. Is there a way I can get permission, so Owen can't turn me back when I walk through your father's fields?'

'Come and ask him. My father, I mean. Come on Sunday afternoon – it's the only time they take a few hours off between feeding the animals and milking the cows.'

She hesitated. 'I'm not happy around farms,' she admitted.

'Much of it is arable. In fact, we grew a few acres of flowers before the war brought a ban. We have cows and a few steers and sheep and the pigs of course. But it's the way of the world and I can't see it ever changing.'

'It changed for me, after seeing so many people slaughtered for so-called honour and duty. Too much killing. I can't take any more.'

'Then you won't come?' He stared at her, his brow creased in a frown. 'Just because you don't agree with what we do to earn our living?'

61

This was another turning point. She could walk away and never see him again or face the fact that his life was raising animals to feed a population of meat-eaters. He would go on doing the same whichever decision she made.

'Thank you,' she said, lowering her head a little. 'I'd love to come.'

Four

When Sophie stepped out of Ryan's van at the gate of Badgers Brook, a small figure stood watching her. 'He's the farmer bloke, isn't he?' he asked.

'Yes, he kindly gave me a lift home.'

'Have you got any cakes in your house? Starvin' I am and Mam's out.'

Ryan had been watching the boy and he reached into his pocket and handed him a shilling. 'Buy yourself some chips,' he said.

Bertie grabbed the shilling and thanked him, then turned to Sophie. 'I'd rather some of your cakes, miss. The shilling will do for tomorrow, I expect she'll be out again then.'

'I haven't seen you for a while. Does that mean you're going to school regularly?'

'Mam said you're tired of me bothering you, miss, so I thought I might as well go.' Sophie smiled and waved to Ryan. 'It seems I have a guest for supper.'

'Don't forget Sunday,' he called as he drove away.

In the kitchen, Bertie dragged a chair towards the sink, climbed up and filled the kettle and placed it on the gas ring ready for her to light. 'I can light the gas, but Mam says I mustn't. So I only do it when she's out.'

Which, Sophie suspected, was most of the time. More than the hours Sarah spent at the factory. She lit the ring and watched as he efficiently set out cups and saucers and plates, then climbed up to the shelf where the cake tin lived. The boy was capable and independent – much more so that a child of his age should be.

'She has to work, see,' Bertie explained, pulling an understanding face. 'That's why she's out so much.'

63

They ate the cakes and Bertie enjoyed several rounds of toast made in front of the fire and covered with home-made apple and ginger jelly. She was careful not to ask too many questions; she didn't want to stop him coming. The only objection his mother had, of her encouraging him to stay away from school, was not valid, and he did appreciate the food she offered. Hungry and lonely were two adjectives that should never apply to childhood, she thought sadly. But in case of criticism she decided to talk to his mother again.

The evening was closing in and it was an excuse to walk him home. This time he didn't object, or pretend the ownership of a new bike, but put on his school coat as she prepared to leave. In the hedge outside he struggled with something, which turned out to be his school satchel.

'Oh, Bertie, what a pity you didn't show me. Have you any of your work in there?'

'Only a pattern I painted. Miss Green was going to put it on the wall, but I took it down.'

'Can you tell me why?'

'Mam wouldn't see it *there*, would she?' he said, as though it were obvious. Sadness overwhelmed her and caused tears to seep into her eyes. He was probably the only one who didn't have a parent visiting the school's exhibition of work.

'Please, Bertie, can I see it? Or would you like your mother to see it first?'

'Mam first, miss,' he replied.

His mother was in and a light shone through the open curtains of the room she rented in Loxton Street. With some hesitation Sophie was invited in.

The room was small and over full. It was as though the move had been accomplished but nothing had been done to make the place into a comfortable home. Although, Sophie conceded, with two people in such a small space, that would have been difficult to achieve even with the best of effort.

Sarah herself looked defeated by life, her expression and the droop of her shoulders showing she had given up trying. Her hair was straggly and in need of washing and a decent cut, her face was shadowed by depression and her voice was low and without energy as she said mournfully, 'Sorry I can't offer tea, but the ration's gone till Friday.'

Sophie didn't know how to reply: with sympathy? Indifference? Or with an attempt to reassure? Bertie answered for her. 'It's all right, Mam, miss gave me tea. Toast and home-made jam *and* cakes. Smashing.'

'Miss?' Sarah queried. 'Are you a teacher then?'

'No. I might have been but for the war. I gave up before I qualified, and joined the WAAFs.'

'There's a vacancy in the school for an assistant. I wish I'd been trained for something.'

'Bertie, show your mother your painting,' Sophie coaxed. Bertie pulled out the bright pattern and offered it to his mother, who looked, smiled, said it was lovely and, far too quickly, put it aside. Sophie felt the child's disappointment even though she didn't look at him.

There was something defeated about the woman and the drab, cluttered little room that made Sophie want to escape. She made her excuses, received an assurance that Sarah had no objection to Bertie visiting, as long as he attended school, and almost ran from the place.

Sarah didn't move for a long time after her visitor had left. This room was too dark and too small for her ever to make into a proper home. She couldn't see a glimmer of hope of an improvement. She'd lost the flat because it had been more than she could afford, and several rooms since because she hadn't paid the rent regularly and had got into arrears.

What a fool she had been to earn the money at the factory and waste it on going out, treating friends in an attempt to forget her unhappiness for a while and buying clothes she never wore. Feeling sorry for herself and neglecting her son. What a dreadful way to live. It had taken the headmistress at Bertie's school to remind her that he needed decent shoes.

She looked at Bertie waiting patiently for her to light the gas ring so they could fry the bit of fish she had bought. 'Bertie, I have to buy you some new shoes,' she said, and was ashamed then angry when his face lit up. 'I can't afford them, we'll have to do without something else, and you'll have to make sure not to scrape them. I won't be able to replace them for a long time. And I'll have to try and buy some clothing coupons as I don't have any left. That's illegal. Costing me a lot of money you are.'

The next afternoon she went and chose new shoes, promising to collect them the following day when she had 'found my mislaid clothing coupons'.

One of the farm vans passed her and regrets welled up inside her. What a fool she had been, giving up a good life at the Treweathers and ending up in a tatty room without a hope of getting out of it.

A group of cyclists stopped then and asked the way to Clements' bed and breakfast, and she pointed the way without stopping. Daphne's next question would have been to enquire about Sophie Daniels, but Sarah hurried on and the chance was gone.

It was few days before Sophie remembered Sarah's mention of the vacancy at the school. At first she shrugged away the idea. She wasn't ready for such commitment, and knew that standing up opposite the curious and lively faces of a couple of dozen children would be difficult – but something convinced her she should try.

She made an appointment to see the headmistress, but her interview was brief once she had explained about her aborted training, and the fact that all her papers had been lost in a bombing raid.

The shake of her head as the headmistress listened convinced Sophie that she wasn't believed. So many families had lost all their papers, so perhaps the excuse had been used by dishonest people and was now automatically met with distrust.

As she stood to leave, she gave the name of the college she had attended together with the dates, and the head agreed to make enquiries. Sophie had the impression she wouldn't bother.

A week later, at the end of June, a letter came offering her the position, to start in September. Better still, she was invited to work two days a week as a temporary class-assistant until the summer term ended. As a trial, she supposed.

She still lacked confidence in her dealings with other people, and, knowing that Owen Treweather disliked her, she was hesitant about visiting the farm uninvited. But she wanted to share her good news with someone and Ryan was the first person she thought of as she held the letter in her hand.

Picking up her basket, planning to gather from the hedgerows as she went, she headed for the farm. She went through the wood, half afraid of being sent back by Owen, and emerged without mishap at the point where she could see the roof and chimneys of the farmhouse. A tractor was working in a field and she watched for a while as the machine changed the colour of the earth to a rich dark brown. She couldn't see from there who was driving so she headed down the hill to the house.

Only the twins' mother was there, making some illegal clotted cream for a special celebration. 'Mr and Mrs Downy's thirty-year-old son is coming out of hospital at last, after a terrible accident. After all this time, an unexploded bomb was unearthed in a field near their house. It went off near him and he almost died,' Rachel explained.

That unkind part of her mind that Sophie tried to deny closed against the joy of the man's recovery. Not everyone had been given a second chance of life, and that reminder made the pain return.

'I called to tell Ryan that I have a job,' she said, trying to push aside her mixed resentment and shame. 'I'm to be an assistant teacher in the school.'

'That's good,' Rachel said at once. Then her face fell as she said, 'Teaching is what Ryan wants to do, but his father and I hope he'll change his mind. If only one of the boys would stay we'd cope, but Ryan wants to teach and Gareth wants to travel. He says the army let him down by keeping him in this country when he'd wanted to see other places. I tell Gareth he's lucky not to have been sent into the worst of the fighting. He might not have lived to see today.'

'You didn't need to be sent into the fighting to lose your tomorrows,' Sophie said, then quickly turned to go before Rachel asked what she meant. 'Would you tell Ryan about my job?'

'As soon as he gets back from town,' Rachel promised. 'I'll tell him about the low wage he could expect as a qualified teacher, too, and the cost of finding a home and everything else, once he leaves the farm where he has everything done for him.' Oh yes, she'd remind him about the job for which he was prepared to put aside generations of the family's history. 'What he needs is a good capable woman who would enjoy the life of a farmer's wife, then he'd change his mind and stay. It only takes the right woman, and that's what Tommy and I are hoping for.'

'It was clear that she was warning me away from Ryan,' Sophie told Kitty later with a grim smile. 'That was as close to a reprimand as she can get without actual rudeness. I've been well and truly told to stay away.'

Walking to school on that first morning, Sophie was filled with trepidation. This community was pushing her along, forcing her into doing things before she was ready. Anxiety almost overwhelmed her as she faced each difficulty, and she always had an urge to run, as she had in the past. But she slept soundly in Badgers Brook and awoke each morning with her latest fears calmed.

Today she would return to a classroom, an environment she had thought never to see again. There would be strangers, curious people asking questions, expecting answers. Inexplicably she wished Ryan had called, congratulated her on the job and wished her well. She would be feeling more confident if he had. His mother must have told him, yet he hadn't been near.

Bertie was waiting at the gate. He was dressed in ill-fitting but clean and well-pressed clothes, his face shining from enthusiastic rubbing with a flannel. He carried a creased paper bag, which she presumed carried his lunch.

'Morning, miss,' he said gruffly, before turning away. She let him go, understanding that he didn't want to bring attention to the fact that he knew her. As he walked away from her a boy ran towards him and bumped into him, causing him to stagger. His paper bag fell on to the ground and he picked it up without a word to the boy, who now stood with a group

68

of his friends, watching Bertie's progress with amusement. Rough play, she thought, nothing more. He was probably too embarrassed by her presence to retaliate.

She spent the morning assisting where she could, enjoying the environment with the enthusiastic six-year-olds and concentrating on learning their names. At play time she was asked to stay in the yard and 'keep an eye'.

She saw Bertie knocked over by the same boy who had pushed him before school, and ran across to him. Bertie refused her help, rubbing his bloodied knee with a dirty handkerchief. She didn't insist, although she did ask one of the teachers to look at it.

Dinner time was an opportunity to visit the shops. She was coming out of the bakery with a lunchtime snack when she almost bumped into Ryan, avoiding him by staggering against the shop window.

'Oh,' she said with a laugh, 'this is worse than the playground.'

'The playground?' he asked.

'I started working in the school this morning,' she explained. 'Didn't your mother tell you?'

'No, I expect she forgot. We're very busy just now.'

'I went to the farm as soon as I got the letter. I took it to show you, but you weren't in.'

'I didn't know you were a teacher.'

'I'm not, quite. I gave up before the final exam when I decided to help the war effort. I was in the WAAFs for a couple of years.'

'I've applied for a place in college for October but I haven't heard yet.

'Good luck,' she said warmly, but a part of her was disappointed at the thought of him going away. They were hardly close, especially since Rachel's lecture on her unsuitability, but he had played a part in her decision to settle in Cwm Derw, and she felt let down that he was leaving before she felt safe and secure.

She went back into the shop with Ryan so he could buy some lunch, and they sat together in the small park in the centre of the town to eat.

69

They were walking out when Bertie ran past, his face red with the effort, his socks around his ankles, bruises and dried blood on his skinny legs. Sophie wanted to follow him, but she had to get back to school. 'I'll talk to him there,' she said anxiously.

Bertie didn't attend school that afternoon. She learned that there had been another incident in the playground and he'd been upset, but had refused to explain what had happened. It was obvious he was being bullied.

When school ended Sophie stared out at the group of parents waiting to collect their children and she panicked. She couldn't walk through them; it had been difficult enough coping with the few staff and the children – but this! She hadn't thought of the curious faces all watching her or whispering together, sharing the little they knew about her. She turned away and escaped through the back entrance across the playing field. Ryan was waiting in the van, and, catching sight of her at the gate, he drove round and offered her a lift.

He saw at once that she was tearful but didn't comment. He chatted casually to fill the silence and allowed her to recover.

'I'm not going home,' she told him eventually. 'I want to talk to Bertie.'

They found him on the street near his one-roomed home, sitting on the curb, throwing stones down a drain. He wore his old shoes, which lacked laces. 'They call me bastard,' he said after much persuasion.

'D'you know what that means?' Sophie asked.

'No, but I know it's something horrible from the way they say it.'

'It might be, but it doesn't apply to you, so try and ignore it.'

He looked up the street and stood up. 'Mam's coming, she'll yell at me for missing school again.'

Sarah Grange came closer and, to Sophie's surprise, Ryan moved away and got into the van. Sarah began to run, shouting, 'You might well hide, Ryan Treweather. Coward that you are. Get away from us. Leave the boy alone!' She reached the van and hit it with the umbrella she carried, then turned to Sophie. 'You too. Stay away from us, d'you hear? Bertie's nothing to do with any of you.' She grabbed the frightened boy by his lapel and half dragged him into the house, slamming the door behind them then drawing the curtains. They heard her shouting, then all went quiet. 'D'you think he's all right? What on earth was that about? 'Do you know her?'

'Of course I know her. It's so long since I saw her I just didn't know Bertie was her son.' His voice was low, and he looked startled.

Sophie waited beside the van, looking at his shocked face through the driver's window, waiting for an explanation.

'Get in and I'll tell you the full unhappy story,' he said.

He drove to the lane near the cottage where she had once lived and stopped the engine. 'We lived here, in the farm-house, when Gareth and I were small. Then, when the new house was built, Owen lived here with his wife. During the war he went away for three months to train landgirls in some of the skills needed for farm work, although most of them just arrived at the farms and learned on the job.'

Sophie waited patiently for the threads of the story to connect with Sarah and Bertie.

'His wife had a child and it was absolutely without doubt that he wasn't the father. Dates didn't add up, you see. She left, but in fairness to Owen I don't think he forced her to. She found herself a flat. Apart from a minimum payment paid monthly, he's had nothing at all to do with her since.'

'So Bertie is legally his son?'

'Well, legally I suppose, but not in fact. Sarah had a fling, an affair, call it what you will, and Bertie was the result. She might have convinced Owen that stories about her having an affair were untrue, nothing more than rumours invented by unkind neighbours, but Bertie arrived, flesh and blood, some-thing that couldn't be hidden or denied.'

'But didn't he try to help the child? Didn't your parents offer help? Bertie isn't the guilty one, he doesn't deserve what's happening to him. Didn't Owen feel at least a moral obligation? "Better or worse, sickness and in health?" That sort of thing?'

'When you're part of a family that can look back over

71

several hundred years . . .' He smiled deprecatingly. 'I know this sounds pompous but to my parents it's a bit like royalty, the pride in the name and the strength of the traditions. They don't feel able to accept someone who bears the name but not the true inheritance.'

'Come on, Ryan! A history going back a couple of hundred years? It must have happened many times before.'

Ignoring the interruption he went on, 'Owen is a member of the family but Bertie is not his son.'

She gave a disapproving groan.

'Mind you, I sometimes think Owen might have forgiven her if it hadn't been for pressure from my parents and his love of the farm and its traditions. All my mother says in response to any thought of meeting the little boy is that Bertie is Sarah's child but not her husband's.'

'And you?' she asked coldly. 'Is this how you feel too?'

'I just went along with it. The problem seemed to belong with Owen, not me. If he'd accepted the child then I would have had no difficulty doing the same.'

'Sarah is not coping well. She's out much of the time, and Bertie seems to feed himself, with the luxury of chips when someone gives him a shilling,' she added, a harshness creeping into her voice. 'He's unhappy in school, a low achiever, and the fact that he has no father is a gift to bullies.'

'I should have done something,' Ryan muttered. 'You make me feel ashamed. I just followed my parents' lead and ignored Sarah and her son – whose name, incidentally, I thought was Alfred.'

'Albert,' she corrected softly. 'Named, so he told me, after Queen Victoria's husband.' She glanced at him, saw the solemn expression in his dark eyes as he struggled with his thoughts. 'So what will you do?'

'Talk to Mam and Dad and Gareth first. Then Owen. There must be something to be done that will make the boy's life easier, without embarrassing Owen.'

'Thank you,' she said, lightly touching his arm.

When he left her outside Badgers Brook he called, 'Come again next Sunday and we'll try to involve the family in a discussion.'

72

'How can I?' she said with a light laugh. 'First your cousin forbidding me to walk through the fields and now you mother telling me to stay away in case I'm a bad influence on you!'

'What?'

She ran up the path and into the house before he demanded an explanation. Let him sort it out. After all, Rachel was his mother.

A couple of hours later she was preparing a bowl of wild raspberries she had found near the edge of the wood when there was a knock at the door.

'Come in,' she called, reaching for a tea towel to wipe her sticky fingers. It was Owen. His words were precise and brief.

'Keep out of things that don't concern you.'

'But Bertie does concern me,' she replied quickly, before he could close the door. 'A child brought into the world to be despised and deprived of a normal childhood – how could anyone not be concerned? Every child has a right to be happy.'

'In a perfect world, yes. But when people don't follow the rules of decency others get hurt and there's nothing anyone can do about it!'

She took a deep breath but he was gone before she could continue to argue. She looked out of the kitchen window and saw him hurrying down the path to the lane, the stiffness of his gait showing his anger.

By interfering she had probably made things worse, she surmised sadly. This was confirmed later, when she knocked on the door of Sarah's sad little room and was told loudly to, 'Please, go away!'

A few days later, during which time she had seen nothing of Bertie either at school or at Badgers Brook, she went around again and pushed a note through the door. On it she asked Sarah to please call, promising only to listen, so between them they might work out a way of helping Bertie. She repeated her words on a second note, to Ryan, to which she added a postscript: *Every child has a right to be happy.*

The following Saturday morning a knock heralded Sarah's arrival, and Sophie invited her inside and lit the gas under the kettle. 'Thank you for coming,' she said. 'Isn't Bertie with you?'

'He's outside but won't come in.'

'Then will you take a few biscuits? He can eat them outside, boys of that age are always hungry, aren't they?'

Obediently Sarah took the proffered plate and went out to call her son, who took the honey and lemon biscuits and sat on the step to eat them.

'What's all this to do with you?' Sarah demanded. 'Five minutes you've been here and there you are, trying to solve everyone's problems—'

'The truth is, I'm trying to solve my own.'

'What are you talking about?' The anger was still there, but Sarah looked at her with curiosity.

'I had a bad war, and I found it difficult to settle. Coming here, finding this place calmed me. It seemed to offer a friendly community that would help me to heal. It's worked better than I'd hoped, and here I am, "only five minutes in the place", and working at the school, making friends and . . . getting into trouble.' She smiled then, and she saw the young woman relax, the stiffness leaving her face. 'So now,' she added, 'I have to find a way of putting right my stupid mistakes.'

'Not stupid, you just didn't have all the facts.'

'Will you tell me, so I don't rush in like a fool again?'

'There's nothing to add to what Ryan told you. I was married to Owen and I had a child.'

'It can't be that simple. Did you love him, this other man? Did he walk away from your predicament?'

'I sent him away, when I realized my mistake. It was Owen I loved. Believe it or not I still do. The other man was only an adventure, a stupid, childish need for danger and illicit fun. It was only later that I realized I was carrying his child, and then it was too late.' She looked towards the door, checking Bertie wasn't there, and added quietly, 'I did think of getting rid of him, but I couldn't, even though it would have saved me all this misery. I love him, even though I don't always show it.'

Sophie heard the kettle spitting angrily, demanding to be attended to, but she didn't dare look away from Sarah, knowing there was more to come.

'I refused to see Owen when he came back after the three

months, and I left the old farmhouse and found a rather nice flat – which I quickly realized I couldn't afford. I didn't give him a chance to understand or forgive as he might have done. He's basically a decent and kindly man. We were married, and there would have been no gossip. I thought my parents would help me, but they were unsympathetic, insisting I went back to Owen, even after I told them about the baby. So, here I am, struggling to survive and making a poor showing of it. Poor Bertie, he doesn't deserve the life I give him.' She stood up, turned off the gas and poured the boiling water into the pot. 'The saddest thing of all is that Owen might have accepted the child, even knowing it wasn't his. He wanted a son so badly, and I've even deprived him of that.'

It was no wonder, Sophie mused, that the man was so ill tempered.

'I promised Bertie new shoes a week ago – even chose them and asked the shop to keep them – but by the time I'd bought some extra coupons I didn't have enough money. I owe a few pounds, you see, and have to pay it back a little each week. Oh, what a mess.'

'I'm good at managing on very little,' Sophie said quietly. 'Will you let me help you?'

'No, I'm almost clear now, just a few pounds to the coalman and the grocer. I'll be able to get the new shoes very soon.'

Betty Connors stood at the door of the Ship and Compass, staring along the road and hoping for a sight of her brother. He was late and there were bottles needing to be brought up from the cellar and a barrel to tap if she wasn't to run out before closing time. Eddie was becoming more and more unreliable these days and she began to wonder if one day he'd forget about his work completely.

With less than an hour to go before opening time, she closed the door behind her and went to the house where Elsie lived. She had never called there before asking if her brother was there and the idea embarrassed her, but she had to have help; she couldn't manage the cellar work and Ed knew this. She heard voices and laughter from inside and imagined him sitting there without a care, while she was frantic to get ready for opening. Irritation made her knock on Elsie's door more loudly than intended.

A second knock was necessary before she heard the sound of someone coming, and she stepped back, trying to decide what to say.

'Betty!' Ed said, surprise and embarrassment written on his face. 'What are you doing here?'

'Looking for you, of course!'

'You haven't the right, banging on the door like a debt collector! People will talk and—'

'How d'you think I'm going to get the pub ready? We're opening in less than an hour.'

'I'm just coming, but don't knock at the front door again, Elsie doesn't like it.'

'Elsie doesn't like it? Pity for her!' she snapped and turned to walk back down the road to the pub, where already Mr Francis and a couple of others were leaning on the wall, patiently waiting for opening time.

She was relieved when Ed followed a few minutes later but irritated when he avoided speaking to her. 'It's you who let me down, so why am I having the dirty looks?' she demanded.

'Elsie's a respectable widow and she doesn't want people gossiping. You knocking at the door like that, hauling me out like an intruder.'

'Plenty of people are already gossiping, mainly because of you sneaking in the back way instead of using the front door,' she hissed in reply. She knew things were more likely to get worse than better and wondered what to do about it. The pub was hers but Ed had helped her ever since she'd been widowed many years before, and she didn't know how she'd cope if the argument developed into an estrangement. She also knew they couldn't carry on like this.

On Sunday afternoon Sophie was hesitant about visiting the Treweathers' farm. The situation with Bertie and Sarah was making her uncomfortable. Rachel's attitude hadn't helped, either. The thought of seeing Ryan decided her. To confirm her decision, Gareth called for her, and, failing cheerfully in his attempt to convince her he was Ryan, explained that his brother had been delayed

To her relief there were others in the big living room beside the family. She heard the buzz of lively conversation before she opened the door.

Geoff and Connie were there, with Stella and Colin from the post office, Kitty and Bob Jennings, and a few others unknown to her.

Rachel greeted her and introduced her to the others. 'Betty Connors from the Ship and Compass, enjoying a little relaxation on her day off,' was the first.

'Between cleaning and doing the books and making out the orders,' Betty added with a smile, 'and we're already friends. Are you settling in at Badgers Brook?'

'I couldn't be happier,' Sophie replied. 'I've already made some good friends and I feel that the house welcomes me every time I return.' She moved closer and whispered, 'Is this a party?'

The reason for the gathering was the wedding anniversary of Rachel and Tommy. Ryan and Gareth had also invited some friends. A few cards stood on the table near the window and Sophie was relieved that she had brought with her a small gift.

'I didn't know this was a special occasion,' she said, 'but I brought you this.' She handed Rachel a jar of crab-apple jelly, ruby red and glowing like a jewel as she held it up to the light. 'Last year's, but I'm sure it will be all right,' she added.

She accepted a drink of cider and sipped it warily; it tasted very strong, not the sweet variety she had expected. Looking around the crowded room she was surprised not to see Owen. Perhaps, being a farm, there was work to be done, and there were few hours during which they could be idle.

'Will you come and help me carry in another tray of sandwiches?' Rachel asked, and Sophie thankfully put down the drink with which she had been struggling and followed her into the kitchen.

'Congratulations, Mrs Treweather,' Sophie said, picking up a tray and removing the white tea towel covering its contents.

'Thirty years married and working together is something to celebrate, isn't it?'

'Not everyone is so fortunate,' Rachel replied, staring at her as though there was more to say. Sophie rested the tray on a corner of the table and waited apprehensively. 'Owen, for instance.'

'I'm sorry about Bertie, but I had no idea that he was related to Owen. I didn't mean to interfere.'

'I know, but I think it best if you stay away from him, in fact, better you stay clear from all the Treweather family.'

'But . . . surely we can remain friends?'

'All right, I'll be honest with you. Tommy and I need for the boys to stay here, working the farm, carrying on from us one day. You aren't farmer's wife material, and if Ryan marries someone like you he'll leave. As I told you before, we think that if he marries the right person, someone strong, hard-working and determined, there's a chance of us getting our wish. Owen married the wrong girl and see where that ended.'

Sophie's face was rosy with shock and embarrassment. 'I don't know why you're saying this. I've seen Ryan about half a dozen times, and I've only lived in Cwm Derw since April! Less than three months, and not a hint of anything more than friendliness between us. So don't be afraid of me, Mrs Treweather. I have no desire to marry anyone and certainly not a farmer. Rearing animals for slaughter is something I'd never cope with. Never.' She put the tray more firmly on to the table and, without waiting to find her coat, ran from the house.

It was raining, fine, warm summer rain, but she was unaware of it as she ran up the hill towards the wood. Panting with the effort, sobs interfering with her breathing as she ran, she stood and leaned against the smooth trunk of a beech and allowed her breath to return to normal. Then, more slowly, she walked on, across the stream and into the lane. Parked outside the house was a muddy van. Ryan had come to find her.

'Why did you run off in such a hurry?' he asked as he got out of the van, carrying her coat and basket.

'Your mother made it clear that I was unwelcome at a

gathering of friends,' she said, snatching her belongings. 'Now please excuse me but I have some art work to prepare for school tomorrow.'

Ignoring her words he followed her to the door and into the kitchen. He said nothing, just watching her as she coaxed the fire into life by lifting the coals with a poker then filled the kettle and slammed it on to the gas stove, her every movement an indication of her anger. She pointedly put out one cup and saucer, but he reached up and took down a second.

'And the cider tasted disgusting!' she said at last and heard him chuckle.

'I don't know what Mam said to you, but you were there as my guest and I'm very sorry if you weren't made welcome. I couldn't call for you as I had to collect a couple of ancient aunts and then I was busy topping up drinks. I'm afraid I didn't give you the attention I should. I forgot many of the guests would be strangers.'

'I knew a few,' she admitted. 'And I was enjoying it once I got talking to a few people, but your mother made it clear I shouldn't be there. So I left.'

'Without finishing your cider?' he teased. The kettle boiled and she filled the teapot. 'I'm sorry, I really am,' he said, turning her to face him.

'All right, it wasn't your fault. It was a nice idea – arranging the afternoon for your parents, and inviting me, although you might have told me it was a celebration!'

He held up in arms in mock surrender. Then reached out and pulled her gently towards him. Without hesitation she relaxed against him and they didn't move for a while, each afraid of what might happen next. He sensed the need for caution, knowing he could harm a growing affection if he rushed her, so he eased away, touched the side of her forehead with his lips. Shyness made her say foolishly, 'I think our tea is getting cold.'

'Still better than Dad's cider, eh?'

He didn't stay long. They were both edgy, aware of each other, knowing that things would never go back to how they had been, and wondering where their growing feelings for each other would take them.

79

Sophie knew she could never cope with the killings on a farm, no matter how valuable and essential that way of life might be. Ryan was kind and gentle, and she knew there might come a day when she could entrust her future to him with utter confidence, but not now, while he worked on the family farm. But if she became involved, seriously involved, at a time when he was considering leaving the farm and behind him, would he one day regret it? Or even go back, expecting her to go with him?

As on so many previous occasions over the past four years she had the impulse to run away, move on before she became strangled with confusion. She felt an attraction for Ryan as she had for no other man; even her love for Geoffrey had had a desperation about it: there had been a need for comfort and the promise of a future during those awful days. But she had to consider Ryan's circumstances.

She stood up and walked around the large kitchen. What was she thinking of? They had only ever spent a few hours together, and touching her forehead with his lips wasn't a kiss, so why was she galloping so far ahead?

Stella and Colin called an hour later, followed by Kitty and Bob. 'Worried we were,' Stella told her. 'One minute you were there pretending to drink that strong cider and the next you were gone.'

'Thought it had done for you!' Colin said with a chuckle. 'Two barrels every year Tommy buys, thrives on the stuff. I don't mind a drop or two myself, mind.'

The last visitor that day was Betty Connors, but she didn't stay, seeming satisfied when she saw that Sophie was unharmed. 'Call and have a cup of tea one afternoon,' she called as she walked back down the path to the lane. 'Usually there after lunchtime closing.'

Sophie stacked the dishes from her visitors and went out for a walk. She needed to clear her head, and that was nothing to do with the cider. She had to admit to herself that the thought of marrying Ryan, of spending the rest of her life with him, had been occupying her thoughts all afternoon, but she had to stop herself thinking about him as though they were more than friends. Anything else would lead to disappointment,

80

and she'd had enough of that. 'Not even casual friends,' she reminded herself, muttering the words aloud. 'Strangers we are and nothing more.'

Betty went home and planned a quiet hour listening to the wireless. She went in and changed into more comfortable clothes and settled in her favourite chair. Ed would be in later for his supper but there was an hour or so before she need worry. She picked up the Sunday papers and began to read. Sundays were the only days when the place wasn't open, but she would still be busy with all the things she couldn't do during the week. Having the invitation to the Treweathers' tea party had decided her to take the whole day off.

She heard the back door open and guessed it was Ed. He was early. Damn, now she'd have to get up and make him tea. He usually stayed at Elsie Clements' place till seven.

'Betty?' he called, then came in and, with an outstretched arm, gestured for her to remain seated. 'I have something to tell you,' he said, and she sat up straight; it sounded serious.

'What's wrong?'

'Nothing. In fact, everything's right. The fact is, Elsie and I want to get married, and I'll be going to live there. She has a few rooms she rents out from time to time and she'll be glad of my help with the maintenance of the house and all that.'

'Like I've been, you mean?' Betty said, her voice choked with shock. 'You're leaving me to cope and going to help Elsie?'

'We're getting married,' he repeated.

'Congratulations,' she said, her voice making the word sound like a reprimand. 'And when is this to be?'

'End of the month.'

'What? And how d'you expect me to find someone else in a couple of weeks? Besides, don't the banns have to be called three times?'

'They were called in Elsie's church last Sunday and again today. I'll still work here for a few weeks, do the usual hours, I just won't be living here, that's all. Just till you find someone.' He spoke quickly, hoping she wouldn't pick up on the fact that he hadn't told her earlier. But she did!

'So you could have told me earlier?'

'Well, yes, but I found it hard to say the words.'

'Making it harder for me to find someone!'

'Sorry, Betty, but it's a chance for a little happiness, and Elsie's a fine woman. I'm very lucky, you must see that.'

'Of course, and I am pleased for you. I just wished I'd been told sooner, that's all. Bring her here tomorrow evening and we can tell everyone and have a bit of a do.'

'Thanks, Betty.'

She stood up and hugged him. 'Good luck, Eddie, I'm sure you're doing the right thing.'

'Pity she hasn't got a brother, eh?

'Yes, a man with muscles like Popeye and the temperament of a saint.'

She didn't sleep much that night, aware of her brother in the next bedroom and imagining living in the old, creaky building completely alone. She had to find someone, and quickly. Common sense meant she needed a man to do all the work Ed had been doing and who'd be willing to live in. Not an easy position to fill. She needed to feel safe, and that wouldn't be possible with a stranger. Her mind sifted through the possibilities and rejected them all.

As the weather grew warmer still, visitors passed through the town on their way to the local beaches or quiet countryside. A short while after Ed's announcement, three young women stopped and parked their vehicles not far from the post office, looking around them for a likely place to eat.

The sight of the café with its crowded tables seemed hopeful, and they went inside but groaned when they saw the queue and how slowly it was moving. One of the women, tall, confident and obviously in charge, loudly demanded of the assistant, 'Is there a fish and chip shop near?'

'Gwennie Flint's, just around the corner,' she was told, and she and her friends trooped out and followed the direction of the girl's pointing finger.

They sat on a seat outside the Ship and Compass and ate their meal. As they were finishing, folding the paper and looking around for a rubbish bin, a huge brewer's delivery lorry arrived and parked nearby. A man got down and knocked on the door, opened it and called, 'Betty? Ed? I'm parked awkward, can you get a move on?' While the delivery man began to unload the crates and boxes and roll barrels expertly towards the cellar doors, the three cyclists heard angry voices from inside.

'Ed, what's the matter with you? You can't leave me to deal with a delivery!'

'I promised and I won't let her down. She's got summer visitors arriving and she wants me there to deal with the luggage.'

'This is ridiculous! You're responsible for dealing with the deliveries. There is no one else. The woman can wait half an hour, can't she?'

'No! "The woman" can't!'

The three cyclists looked at each other, suppressing smiles as Ed walked out of the door, and, without acknowledging the delivery man's greeting, walked jauntily off down the road. Betty came to the door and called, 'Sorry, but you'll have to just leave it out there. One of my regulars will help me later – I hope.'

'Come on, girls, let's see how strong we are.' The tall girl, who appeared to be in charge, waved to Betty and called, 'Don't worry, landlady. WAAF-trained we are, and we'll help with this. Go and open up the cellar for the barrels and we'll carry in the rest, won't we, girls?'

Without waiting for Betty to agree, the tall girl began organizing the delivery. Within less than half an hour the barrels were safely in the cellar and the rest of the crates and boxes were placed where a bemused and grateful Betty directed. When she offered tea and cakes, the tall girl shook her head. 'A shandy and a sandwich would be better, we're still hungry after our fish and chips.' She offered a rather grubby hand. 'I'm Daphne Boyd and these are Gloria and Frieda.'

It was as they were eating the sandwiches that Daphne mentioned Sophie. She didn't hold out much hope, having passed that way earlier in the year, but explained her quest to find her friend.

'We have a newcomer to the village who served in the

WAAFs' she told them, 'Sophie – er – something, her name is. She's moved around a lot, living like a tramp sometimes, I understand, but she seems to have settled in Cwm Derw.'

'Not Sophie Daniels?' Daphne gasped. And when Betty agreed that was correct, she said, 'I've been searching for her for four years. I'd given up hope of finding her. Close friends we once were, but after demob she just disappeared. I've no idea why, so I'd better be careful how I approach her, eh?' With great excitement she wrote down the address and hoped the name wasn't just a coincidence. The quiet girl Betty described certainly didn't sound like the Sophie she had known.

Sophie received very few letters. There was no one in her past who knew where she was living, no one who would bother to write if they had known. So it was with curiosity that she stared at the hand-written envelope that had been pushed through the letter box. She picked it up and studied it, trying to identify the writing, but the rather flamboyant style mystified her. Large, bold and with letters generously flourished with loops and fancy tails. She opened it, took out the good-quality paper and gasped with surprise. Daphne Boyd! How on earth had she managed to find her?

To get this unexpected reminder of her past was exciting but also alarming. She had thought she was safe from anyone she had known finding her. Again there was the almost over-whelming impulse to run away and find somewhere else to hide.

To meet, as Daphne suggested in her note, would mean talking about all that had happened, and that was never going to be easy, however long she delayed. Daphne would be a difficult person to discourage from asking questions. She wasn't the type to take a hint! Perhaps this was another example of how life was pushing her along, forcing her to take strides towards the day she finally opened up and faced the trauma. She sat down and replied straight away, and posted the letter on the way to school before she could change her mind and throw Daphne's letter on to the fire.

They had been such close friends before duties had sepa-rated them. Daphne would have been her bridesmaid if her wedding had gone ahead. She must have wondered why she hadn't kept in touch.

A second letter came from Daphne explaining how she had found Sophie, and asking if she might visit her. A week later they met, Daphne – to Sophie's alarm – arriving with a small suitcase and a request to stay for a few days. 'While I cool off,' she said in her loud, confident voice. 'If I don't get away from home soon, I'll go crazy.'

Everything about Daphne was large. She was almost six feet tall and was no beanpole. She did everything at breakneck speed and spoke loudly without worrying about anyone hearing her, even when she was criticizing someone for being in her way, or being slow doing whatever she had asked. Shop assistants, bus passengers, pedestrians on the crowded pavements – she bustled them along, but in a good-natured way that had them smiling rather than taking offence.

After a brief stay to drink tea and eat a sandwich, she wanted to explore. Striding along, with Sophie giving an occasional hop to keep up, they went to the main road to inspect the shops and café. 'To the post office first,' Daphne said, pushing people aside as she entered the small, crowded shop. 'Keep my place in the queue while I choose a card to send to Mam and Dad.' Ignoring the curious and amused glances, she kept up a running commentary on the card before selecting one of the park. 'You'll have to take me there, Sophie. I must see the place before I send this or it'll be a cheat,' she announced.

'Where d'you find this one?' Stella asked with a sideways nod towards Daphne, as Sophie reached the counter and bought a couple of stamps.

'A friend from long ago,' Sophie replied. 'Daphne Boyd, meet Stella Jones.'

'Bring her to have tea in my country cottage,' Stella invited. 'You know how to find it. I'll be there on Wednesday.'

They walked around, stopping occasionally when Sophie met someone she knew and Daphne insisted on being introduced, then Sophie suggested tea in the café. Daphne pointed to the Ship and Compass. 'Pity the pub isn't open, I could do with something stronger than tea, couldn't you?'

'I have some elderflower champagne at home,' Sophie offered.

'Sounds good to me.'

After they had eaten, and Sophie planned to settle down to read or listen to the wireless, Daphne jumped up, dealt efficiently with the dishes and announced that they would go for a stroll, which meant something different from Sophie's idea of wandering through the wood. Daphne walked briskly along the lanes and roads, asking questions, getting her bearings, working out a different way home from the one Sophie suggested and getting it right.

At her suggestion they explored the allotments to find Stella and Colin's country cottage. Daphne discovered it to be a very well-kept and elaborately painted garden shed. Through the shiny windows they saw it was furnished and had a paraffin stove and a kettle. 'All ready for making tea.' Daphne laughed her rather loud laugh and said, 'I can't wait for Wednesday.'

By bed time Sophie was exhausted. Being alone for most of the time, visitors tired her – the conversation, the feeling of being on duty and not being free to relax and do what she wanted was even harder with the energetic Daphne. Had they really been such friends? If so, which of them had changed? Had she really shared the enthusiasm of this strong character? She must have, so it was she who had changed, the four years alone had taken away her spirit, left her weary and empty. Perhaps a short visit from Daphne was exactly what she needed. If she survived it!

Five

Gareth came off the phone to find his mother standing near, staring at him with disapproval on her face.

'Brian Powell again?' she asked.

'Yes, Mam, and you might as well know, we are considering buying a place together. He and his wife are selling their house and I will contribute by getting a loan, and I've found a job to pay it back. Right?'

'I can't understand why you have to leave here. For heaven's sake grow up, stop this nonsense about travelling and moving away and take up your responsibilities here. There's everything you want right here. How can you walk away from what we've built up? We've done it for you and Ryan and you can't let us down like this.'

Gareth stood while she became more and more angry, her voice rising, her eyes filled with frustration. When she paused he said simply, 'Mam, it's all arranged. You must advertise for some help. Whatever you say, I'm leaving.'

The door opened and Tommy walked in with Owen behind him.

'What's going on? he demanded.

'It's me, Dad. I've just told Mam that I'm going into partnership with Brian Powell and his wife. And before you start, it's all arranged and you won't change my mind.'

Without turning around Tommy said gruffly, 'Go away, Owen. This is family business.'

Owen left and closed the door, but he didn't go far; he stood listening as the three of them ranted, all shouting at once, each insisting they would be heard, their voices getting out of control. When he heard footsteps coming towards the door he darted around the corner of the house and hid in one of the barns. He was smiling. This disagreement and Gareth's determination to leave was heaven sent. It would take Rachel and Tommy's mind away from what he was doing.

Later that day, he transferred a small amount of money into the new account he had opened in the name of George Treweather, George being his middle name.

Bertie walked through the lane and entered the wood, wandering aimlessly, killing time, knowing his mother wouldn't be home for at least another hour. He climbed to the top of an oak tree, imagining himself on a ship in a stormy sea, then slid to the ground, unaware of losing a button from his coat. The sound of a pigeon flapping its way through the branches startled him, then he used the sound to pretend he was being chased by a dragon. He ran across the ivy-covered ground and squeezed himself into the hollowed-out trunk of an ancient ash, pretending to fight off an enemy with a stick. After a moment or two he stayed still, as the spurious excitement faded. Games weren't much fun without companions and his friends were all home eating their tea and chatting to their families. When it was time to get out, he found he couldn't move. He was stuck.

He struggled for a while, then began calling, shouting, then sobbing as no one came. He lost all sense of time but he was dreadfully hungry and thought he would be dead before morning. Intermittently shouting then quietly sobbing, he was silent when he heard the sound of someone coming. At once he began shouting again and a man appeared, a dog at his side, a gun broken over his arm.

'Hush,' he said, 'you're frightening the pigeons away.' But he didn't sound angry.

'I'm stuck,' Bertie said, trying not to sob.

'Take off your coat, that will help,' the man said. Carefully and with infinite patience the man helped him to free himself – a leg, an arm and gradually the rest of him popped out – then he asked the boy where he lived.

'With my mam,' Bertie replied.

'All right, who is your mam?'

'Sarah Grange. She'll be home by now so I'd better run.'

He turned and ran off, dragging his sorry-looking coat behind him, his feet slipping in the too-large shoes. Tommy Treweather watched him thoughtfully until he was out of sight. Sarah's son, so dirty and unkempt he hadn't recognized him. What a disgrace Sarah had turned out to be. Ruining her marriage and not even caring for the innocent reason for it. Such a shame Owen was so pig-headed. The boy couldn't have much of a life living with his mother; the last he'd heard they were living in one room. If Owen had been more forgiving the boy could have had the freedom of all the space he needed and a family, the feeling of belonging at Treweathers' farm. And the farm was in need of young blood – even if it wasn't Treweather blood.

Perhaps he ought to have a word with Sarah. If they happened to bump into each other. He needn't tell Owen, just a quiet word with Sarah when an opportunity offered, to see if she needed help.

Poor little boy. He hadn't thought of him overmuch lately, and if he thought of him at all it was to imagine him as the baby who'd been born by mistake and ruined lives. Now, seeing the unkempt child wandering with no one who cared enough to worry about where he was and if he was safe, he felt a creeping shame.

An hour later he decided not to wait any longer in the hope of accidentally meeting Sarah, but to go and find her. More guilt, as he realized he didn't even know where they lived. He'd simply followed Owen's lead and put Sarah and her child out of his mind. He went to Stella Jones at the post office; she'd know where they lived. Everyone used the post office for one thing or another.

The house, when he found it, was a disappointment. It looked shabby, with ill-fitting curtains and unwashed windows. The garden was filled with clutter: abandoned and broken toys, a bicycle red with rust and missing a wheel, paper strewn on bushes where wind and rain had reduced it to pulp, even a few clothes piled up and forgotten, covered with leaves and rotting away. There was no reply to his knocking and he went away, frowning and wondering what he should do about it.

89

Bertie had been hiding, convinced the man had come to complain to his mother about his being in the woods. He didn't come out until the van had driven away.

Tommy went next to the school, in case Bertie was hiding his absences by pretending to come out of school at the right time. He smiled as he remembered Gareth doing just that when he became obsessed with fishing. The school was closed and there was no one hanging around the gates.

He knew Sophie had befriended the boy and went to Badgers Brook, but again there was no one in. Anxious now, he went back to make sure the boy hadn't returned home, then drove back into town and stopped a young woman walking with two small children.

'Try the café,' she suggested. 'That's where you'll find her for sure.' He remembered then having seen her there on more than one occasion.

He spotted her in a corner, with teas and cakes on the table in front of her, talking to friends, factory girls by the look of them, turbans on their heads, overalls visible beneath their coats.

Anger towards her and sympathy for a neglected little boy boiled over. He pushed through the door and put both huge, brawny hands on the table beside her. 'At last! Looking for you, I've been.'

She tried to stand up, startled at his sudden appearance and the fury of his expression. 'I've just found your son, in the woods, stuck and in danger, while you're here idling time that should be spent with him!' He didn't lower his voice, but leaned lower on the table she was sharing and spoke loudly, his anger increasing. 'Get home and look after the boy. It isn't his fault you made a mess of your life!' Unaware of the faces turned to stare, furious at the woman's stupidity and thoughtlessness, he stormed out and drove off in the mud-spattered farm van.

Without another word, Sarah ran out of the café and headed for home. Tommy Treweather was right; she was neglecting her son. He was the only person who needed her in the whole world and she was treating him with complete disregard.

He wasn't there. Deeply frightened, she walked around,

90

calling his name, searching in wider and wider circles, sobs threatening. She found him at Badgers Brook, where Sophie and Daphne had washed him and were mending his coat and feeding him with beans on toast.

'Come on, Bertie, thank these kind ladies for looking after you, but I'm here now and I'll take care you.' He muttered a polite 'thank you', and followed his mother out.

'Perhaps this time she means it,' Sophie whispered to Daphne, without conviction.

At school over the next few days Bertie avoided her, and Sophie knew that it was from embarrassment at his mother's behaviour. She spoke to him but didn't encourage conversation; he'd come to her when he was ready. He spent playtimes and dinner hours sitting on the wall near the gate and looking along the road. She knew he was keeping out of the way of the boys who tormented him, and wondered what he was thinking, guessing he was wishing that a previously unknown uncle or a grandad, or even a dad, might miraculously appear, to love him and make life better.

Walking through the curious mothers who waited at the gate after school was still a dread for Sophie, with the fear that they would attempt to begin a conversation and ask the inevitable questions. Her heart raced as she pushed her way through them with her head down. Sometimes, when she couldn't face them, she would wait, talking to the cleaners, until they were gone.

Today she looked out and to her relief saw Daphne waiting for her to go to Stella and Colin's country cottage. She was grateful for the excuse to ignore the other women. She ran through, apologizing but not stopping, as though dashing through a field of dangerous animals. She was breathless when she reached Daphne and hurried her away from the gates and the curious glances.

As they walked, Bertie passed by, and she asked, 'We're going to see Mr Jones's allotment, want to come? I know they'd love to see you.'

He shook his head and ran off.

The shed was open when they arrived at the field, and Stella and Colin were sitting outside on folding chairs, sipping tea. Beside them on a neatly set small table were plates filled with biscuits and a few small cakes and some sandwiches.

'Oh, good, you've come,' Stella called out when she saw them. Within moments she had poured teas and provided plates and instructed them to 'Help yourself, there's always plenty.'

They discussed Colin's neat plot and, having some experience from her father's garden and the time she had lived in Badgers Brook, Sophie made the right comments and Daphne asked all the right questions. They also admired the 'cottage', Daphne flattering the woman, complimentary about her imaginative efforts. Sophie was impressed at the way Daphne coped with strangers. She was talking to Colin like an old friend and even offered to come and help when he was doing his autumn digging. 'So you can teach me the proper way to turn the soil,' she added.

Although pleased to see her friend so easy with the people she met, Sophie began to wonder whether Daphne would ever leave. The original invitation, for two or three days, had stretched past the weekend and halfway through the next week and she was still making no move to return home.

'The trouble is,' Daphne explained when she broached the subject, 'I'm bored out of my mind. Returning home and going back to the office where I dealt with allocations of foodstuff was interesting enough for a time, but now, having travelled, seen other places and met new people, I feel trapped. So I've decided to leave. I've written to telling them of my intention, and I'm hoping they'll agree to my working out my notice during the holiday. It will only mean going back for a week if they don't, and I wasn't that good,' she admitted with her loud laugh. 'I just can't go back to everything I've left, everyone expecting me to settle back in again.'

'It was the opposite for me,' Sophie explained. 'No chance for me to settle back into how things were before. I came back to nothing and no one.'

'Hardly no one, surely?' Daphne asked curiously, but her words were ignored.

'I needed a base,' Sophie went on, 'and I think I've found it here. But I don't think Cwm Derw offers what you need.

It's hardly a place of variety, of excitement. Boredom is never far away.'

'Would you mind if I gave it a try?' Daphne asked and at once added, 'Not here, sharing your home. But if I could find a place to stay, would you find my presence an intrusion? Please tell me, I prefer people to be straight.'

'I'd love it if you were near, so we could meet and share some time together, but no, you're right about my not wanting you to live here. I need the solitude. Besides, I'd have to ask my landlord, and Geoff might not approve of my inviting someone to share.'

'Betty Connors wants someone to live in at the Ship and Compass. Just company through the nights, no work. So I'd have to find a job, and pay her rent. Shall I go and talk to her?'

'What a good idea!'

Betty agreed immediately and, with relief and some regret, Sophie waved goodbye to her visitor and settled back into her quiet days.

The garden was producing an amazing amount of food, and, although the arrangement was for Bob to work it and take all he grew, he was generous with Sophie, leaving vegetables and salad stuff on the doorstep for her most days. On the days she wasn't at school, she helped, finding pleasure in working the ground and nurturing the new growth.

On Saturdays Bertie began to appear again, and Bob gave him some simple tasks, enjoying the boy's growing interest.

'Tell him a thing once and he's got it for ever,' he said one late evening, as Bertie ran off home, clutching some young carrots and a sixpence. 'He seems to have a great interest in the land. Such a pity he hasn't grown up on the farm, eh?'

'Life isn't always fair.'

'A father who doesn't even know of his existence and a mother who's too unhappy to cope. What chance does he have to grow into a well-adjusted man?'

'A better one with you taking an interest, Bob,' Sophie told him. 'The saddest thing is that I have the feeling Owen would have been happier, too, if he'd accepted him and been a father to the boy.'

'Too late now though.'

To Sophie's surprise Sarah called to see her a few days later and asked for her help.

'I'll do anything I can,' Sophie promised, wondering what was to come.

'It's Bertie. I've made a career of self-pity and I've neglected him. He needs more than I'm giving him and I want to change things, so I can improve our lives. Working in the factory and spending so much time away from him has become such a habit, I've hardly been aware of how cruel I've been.'

'Not cruel! Don't be so hard on yourself. You've tried to do what's best for him. He knows you love him.'

'I've tried to make a fresh start several times. Moving to a cheaper room was always done with the intention of saving, getting us somewhere decent. But I seem incapable of managing however low the rent. I borrow and still owe arrears on the bills. I don't know why it happens, but this time I want to get it right, The room is awful and Bertie deserves better.'

'He understands, even though he's only a child.'

'But he'd like to run home from school and find me waiting for him?'

'Of course. He wouldn't call on me if you were there, believe me.'

'All this time I've earned a good wage, but I've wasted it being sorry for myself, going to the pictures, buying clothes I don't need, meeting friends for a good moan, you know what I mean.'

'We can all fall into that trap,' Sophie said with a comforting smile. 'So, what's the plan?'

'I saw an advertisement for a part-time sales assistant at the dress shop and wondered whether I should apply.'

'Have you worked in a shop before?'

'Oh yes. I was a manageress before I married. Not dresses, mind, but selling is selling, and I was quite good at it.'

'What did you sell?'

Sarah looked a bit embarrassed. 'Pots and pans, kitchen goods, in a department store,' she said with a grin.

'Well, selling is selling,' Sophie agreed with a laugh, and Sarah joined in.

Sophie stared at her. In some inexplicable way the decision to leave the factory and work fewer hours so she could take better care of her son had changed Sarah. It was as though she had stepped out of the shadows. She looked younger and far more attractive: the smile had eased away the frown lines, her hair was freshly washed and shinning like gold. Perhaps, like Bertie, she had needed to know someone cared enough to help. The little Sophie had done, and perhaps the intervention of Tommy, had been enough.

They talked about the possibilities for a while, and Sophie promised to be there whenever she was needed. 'Between us we can make sure Bertie is safe,' she said, brushing aside Sarah's thanks. 'I'll be at the school, at least for a while, so I'll be in a perfect situation to keep an eye on him, although, like you, I feel the need for something to change.'

'Go back and finish your training then.' Sarah laughed again, relishing the friendliness of this quiet, gentle woman. Then, her eyes shining with merriment, she added, 'Oh, just listen to me! Talk about cheek! The thing is, I feel so different about everything, I feel I can solve everyone's problems as well as my own.'

'Good luck at the dress shop,' Sophie said.

Sarah dressed with care on the day she was to see Nerys Bowen, the owner of the dress shop. She looked with dismay at her wardrobe, which lived in boxes pushed under the bed. She had bought so many garments that were completely unsuitable. How could she have been so stupid, and for so long? She borrowed the householder's iron and set it on the fire to heat, having chosen a pink blouse and a floral dirndl skirt. She also ironed two of Bertie's shirts and wished she'd spent money on buying him something decent instead of second-hand clothes that were never a good fit. But her eyes were opened now and things would be different from today.

She hid her anxiety and, exuding confidence, she breezed her way through the questions with ease. Nerys Bowen seemed content with her replies and laughed with her when she cheerfully told her she had previously sold saucepans. It was clear the two women would work well together and Sarah was told straight away that the job was hers.

She told Nerys about being a mother on her own and quickly explained that she was no honourable war widow but a woman separated from her husband because of her own stupidity.

'Do the job and that part of your life is your own business,' Nerys said.

'Bertie will be pleased I won't have to leave him on his own so much. Factory hours have been hard on him.'

'A boy needs his mother,' Nerys said softly.

And a father, too, Sarah thought, but she didn't speak the words aloud. It was too late for that.

The subject of their conversation ran home and burst in through the door, telling his mother about his latest gift. 'Real carrots, grown in Sophie's garden,' he called, then his voice fell away as he saw that the room was empty.

He washed the carrots under the tap in the shared kitchen and chomped his way through them as he sat and waited for his mother to return. He heard her humming a favourite tune as she came in, adding words occasionally: 'Sing a song of sunbeams, let the notes fall where they may, la, la la, la la, la, Oh it's such a lovely day.' She added her own words, as she often did. 'Hello, Bertie, where have you been?'

'Sitting waiting for you,' he replied grumpily.

'I'm glad you're here. I've news for you. I'm leaving the factory and the awful hours spent away from you, my darling boy, and I've got a new job. Isn't that great? No more awkward shifts. I'll be here when you come home from school. What about that, then?'

'What job?' he asked huffily.

'A dress shop, would you believe? I'll have to spend a bit on clothes – I wasted so much on things I'll never wear. I can't wear my usual old stuff, it won't be hidden by an overall any more.'

'Can I have those shoes?'

'Yes, with this week's wages, and that's a promise.'

'Anything to eat?' he asked.

'Not much, love, but once I get us sorted we'll be fine.'

'Will we be able to move from here?'

'One day. One day soon. I'll be earning less but I'll manage on what I earn and put aside what – what goes into the bank for us – and before you know it we'll be rich enough to move to somewhere with a garden. We might even have a dog, what about that, eh? I've really made up my mind. You'll see.' She didn't tell him she had also agreed to clean the floors and brass in Betty Connors's public house. It would be hard and would mean being out of the house almost as much as before, although at more reasonable times, but they'd need the money if she really was going to make things better for them both. And she would. 'This time I've really made up my mind,' she repeated firmly.

They went to the shop on Saturday morning and bought the new shoes for Bertie. Unthinkingly, she moaned all the way home about how expensive they were, and how buying them had prevented her paying off the arrears owed to the coalman and milkman. He felt so guilty it was hard not to cry.

At school on Monday morning he was teased about his shoes, and on the way home he slipped into a muddy ditch with water up to his knees. When he got home he took them off and put them in the hearth, washed his feet as well as he could in cold water, and sat waiting for Sarah to come home.

She was about to shout and rage at his stupidity but a glance at the over-filled boxes protruding from under the bed reminded her how much she had wasted. She handed him the ration book and said, 'You go to the shop and get a tin of soup and I'll try to clean them up, OK?'

Feeling the need to tell her estranged family about her change of occupation and determination to improve her life, she went to the farm after walking Bertie to school one morning. As she had hoped, Owen wasn't there. Only Rachel, sorting out some overalls that needed repair, and Tommy, who could be heard swishing water through the milking sheds some distance away.

'What d'you want, Sarah?' Rachel asked without warmth.

'I wanted to tell you I've left the factory and intend to be at home when Bertie comes home from school. Tommy found him in the woods one day and it made me realize I needed to be home more than I have been. Tell him, will you?'

'I'll give Mr Treweather your message,' she replied pointedly. 'And if you've come to ask for more money from Owen, you'll have to see him about it.'

'I have a job. Two, in fact. And although both together they won't pay as much as I earned at the factory, I'll cope. Tommy made me realize how I've neglected my son, and I won't make that mistake again. Tell him, will you?' She turned from the door – obviously she wasn't going to be invited inside.

'Come in, if you've time,' Rachel called and, surprised, Sarah stopped, a harsh remark at the tip of her tongue. Then she saw the expression on Rachel's face and held it in check.

'Five minutes,' she replied; she didn't want to appear grateful.

The heavy kettle was always simmering on the edge of the fire on the large oven range, and Rachel slid it closer to the heat. When it boiled she tilted it to fill the teapot. Sarah sat in silence as tea was poured and a slab of cake cut into slices.

'I've found a job in Nerys Bowen's shop, part time, so I'll be there for Bertie a bit more,' she said when Rachel sat in the large armchair close to the fire.

'Selling clothes? But you haven't had any experience.'

'I've sold saucepans.'

At last, a hint of a smile. 'Different sales patter needed then?'

'I'll learn. And I'm also cleaning in the Ship and Compass a couple of mornings, while Bertie's at school. I'll have to think of some arrangement for school holidays, but Sophie at Badgers Brook has promised to help.'

'Do you have to do both jobs?'

'Of course. As I said, even with the two jobs I won't be earning as much as the factory work, but looking back I'm ashamed of how much I wasted. I'll have to be more careful if I'm to get us out of that sad little room to somewhere better. Bertie deserves it and I'm determined to find somewhere before the year is out.'

'I wish you luck.' It wasn't said unkindly and Sarah thanked her. 'Your son, he's well, is he?'

98

'Physically he's fine, but I don't think he's happy. The children at school tease him. Having no father is a heaven-sent gift for bullies, and he hasn't been dressed as well as he should be. My fault, all of it.' She stood to leave, wondering why she had succumbed to the ever-present need to talk to someone and confessed her failings to the very person she shouldn't, who would never ever see her point of view or feel even the slightest sympathy.

To her surprise, Rachel stood and helped her on with her coat. Keeping her hand on Sarah's shoulder, holding her there a moment longer, she said, 'Owen was dreadfully hurt by what happened while he was away, and he was too stubborn to forget. And you didn't help, mind, running away before giving him a chance. No one need have known if he'd been able to accept it. Believe it or not, Sarah, I tried to persuade him to reconsider his rejection of the boy. He isn't Bertie's father, and nothing will change that, but I pointed out that he is half yours, and that won't change either.'

'Thank you,' Sarah whispered as she hurried through the door, fearful now of seeing Owen, or even Tommy, and being warned once again to stay away.

Elsie and Ed's wedding had not taken place. Twice the service had been arranged but each time Elsie had been unwell and it had been cancelled. Ed spent a lot of time at the B&B, and Daphne slipped into the role of Betty's assistant. After going back to work her week's notice, which her boss had insisted upon, she had found work in the offices of a garage and had bought herself a car, which she offered to Betty for occasions when Ed was using his car, to which Betty had previously had access.

Settling in the town of Cwm Derw and living in a public house was something that amazed her sometimes. When she wrote her weekly letter to her mother and told her what had happened during the week it all sounded so dull, yet she had never been happier. The only disappointment was the departure of Gareth Treweather. She had begun to imagine that they might become close one day.

*   *   *

99

Learning that Sarah had left the factory and its beguilingly high wages made Sophie consider her own situation. She had enough money to live on, and she earned a little making her preserves, but looking ahead, she knew it wouldn't be enough.

Everyone was getting settled and it was time she did the same. But what could she do? Returning to college and completing her training seemed so long term; she wanted something now. Ideas drifted through her mind but none stayed. The school seemed the right place for the moment.

She had her base; Badgers Brook had welcomed her like a much-loved, secure haven, but there had to be somewhere outside where she would felt needed and useful. She enjoyed the hours she spent in school and it was there she would stay until something more enticing appeared.

Owen came in from the fields where he had been checking on the sheep and heard loud, angry voices coming from the parlour. He stopped, calling back the dogs, who had followed him into the kitchen, and, shutting them outside, closed the door as silently as he could, without fastening the latch. Then he crept into the hall and close to the parlour door to listen.

'I thought now Gareth had gone you'd stay. You can't really be planning to leave us without help? Owen and a couple of untrained boys, that's no way to run a farm. It's a family business, you've always understood that. You can't walk away from your birthright.'

'But you've known for months what I've been planning!' Ryan said, his voice loud with exasperation. 'I'm leaving to train as a teacher. I realized while I was in the forces that farming isn't what I want to do with the rest of my life. Rearing animals and sending them off to be killed – there has to be a better way.'

'It's that girl. Those are her words. She's confused you,' Rachel said.

Ignoring the remark Ryan turned to his father and said, 'Look, I'll be away during the week but home most weekends. I'll do what I can to help then, but that's all I can promise, right?'

'Don't bother!' Tommy shouted. 'If you can't be here during

the week, you're no use to us. If you go you can stay away all together.'

'Tommy!' Rachel's softer voice pleaded. 'Don't say things you'll regret.'

'Regret? I regret that the boys came back when the war ended and made us believe everything would go back to normal. That's what I regret!'

'Oh, why don't you sell up?' Ryan shouted. 'Building land is in demand at the moment, so take the money and enjoy a few years of ease.'

'I might just do that.'

'Good.'

'Tomorrow I'll see about getting the place surveyed and valued. Right? Why should we work all the hours of daylight just for you to inherit it all when you don't care. Tomorrow I'll start things moving. Your home, your inheritance, will go on the market. How d'you feel about that, eh?'

'It's fine, Dad. Sell up, buy a small place and use the money for you and Mam to have a good time. It really will be for the best.'

'You wouldn't get anything out of it, mind, so don't think you will. Any money will go to charity. No one in this family deserves anything – your heart isn't here so why should you benefit?'

'Just enjoy it, spend it all. Gareth and I can make our own way.'

'Don't talk rubbish,' Rachel interrupted softly, her face creased with distress.

Tommy stood up and glared at her. 'I'm not the one talking rubbish. Look to your sons if you want to listen to rubbish, giving up on everything we've worked for, keeping it going through the war, and for what? Two useless, ungrateful—'

'It's a waste of time talking to you,' Owen heard Ryan say. Then he heard the scuffle of feet on the wooden floor and moved swiftly towards the back door. He rattled the latch loudly, and, calling the dogs waiting outside, walked through the kitchen and into the hall again.

'Anyone home?' he called. He had to move to one side as Ryan left the parlour, pushing past him, hardly aware he was there, his eyes staring straight ahead, glazed with anger. 'What's happened?' Owen asked, going in to see his aunt and uncle staring at the door through which Ryan had just stormed out.

'Nothing,' Tommy snapped. 'Nothing to do with you.'

Owen looked away, trying to ignore his uncle's angry words. He forced a smile and looked at Rachel for an explanation.

'Just another spat between your uncle and our Ryan,' was all she said.

'Come on, it's more than that, surely?'

'Oh go away, Owen, it isn't any of your business,' Tommy snapped. 'Have you checked the hedges at the top of the field near the power pylon?'

'Not yet, I thought I'd have a cup of tea first.'

'Go and do it then, will you?'

Rachel led him out. 'Best you go, this isn't the time to talk to him. Come for your dinner at one, all right?'

'If it's to do with the farm, shouldn't I be told what's going on?'

'Nothing's going on, just an argument, that's all.' She hushed away his protests, insisting it wasn't anything that concerned him, and he went out, carrying the gun without which he rarely went on to the hill, and stormed up to where the pylon stood like a giant meccano toy. He half-heartedly checked the hedge, marking with string the areas that might need attention, then sat on the bank and looked around him.

This land was as much his as Gareth and Ryan's, yet they talked about selling without even discussing it with him. As he sat listening to skylarks singing their summery songs and the contented sound of sheep chewing the sweet green grass close by he calmed down. Perhaps thinking of selling this beautiful place was nothing more than momentary madness, a way of adding force to an argument, fuelling a bitterness that was intended to hurt. Well it certainly hurt me, he thought.

One of the routines of running the farm was to have a weekly discussion, where grievances could be sorted, and problems solved. To Owen's chagrin, many other meetings took place to which he was not invited. Perhaps he might bring up the idea of selling at the next meeting he attended,

102

pretend he'd heard a rumour in the town. That would be easily believed. Rumours grew like mushrooms but lasted longer. He might even start one himself; that wouldn't be difficult, either.

The following day he went to the post office. The queue was often out into the pavement, especially on pensions day, but today it waggled its way down past the row of houses and around into a side lane.

'What's going on?' he asked a young woman hurrying out of the shop carrying a few small packages.

'Sweets are going on ration again on the fourteenth and Stella is selling all she has before the restrictions start.'

'But they only came off ration in April.'

'Too many greedy people with plenty of money, I suppose,' the young woman said as she hurried off.

Owen went into the café and sat nursing a cup of tea, hoping the queue would soon disappear. To his embarrassment, he saw Sarah coming in. He didn't recognize her at first, used to seeing her only rarely and then dressed shabbily in overalls, her hair untidy after being fastened in a scarf or safety hat from the factory. Today she was dressed in a pretty summer dress and talking animatedly to Nerys Bowen from the dress shop. His stomach jerked with what could only be jealousy as he wondered if she had found a man friend for whom it was worth making an effort.

Leaving his tea unfinished, he waited until Sarah and Nerys were busy studying the menu and sidled out. The queue at the post office had dispersed and he went in and asked for a postal order to send off for some ex-army boots that he hoped would be suitable for the autumn days to come. He looked at Stella and gave a half-hearted laugh. 'I'm amazed at the gossip that this town comes up with.'

'I'm not, nothing surprises me any more,' Stella said, handing him his purchases. Her eyes brightened as she asked, 'Come on, what's the latest then?'

'I've heard from two sources that my aunt and uncle have agreed to sell Treweather Farm for a company to build an estate of houses.'

'Never!'

'Two different people asked me if it's true.'

'And is it?'

'If it was I daren't tell you, Mrs Jones. Rumours can do so much harm, can't they?' He left the shop, and when he glanced back inside Stella was already on the telephone, her eyes brighter than ever.

When he reached the farmhouse, a meal was almost ready and Rachel, red faced from the heat of the fire, was placing the last of the serving dishes on the huge table, where a silent Ryan and Tommy sat. Owen went to wash his hands and when he returned the tableau hadn't moved.

'I heard a stupid rumour this morning,' he said brightly. 'Someone reckons Treweather Farm is up for sale to one of these firms who build dozens of houses all close together like in towns. As if anyone would want to live in a place like that. Daft, eh?'

In silence, Ryan and Tommy began to eat.

When it was time for Ryan to leave, he was still not speaking to his father. He had hoped to have a party, invite some of his friends for a cheerful send-off before attending the summer school where he would 'sit in' on lessons and prepare for college that autumn. But the atmosphere in the house made that impossible, so instead he invited Sophie out to a restaurant a little way out of town.

Just before the time he'd arranged to call for her, he went to get the van, but it wasn't there.

'Owen?' he called, running up the stairs to where Owen slept.

Owen opened his door and when Ryan asked where the van had been parked he said, 'It's at the garage. Your father said there was an oil leak or something. Why, did you need it? I thought you'd be too busy packing to need it today.'

'I was taking Sophie out. Now I'll have to cancel.'

'Buses?' Owen said with slight sarcasm.

'I'll cut through the wood.'

'Not in those shoes, I hope? Or that suit. Demob suit, isn't it?'

Giving no reply, Ryan hurriedly changed into wellingtons

and a donkey jacket and, carrying his shoes, walked up the hill and through the wood into the lane.

'Why don't we stay here?' Sophie suggested when he had explained. 'I have soup, my cheese ration, fruit, some home-made bread and even a bottle of last year's elderflower champagne. It's too soon for this year's bottling.'

'It sounds perfect,' he said, kissing her lightly on the cheek. He was aware of her pulling away from even that most inno-cent of salutes and felt chastened. And disappointed. He had hoped to reach an understanding with her before leaving; the promise of having her to return to whenever he had a free few days.

'Dad and I have seriously quarrelled,' he told her later as they sat in the garden and sipped the delicious wine as the day cooled. 'I won't be going home in my free time.' He felt her start. Surely she wasn't expecting him to ask if he might stay there?

'I've arranged to stay at Elsie Clements's guest-house,' he went on. 'Perhaps we can meet when I come back, and get to the restaurant I booked, eh?'

'That would be lovely. I hope you enjoy the work and meeting new people. It will be very different from the semi-isolation of the farm.'

He stood, believing he could hear beneath the words a gentle dismissal. 'I'll write and let you now how I get on, shall I?'

'Please, Ryan. I'd like that.'

She was edgy, and when he leaned forward to kiss her she backed away again. Embarrassed he picked up his wellingtons and old jacket and carried them, not wanting to stay and change in her presence.

She had seemed friendly, almost affectionate, but as soon as he had moved close she'd been afraid. Unsettled, he walked through the woodland for a long time before going back to the farm.

The next morning he left, Owen insisting he was unable to give him a lift, and, not willing to ask his father, he ordered a taxi. When he turned back to wave, only Owen was there to see him off, and he was smiling with what appeared to be delight at his departure.

Six

Sophie felt strangely bereft knowing Ryan had gone. There was embarrassment, too, remembering the way she had behaved, shrinking away from what must only have been a polite, friendly kiss, a farewell, a promise to keep in touch. What was the matter with her that she was so afraid of getting too close that she acted like a child?

She kept busy, trying to wipe out the fear of a lifetime of loneliness that was of her own making. How could she miss him? They hardly knew each other, and he hadn't written, so he must have forgotten her once he made new friends among the students.

The weather was warm but with a threat of showers, and to cool off after a few hours working in the garden she took her basket and walked through the woods. The clouds darkened the air, and when she came out above the old farmhouse she hesitated, wondering whether to go down or head back home. Tempted by the possibility of some wild strawberries she went down.

The rain when it came was fast and furious, hitting the dusty ground like tiny arrows and making her run towards the farmhouse. To her surprise the door opened under her gentle push, and she went inside.

'Who's there?' a voice called, and, looking up, Sophie saw Sarah coming down the stairs smiling a welcome. 'Are you sheltering from the rain too?'

The rain brought its chill and they stood at the door clutching their cardigans around them, watching as the ground gradually became covered with water, creating a stream that headed for the lane.

'You used to live here, didn't you?' Sophie said. 'Are you reliving old memories?'

'It's hard for you to imagine Owen being anything but ill-tempered and solitary, but he wasn't like that then. We were happy, until I messed everything up.'

'We can usually overcome the consequences of our mistakes, but it was difficult in your case. If you'd talked about it you might have sorted things out.'

'You've seen how he is with Bertie. And having suffered too, you'd think he'd at least be understanding towards the boy, even if he never forgave me.'

'I thought he was a cousin and had lived with Rachel and Tommy all his life. How could he have suffered?'

'They've always treated him the way he behaves towards Bertie, constantly reminding him of his place and the favour he owes them. They exclude him from meetings where decisions are made about the running of the farm and the only responsibility he has is for the accounts, which he takes to the accountant once a month. Even there he's treated with suspicion. Tommy goes through every transaction as though Owen is likely to cheat them.

'When I was with him we treated it as a joke, but after these years alone his resentment is growing. So why doesn't he sympathize with a child in the same situation? If he'd really loved me he would at least have tried.'

Sophie was curious and longing to know more. But Sarah pushed open the door and saw that the summer shower was over. 'Come on,' she said, 'best we go before it starts again – or my dear ex-husband complains about us being here, walking on precious Treweather land.'

At the edge of the wood, a place where he often came to stare down at the place where he'd last been happy, Owen watched the two women leave the house and go their separate ways. Sarah had changed back from the dowdy woman working in the factory, careless about how she looked, into the attractive woman he had married. He stood for a long time after both women had disappeared, wrapped in dreams and memories, before turning and making his solitary way back to the farm.

Sophie had stopped to gather a few of her favourite herbs and picked a saucerful of the tiny wild strawberries growing against the hedge. As she wandered home through the dripping trees she thought about Owen. He was treated by the Treweathers more like a casual labourer than a member of the family, but she hadn't realized how resentment had stirred his temper and aggressive attitude. If he'd had a childhood lacking in warmth, Sarah was right, it should have made him sympathetic to Bertie, who was jeered at, teased and called names he didn't understand. Knowing of his sorry start in life, mothers discouraged their children from playing with him, as though he were tainted by his mother's behaviour. So, seeing the child suffer as he had done, why did Owen show nothing but contempt? Unaware of being watched by the subject of her speculation, she walked home.

Sophie enjoyed helping in the garden, with Bob and occasionally Colin explaining what they were doing, and why. She usually helped with the never-ending task of weeding, sliding the long-handled hoe under the weeds – which she called wild flowers – snapping them as the ground was worked. Bertie was often there, too, especially on Saturdays when Sarah helped at the dress shop. He enjoyed sorting out the dandelions and plantains, ragwort and sow-thistle, pulling at them and occasionally falling backwards as they gave under his determined tugs.

She continued to watch over him at school, although he more or less ignored her there – afraid of teasing, she guessed. She enjoyed working with the children more and more but was still unable to respond to friendly approaches from the teachers and mothers. She tried to analyse how she felt and knew it wasn't lack of confidence, just a determination never to be close enough for the questions to be asked. She couldn't imagine ever being able to talk about the deaths of her family. Except maybe one day with Ryan. The only certain way of ensuring that she did not have to was to avoid more than the most brief and casual conversations. Bertie was an exception – she relaxed in the company of children too young to be aware of the horrors of war.

She was pleased to see that he was dressed better, and his shoes, although no longer smart and new, were at least a good fit. He had 'daps' – the local name for plimsolls – for PT and games and he carried his lunch in a neat box on a shoulder strap that had once been used to carry a gas mask. Even the teasing seemed less unpleasant. His knowledge of wild flowers and birds and the larger creatures of the woodland gave him a little prestige, which the teachers encouraged.

Bertie was walking to Badgers Brook after school one day when the dirty old farm van stopped and Owen offered him a lift. His first instinct was to run, then he said, 'I'm not going home, I'm going to Sophie's.'

'Hop in and I'll take you.'

'No thanks, I expect she'll be walking up the lane to meet me.'

'Tell your mother I'll call and see her, will you?'

'We don't like visitors,' Bertie said firmly. 'There's nowhere for them to sit, see.'

With mixed feelings Owen drove on.

He was waiting outside Nerys's shop at closing time and he opened the van door and called to Sarah. Her hair flowed around her shoulders, a scarf was tied about her head with the ends hanging down on one shoulder and her face was carefully made up. She was wearing a pretty pink summer dress with a second long scarf around her neck. White sandals and a matching handbag, which she had been given by Nerys, added to the perfect outfit for a summer's day. Owen found he was breathless, and his voice dropped to a whisper.

'I'm going your way if you'd like a lift. Badgers Brook?' he added as she hesitated.

She brushed the seat before getting in and he smiled in a surprisingly warm manner as he leaned over and made sure the door was firmly shut. 'I remember how careless you were about car doors,' he said.

He said nothing until they were past the shops and turning into the lane. 'How do you feel about this divorce? he asked, slowing the van and pulling onto the grass verge.

'After all this time it doesn't make much difference, does it? Unless you want to marry – I've heard you and Daphne Boyd are friendly.'

'The trouble is, Sarah, I still consider us to be married.'

109

'You living in utter comfort at the farm and Bertie and me managing in one dreadful little room? I can't say I agree with you. You and I stopped being man and wife when I left and you did nothing to stop me.'

'Would you believe me if I tell you I regret that?'

'No, I wouldn't! After nine years? You must think I'm stupid. What's the real reason for this conversation, Owen?'

'All right, I'll tell you, but you must keep it to yourself.'

She reached for the door handle, preparing to get out. 'I don't want your confidences.'

He touched her arm and held her back, and she stayed, leaning towards the door as stiff and unyielding as a poker, and listened. Bertie came up, obviously intending to meet her, and he ran towards the van.

'Go away, boy, I'm talking to your mother,' Owen said. Bertie stood near the hedge, pulling leaves off and dropping them on the ground.

'There are going to be some changes at Treweather Farm. Neither of the boys wants to carry on and it's likely the place will be sold. When it is I'll be out of a job and a home. I just wondered whether we might make changes all round and try to patch up our marriage instead of going ahead with a divorce. I'll have the money to make a fresh start, somewhere far away from Cwm Derw. What d'you think? Will you think about it?'

Still with her hand on the door, she turned and glared at him. 'I won't have anything to do with a man who could see a small child in such difficulties and do nothing to help him. Knowing your own situation makes it even worse. Your self-absorption has made you evil, and I feel touched by it simply sitting beside you.'

Leaving the door swinging she ran out, hugged Bertie and hurried off down the road, back the way they had come.

As term reached its end, there was a presentation for one of the teachers, who was retiring. The children were at the morning assembly, and when the reading and the hymns finished they were told to wait. Sophie stood near the front row of children and glanced around until she found Bertie.

110

He wore a new blazer and a clean shirt and she smiled with relief. Sarah was certainly doing her best for him now. She half smiled at him when he looked at her but he turned away quickly.

Murmurs and foot shuffling in the room increased as the children became restless; then they were called to order and Miss Evans was invited up on to the stage. There was a brief announcement that Miss Evans was retiring, then the head-mistress made a speech, talking warmly about Miss Evans's contribution to the school and giving her a bunch of flowers and a rhinestone necklace that sparkled and sent colours darting around the wall. When they all trooped out to the rousing sound of a Sousa march, Bertie was watching Sophie, a frown on his face. Why hadn't she been given a necklace?

With both Ryan and Gareth gone, the farm was short of help, even though Tommy had employed a full-time labourer, Harry Sutton. Harry was over sixty and had retired when the farm on which he worked had been sold. Since then he had helped in a kennels a couple of mornings a week and was grateful to be invited to return to the work he knew. Owen worked long hours dealing with everything he could and making sure Tommy knew about it, hoping for praise or at least some credit for the hours he put in. He even helped Rachel prepare the meals, which were simple and not up to the standard of her usual fare.

One warm late-July evening, after a humid and exhausting day, Owen drove down to the main road and went into the Ship and Compass. Daphne was in the bar, helping Betty on occasion, and sitting near the bar when she wasn't needed. Owen sat near her and asked if she would like a drink.

'Cider, please, but not as strong as that stuff your uncle serves,' she said with a groan. 'A headache that lasts twenty-four hours is what that stuff costs.'

She chattered easily and flattered him when he told her that since the boys had gone he was left with a part-timer who had to be told everything and his uncle, who was in a foul temper over the abandonment of his sons.

'Doesn't Tommy pull his weight?' she asked.

'He's in such a mood that I hardly dare speak to him. I just

111

get on and do as much as I can without bothering him.' He deliberately spoke lightly, almost with amusement. He didn't want Daphne to think he did nothing but complain. 'I started at five this morning,' he said as he paid for their drinks, 'and finished an hour ago, after peeling potatoes till they looked like marbles and shelling some peas.'

'I don't suppose I can help, can I? Feed chickens? Count sheep or whatever it is you do with them?' Her eyes were sparkling with humour, then she said more seriously, 'I'd love to help if I can. I don't work at the weekends and I'm at a loss sometimes to fill the time. Even your new man must have a day off. As you can see, I'm no fragile flower.' She stood up and stretched to her full height. He remembered that she topped him by several inches, and guessed that in weight, too, she was superior, but it didn't matter. What was important was how well they connected in attitude and humour.

He found her easy to talk to, and they were both unaware of the locals in the crowded bar nodding in their direction, nudging each other and smiling knowingly.

When he invited her to come to the farm and see what was being done, she accepted.

'Would you like to come?' she asked Sophie later, but Sophie shook her head. 'Best I stay away. I was never Rachel's favourite person,' she added with a wry laugh. 'In fact, she blames me for Ryan leaving. As if I could influence him! Nothing more than friends, and hardly that. I only saw him a few times.' She gave away her disappointment by adding, 'He hasn't even bothered to write.'

'Have you?'

'Well, no.'

'Idiot!' was the retort.

After that first visit, when she impressed Rachel by the way she dealt with dishes and helped prepare food as though she'd lived there all her life, Daphne went whenever she had a few hours to spare. She walked around the fields with Owen, holding posts while barbed wire was fixed; she fed hens, gathering and washing their eggs, hardly needing to be told what was necessary; she watched and learned and loved it.

* * *

112

Bertie turned up at Badgers Brook after school on the final day of term and offered Sophie an untidily wrapped package. 'What's this? A present for your mam? Is it her birthday?'

'No, miss, it's for you, a leaving present because you left school for the holidays. Sorry it's late.'

'But I'm not leaving, I'll be there next term. Who is it from? Did your mother send it?' She thought it might be a thank you for looking after Bertie on Saturdays and was worried, hoping it wasn't too expensive. He looked anxious as she carefully unwrapped it: string, then crumpled brown paper. Nestled in tissue paper was a brooch: flowers made of rhinestones similar to the necklace the school had given to Miss Evans.

'Bertie! It's beautiful, but tell your mother I can't accept it. It's far too expensive. What a lovely, kind thought. I'm thrilled with it, but please, take it back and explain to your mam that I love having you and I don't need anything to thank me for looking after you, will you?'

'It wasn't from Mam, it's from me,' he said, head down, staring at his shoes.

'I don't understand. Where did you get so much money from? It must have cost quite a few shillings.'

'It's my money, my dad sent it.' He called the words as he ran off and Sophie stared at the gift with growing concern. Contact from his father was nothing more than a dream, like his new bicycle had been. She rewrapped it, and, next morning, while Bertie was busy helping Bob and Kitty to paint their fence, she set off for Nerys's dress shop. Better to talk to Sarah without Bertie being around, in case what she suspected was true and he had stolen either the gift or the money.

Nerys gave Sarah ten minutes to go with her and drink a coffee in the café after Sophie quietly explained what had happened.

'What should I do?' Sarah asked helplessly.

Inside, Sophie felt her muscles tighten. Uninvited came the memory of her persuading her family to stay together under the same roof; that was the advice she had given, breezily confident, and they had all died because of it. A sort of panic filled her as Sarah looked to her for a decision. There would be no advice from her, no slick answers, never again. 'That isn't for me to say. But I'll help if I can. You tell me what you want to do and I'll help, but the decision must be yours.'

'You're a teacher, you tell me.' Sarah's eyes were filling with tears.

'Think about it, talk to your friends, but don't be hard on him. He's just a child.'

She handed Sarah the brooch and saw her flinch as she gripped it, locking it into her hand, her fingers white with pressure. 'I could kill him, the idiot. Stealing! Why did he do such a stupid thing? And for you. Not me – his mother – but you!'

Sophie started with shock, the hint of accusation making her heart race with a guilt she knew she didn't deserve. 'Take it home and talk to him.' She didn't dare say more, although she wanted to tell Sarah to hug the child, tell him she wasn't angry, just concerned because she loved him. The faces of her dead family ran across her mind. Her advice might lead to worse trouble and she couldn't take the responsibility.

Knowing that her friend Daphne was seeing a lot of Owen, Sophie told her about the brooch and the mystery of where Bertie had found the money to buy it, hoping she would mention it to Owen. She doubted that he would care, but perhaps, just perhaps, he might try to help. Sarah was on her own and had to face the various problems that arose in dealing with Bertie with little money and without any support.

Owen's response surprised Daphne. Having so recently been told he was evil by Sarah had been a shock that wouldn't leave him, and Daphne could see he was upset. She knew that Bertie was not his child, but, after lunch, he led her to a barn and, sitting beside her on hay bales, told her the full story. 'The worst part was Sarah leaving without giving me a chance to consider what we should do. I hated the gossip and being a joke, a husband who had been cheated on. If she had stayed, well, I might have decided it was better to keep the child, easier to bear than ridicule, d'you understand?'

Daphne touched his hand and nodded.

'And now,' he said, 'knowing there won't be any second chances, I'm going to see a solicitor about a divorce. It seems

114

the sensible thing to do, tie up all the ends, make our long separation a permanent one in the eyes of the law, giving us both our freedom to build a life again.' He looked at her, his eyes mysterious in the shaded light of the barn. 'Then I intend to restart my life, begin to live again after almost nine years of teetering on the edge.'

'And Bertie?'

His voice was harsh as he replied, 'He's never been my responsibility. Sarah walked away taking the child with her without a moment's discussion, making it quite clear that I wasn't involved. Nothing has changed there. I couldn't help, even if I wanted to.'

'And do you want to?'

'I might have once, but not any more.'

Daphne waited, knowing from his tense expression that there was more he wanted to say.

'D'you know, Daphne, although I've lived with my aunt and uncle since I was about five, I'm still an outsider, treated with little more respect than a casual labourer. When I offer suggestions about the farm, like adding land drains to give us better fields, or the best position for a new barn, I'm ignored.'

She reached out and put her hand over his and he muttered, 'Thanks for listening. I don't usually complain. My father left me when I was a child and I should be grateful for them giving me a home.'

'You were without a father? Like Bertie?'

'No, not like Bertie! My circumstances were very different.' He stood up and walked away from her and she was furious at her stupidity. Why had she reminded him of Bertie? Now he'd never confide in her again.

It didn't take long for Sarah to discover where Bertie had found the money. She went home, anger building up as she half ran in her eagerness to solve the problem. She grabbed his shoulder and showed him the brooch, held out in a shaking hand, and demanded to know where he'd bought it. She shook him angrily, insisting on answers, and finally he admitted he'd taken five shillings from Kitty and Bob's house and the rest from her own cash box where she kept money for paying the bills.

She turned him over her knee and spanked him, trying to control her fury and dismay, knowing she was in danger of hitting him too hard. He didn't cry, just jumped on to his bed and hid himself under the covers. Sarah left him there and, more slowly, walked back to the dress shop trying to hold back sobs that were more guilt than anger.

She still held the brooch and didn't know what to do with it. Would she get a refund? The bills would have to be paid and Kitty's money returned. There was money in the post office but she hated the thought of using some of her oh so slowly growing savings.

Bertie rose from his cocoon of blankets, his face red and his eyes bright with humiliation and tears. He knew he had been stupid, but, childlike, managed to find someone to blame. He went to Badgers Brook and threw mud and stones at the kitchen window, then leaned on Bob's newly painted fence until something snapped.

Sarah needed to explain her long absence to Nerys, and, when the shop was quiet, she told her exactly what had happened. Aware of the woman's distress, Nerys told her to go at once to the shop where it had been bought and explain. A refund would be the best solution.

After some argument, the item was accepted back and a refund given. While in the same determined mood, Sarah went to see Kitty and Bob. Bob was outside examining the fence, which had a broken support. They went inside and the five shillings was repaid.

'I won't say anything to the boy,' Bob said. 'He's had his punishment. We don't believe in a child having more than one; a telling off, a smack, a loss of pocket money, no sweets – sometimes people don't know when to stop. A smacking and knowing you're upset is enough. '

'It sounds as though he thought it unfair that Miss Evans had a gift and not Sophie,' Kitty added.

'I'm so sorry, I never dreamed he'd do anything like this.'

'Don't worry, I don't think it will happen again,' Kitty said. 'Our boys stole apples from Treweather Farm a few times, and once they came home with a chicken they insisted was

116

wandering and had followed them home. And there was a favourite library book hidden, which they swore was lost.' It was all said to make Sarah feel better.

Sophie called to see Bertie but, although Sarah coaxed him to speak, he sat on his bed, looking down at his boots, red faced, and refused to move. Sophie was just leaving when there was a knock at the door. With a frown Sarah stood up. 'I hope this isn't more trouble,' she muttered, then Sophie heard her invite someone inside and she stood to leave. It was Owen.

'Hello, Owen, I'm just leaving,' she said, patting Bertie's shoulder as she headed for the door through the over-filled room.

She heard Sarah demand, 'What do *you* want? I didn't think you even knew where we lived.' The door closed behind her then quickly reopened, and Bertie darted out.

She managed to grab him as he passed her and held him. 'Bertie, come back with me, will you?'

'No, miss, I hate you.'

'I don't hate you, you're my best and kindest friend.' But he pulled free and ran off.

Sophie hoped that with the school holidays starting he wouldn't be difficult about her looking after him. Sarah didn't want any problems now she was beginning to sort her life out.

Having coldly discussed with Sarah his intention to seek a divorce, Owen made an appointment with his solicitor for the following Monday. When he explained what he wanted to discuss, Mark Lacy was surprised. 'With Gareth and Ryan leaving the farm, I thought you'd come to discuss selling up. There's a growing demand for building land and it's easier now to get planning permission.'

'We aren't selling. I run the farm and with very little help from Gareth and Ryan. Their leaving has made little differ-ence,' he replied shortly. 'Now, after such a long separation, my divorce shouldn't be a problem, should it?'

'If you're going for adultery, what took you so long? Where is the other man? Who is he, do you know? He'll be difficult

117

if not impossible to find after all these years. He hasn't supported Sarah, has he? If we find him will you demand he pays maintenance? Do we have an address? If he can't be located, you do intend to continue your support for the child, don't you?'

The questions came fast and Owen answered abruptly when he answered at all. 'Just do what you think best. I want to be free again, as soon as possible, right?'

'Is there someone on the scene?' Mark asked encouragingly.

'Maybe, it's too soon to know.'

'Then I wish you good luck, Mr Treweather.' The poor woman will need luck, too, if she marries a misery like you, Mark thought, as he saw Owen out and promised to be in touch.

Sophie was at the hairdresser having her hair cut. Elsie Clements was there, discussing her much delayed wedding with a few friends. She had her hair held in tight waves by the grippers that curved half around her head, and the hairdresser, Lucy Calloway, was arranging curls all around the edges. Weddings being such a popular subject, Sophie was quickly included in the conversation.

It will be our third attempt to tie the knot,' Elsie preened. 'Poor Ed, he's been so patient, and me having to make him wait.' Elsie giggled like an eighteen-year-old.

'I do hope all will be well next time. When is it to be?' Sophie asked.

'Very soon,' Elsie said coyly.

'What was the trouble? one lady asked. 'You look very well at present, so everything should be fine next time.'

'Only a trapped nerve but it was very painful and we didn't want anything to spoil our day.' A young girl came out from behind a screen and handed Elsie a cup of tea. 'Thank you, dear, will you put it down for me?'

'There isn't anywhere handy, Mrs Clements, it isn't very hot.' Ignoring the woman's protests the cup was pushed into Elsie's hand and at once her hands shook and the tea spilled over her knees and on to the floor.

On her way home Sophie saw Brenda Morris, the district nurse. 'Is Mrs Clements still at the hairdressers? I was making my usual call but she isn't at home.'

'Yes, she's just spilled a cup of tea. Such a shame about her problem, isn't it?'

Presuming she was aware of the facts, Brenda said, 'The saddest thing is that it will get progressively worse.'

Shocked, sucked into the secret, Sophie didn't want to embarrass Brenda by making her realize she hadn't known, so she said, 'She's very brave, calling it a trapped nerve.'

'A lot of sufferers try to pretend it isn't happening,' Brenda said. 'She'll need a lot of care and very soon.'

'She does know how serious it is?'

'Of course. I think Eddie Connors must be a saint, don't you?'

'A saint,' Sophie agreed.

Now what should she do? Tell Betty that Elsie was suffering more than a trapped nerve? Worst of all, what if Ed didn't know? Should he be told? Why had she allowed herself to become involved with these kindly neighbours? Why hadn't she stayed outside the community, stayed solitary and lived an uncomplicated life? But when she thought about the years before she had found Cwm Derw she knew she could never go back.

It was when Rachel went to the post office that she first heard the rumours, and Tommy was approached later that day when he called into the Ship and Compass for a lunchtime drink. 'Of course we aren't selling,' was the reply they both gave, but still the story spread. They even had a few enquiries from would-be purchasers. They questioned Owen but he told them to ignore the gossip. 'Because that's all it is, people putting two and two together and presuming that because Ryan and Gareth don't want the farm you'll be selling up. I explained that I'm not going anywhere, and we can cope perfectly well without them.'

'It isn't a case of being without them,' Tommy said sadly. 'It's the continuity. I didn't dream that they wouldn't want to carry on the tradition. Treweathers have been here for so long, I thought we were a permanent fixture.'

119

'I'm here,' Owen said. 'I'm a Treweather. It was *my* grand-father who worked this land. He was my grandfather as well as Ryan's and Gareth's, remember.'

'It isn't the same!' Tommy spoke irritably. 'Father to son, that's how it works. The eldest son taking over. Your father was the youngest and he didn't want to stay. He cleared off years ago and went to America to follow his dream. And died there. It's our sons who we need running the farm, not strangers.'

He was thinking of Harry Sutton and the other casuals, but Owen took it that Tommy was referring to him. He said nothing, but his anger was almost impossible to contain. He stood up and left the room. 'I'll see that the hens are locked in,' he called back.

Even at Maes Hir market, where Rachel and Tommy had gone to pick up supplies, they met the same comments – this time from other local farmers.

'Selling up, I hear. Don't blame you.'

'Kids, eh? They let you down, don't they?'

'What will you do when you sell?'

'Ill health, is it?' And so it went on, making Tommy more and more angry as he described the rumours as rubbish and insisted that, 'Treweathers will be here for generations yet.'

When he could stand no more, he hurried Rachel through the last of her shopping then almost threw the parcels into the van and started the engine.

'Slow down, Tommy,' Rachel warned as he turned a corner dangerously fast.

'Don't you start!' He turned to glare at her. 'Think I'm too old, do you? Unfit to drive?'

'No, but I'd prefer that you look at the road and not try to pick a row with me.'

He pushed the accelerator harder and the trees rushed past, the van swerving on the narrow, winding lane. 'Stop, Tommy! You're not in a fit state to drive. Get out and I'll take over.'

'Take over? Certainly! I'll walk.' He skidded to a stop, his hand on the door ready to open it, and misjudged the bank at the side of the lane. The van tilted and almost rolled over, tipping Rachel out of her seat. The driver's door swung open, and, with the van still moving, Tommy fell out, his leg caught under the scraping metal. Inside the car Rachel's arm was between the seats, and when she moved the pain was intense.

She called to Tommy, who groaned and called for her to fetch help.

'I don't seem able to move,' she replied. They stayed where they were, attempting to free themselves from time to time, but without success. Rachel tried to find out where Tommy was and how badly he was hurt, but he seemed to be numb. The fact that he couldn't move and lacked the desire to try was alarming. She knew her arm must be broken. She couldn't move it, and when she tried the pain was excruciating.

She had no idea how long they were there but at last they heard the sound of an approaching engine and Rachel began to sob with relief. 'It's all right, Tommy, love, someone's coming. You'll be all right now.'

Owen was on the hill with the sheep when he saw the police car driving towards the farm. Whistling for the dog to follow, he hurried down. Tommy and Rachel were in hospital, Tommy with a broken leg and Rachel with a broken arm. His first thought was how he could make use of the situation to further his own plans.

At the hospital he made all the right noises, sympathized with them and promised to keep everything on track while they were away. It wasn't until he was driving back that he began to smile.

Once he had finished the routine work, which he dealt with in remarkably good humour, he went to the Ship and Compass and asked to see Daphne. 'Are you enjoying your job?' he asked peremptorily.

'Not really. A greasy garage isn't really me, but there isn't anything else I want to do at present,' she replied, wondering what was behind the abrupt question.

'Would you consider helping at the farm? Tommy and Rachel are in hospital and I need someone I can rely on to help run things. What d'you say?'

'Can I think about it?'

'No. No time.'

121

'I need to give a week's notice.'

'Not if I talk to your boss and explain my difficulty. I'm sure he'll agree and probably keep your job open for when things get back to normal if I ask him. Well? Will you help?'

She held out her hand, her loud laughter giving him his answer, and he went at once to see her employer and demand her freedom.

Betty was sorry to see her go. 'You're leaving the Ship? I thought you were comfortable here with me?'

'I am, Betty, and as soon as Rachel and Tommy are fit, I'd like to come back.'

'I got used to you being here.'

Daphne thought about it for a while, then said, 'All right, I don't see why I have to sleep at the farm, I can be there in ten minutes. All right if I sleep here and work there? I won't disturb you, getting up at some ridiculous hour, will I?'

'I'll even get up and make you a cup of tea,' Betty offered. She had never slept in a house alone, and, like many people, imagined the emptiness, the silence, and felt afraid.

Owen went to the hospital and again reassured his aunt and uncle that everything was running smoothly. 'Daphne is dealing with the house and the jobs you do, Auntie Rachel, and Harry Sutton and I can manage the rest.'

'It's only until Ryan and Gareth get back. You have written, haven't you?' Tommy demanded.

'Of course and I'll write again now I know exactly what's happening.'

Tommy had a list of instructions and Owen listened and nodded at each item, telling him that everything was being done exactly as he would want. 'You don't have to tell me every little thing, Uncle,' he said, managing a smile. 'Who d'you think's been doing it all these years? We'll manage fine.'

Tommy didn't quite believe him but grunted his thanks. 'I'll be home in a day or so and then I can keep an eye on things,' he muttered.

'No rush, I'm coping perfectly well. I've worked with you all my life, remember.'

He took Daphne with him when he went to see his aunt in the women's ward, and again there was a list of questions and demands. Daphne encouraged laughter, telling Rachel what she had done, admitting a few disasters, asking advice on how to deal with things and making sure Rachel knew she was needed.

'Don't rush to get home,' Owen said, 'I'm sure the place won't fall apart in a few days.'

'I'll be glad when you're back, though, even if it's sitting in a chair and giving instructions,' Daphne added. 'I'm such a duffer when it comes to running a busy house.' Daphne knew she was leaving Rachel feeling content. She was needed, but in the short term she knew Daphne was doing a satisfactory job.

Rachel waved as the two of them left the ward, and her thoughts wandered to Owen's future. He might do worse than place it in the hands of the cheerful, loudly confident Daphne. She was unaware that Owen's thoughts were similar.

In the main street later that day Owen went to the post office, where there was the usual queue of people wanting postal orders for sending off their football pools entries. The shop hadn't reopened after lunch hour and someone was banging on the door and shouting irritably.

Accompanied by Stella's retorts, a lively discussion about who was actually first, and the barking of Stella's dog, Scamp, the bolt was pulled and the postmistress scuttled back behind the counter. 'Next?' she called loudly, as though she had been the one waiting.

Owen waited patiently in line, the two letters he'd written in his hand. He had delayed writing to his cousins for as long as he dared, and altered the addresses slightly to delay them further, although he suspected that Gareth's address was out of date, as he had been travelling. This was a perfect opportunity to show his uncle he didn't need Ryan and Gareth to run the farm. He hoped they wouldn't hurry home, even when they did hear about the accident – which he had played down, avoiding too many details. He needed them all out of the way for a week at least.

As he stepped outside he almost bumped into Sarah. She

was on her way to the dress shop and wore a smart black skirt, a little shorter than was fashionable, and a white blouse that was open at the neck, revealing the swell of her breasts. She wore make-up and her hair had been cleverly cut so it swung round her face, shining like silk. He felt his breathing falter.

'All dressed up, aren't you?' he said, staring at her, a frown on his face in an attempt to hide his admiration. 'Some new man in your life?'

'It's none of your business, Owen. In fact, it stopped being your business years ago. Excuse me, I have to get to work.' She pushed past impatiently, glaring at him with carefully made-up eyes. 'Out of my way, and stop glaring at me!'

The sweetly clean, soapy scent of her startled him with its effect. He didn't walk back to the van, but followed until he saw her step into Nerys's shop. So she had given up the factory and was a shop assistant. It certainly improved her appearance, if not her temper, he thought with a smile.

Every time Owen went to see his aunt and uncle, their first question was whether he had heard from their sons. He spread his arms in a gesture of dismay and promised to write once again. They had asked him to bring notepaper and their addresses, but he conveniently forgot or couldn't find them. By the time they were told they could soon go home, there had still been no contact.

'This accident has been a shock for us both,' Tommy told him. 'It's made us realize the need to get our affairs in order.'

'What d'you mean? You've made a will, haven't you?'

'It needs updating.'

'Don't worry, I'm sure there's no need to bother just yet. It will make you nervous thinking about it. Let it wait.'

'The farm is left equally between Ryan and Gareth, of course. No need to follow the eldest-son rule any longer. There's a good living there for them both.'

Owen hoped the shock didn't show as he nodded and murmured a reply.

'We'll keep it running as you'd wish.'

'Oh, and there'll be something for you, Owen. A plot of

land where you can build yourself a house. You've applied for a divorce and you'll marry one day and make a good life for yourself.'

Owen stumbled from the hospital and, almost unseeing, drove to a small beach. It was almost time for milking and for once he didn't care. Harry was there. Let him do it. He thought about his uncle's words: the farm divided two ways, and he was to have nothing. He'd worked on the place all his life, and much harder than the twins, and he was to be rewarded with a plot of land.

He stared out over a choppy sea where the tide was rushing in on both sides of the small island that was cut off at high tide, with a rocky path allowing access when the water went back. He had often crossed the slippery rocks and spent hours out there fishing when he was younger – until the farm had taken all his spare moments, he thought bitterly. I'm thirty and I've given most of my life to Treweather Farm, and I'm still thought of as no more than a farm labourer.

A plot to build a house. Damn it all, the cows were better thought of. Where would the money come from to build it? A piece of useless land. What thanks was that for all the years? Coldly and calmly he got back into the van to drive home. Although, he muttered angrily, it wasn't a home at all, just accommodation provided with the job. His mind was made up, all doubts gone. They owed him and he was going to take what he deserved.

With luck, Ryan and Gareth wouldn't be home for a while, and if he could persuade his aunt and uncle to go away for a couple of weeks, that might just give him time to do it. If he failed and had to leave, well, he wouldn't lose much, just a piece of land, which was probably useless, anyway! It was a gamble and the possibility of being found out was an added excitement.

A van was approaching down the narrow lane and he waited for it to pass. It was Geoff and his wife. What could they want at this lonely beach?

'Hiya,' Connie called, 'Want a cup of tea and a sandwich? We always come here when we've an hour to spare and there's enough for three in the picnic bag.'

They parked awkwardly so he'd have difficulty passing them, and he stopped and jumped out. 'I hope you don't want me to walk over to the island for it!'

'No fear, we never risk that, even though Geoff says there's plenty of time if you catch the tide right.'

The two men discussed their younger days and the fish they had caught, while Connie set out the food. 'Is there any truth in the rumour that the Treweathers are selling the farm?' Geoff asked.

Owen laughed as though it was a huge joke. 'Nonsense. It'll be left to me and the twins after Tommy's days, won't it? Treweathers will be here for a long time yet.' His laughter was false, his uncle's words ringing mockingly in his ears. He needed to prepare his own inheritance, and the sooner the better.

When Daphne told Sophie about her work at the farm, she asked her if she would like to help. Sophie happily agreed, especially since, as she wasn't yet officially a part of the staff at the school, she was earning no money during the holiday.

'I'll have to bring Bertie, will that be a problem? I've promised to look after him, remember.'

'I don't think Owen would complain. Just come and see what happens. They have to face each other sometime.'

Sophie and Bertie arrived at the farm every morning before eight and she started at once preparing breakfast. Feeding the men with sausages and even bacon once a week was something Sophie found difficult. How could they treat pigs and lambs like pets, admire them, care for them, then eat them? She soon found a way of doing something else, happily leaving the cooking to Daphne. She preferred washing dishes and cleaning muddy floors to watching meat being enjoyed.

She said nothing of her abhorrence to Bertie but noticed that he, too, managed with toast and home-made jams. Perhaps loyally following her lead. He was inclined to copy her and listen to her views, which was why she carefully avoided mentioning it.

Owen worked long hours and Daphne, true to her word, arrived soon after five a.m. and helped with the routine chores before getting breakfast for the men. She was very tired, staying to prepare supper before she left to go back to the pub.

Despite all he had to do, Owen helped when he could, and flattered her frequently, singing her praises in front of Rachel and Tommy.

'What d'you think of the idea of sending my aunt and uncle for a short holiday?' Owen asked Daphne one day. 'Before they get back to work properly, a rest would be a good idea. It's just that I worry about you. I know it's been hard for you these past weeks and I know I'm asking a lot for you to continue for a while longer.'

'Another week wouldn't hurt me. I'm getting over the tiredness – my body's used to the work now. Yes, I think that's a good idea. But can I ask Sophie to continue to help? I don't think I can manage without her.'

'I'll ask her myself,' he promised. 'And thank you, you're a blessing.'

Daphne laughed her loud laugh. 'Never been called that before!'

Bertie was there when he called at Badgers Brook; he could see the boy near the sink obviously standing on a chair, and he almost turned away, but Sophie had seen him coming and called to him as he hesitated.

'I wonder if I can ask a big favour, on Daphne's behalf really.' He stopped a few feet from the open door.

'It sounds intriguing, come in.'

'No, I won't come in, I'm in a hurry and—'

'Oh come inside, Owen. Neither Bertie nor I will bite!'

He stepped in, trying not to look at the boy, who appeared to be washing jam jars.

'I hope to persuade my aunt and uncle to go away for a holiday before getting back to a full day's work. Daphne wondered if you'd consider helping her for a few more weeks. I don't know what she wants you to do, you'll have to discuss it with her.'

'I have to look after Bertie while his mother is working. If he can come too, and he would like to, then, yes, of course I'll help her.'

127

'I'll let her know.' Owen backed out and, still not acknowledging the boy, hurried down the path.

Sophie smiled sadly.

'It's you and me or neither of us, eh, Bertie?'

'Have you got any more jars to wash?' he asked, ignoring the remark.

'Come on, Bertie, let's go and see Daphne, shall we? She might have some cake and a drink of pop.' She saw him hesitate, knowing Owen Treweather didn't like him, but not understanding why. 'Come on, there might be some chickens to feed.'

'You'll be staying with me, won't you?'

'We'll go together and come home together. Unless the bull tosses you over the wood and into the garden!' she teased, handing him his coat.

There had been no letters from Gareth. He hadn't given them a new address, as he was travelling around France. He sent an occasional card but there was no way they could get in touch to tell him about his parents' accident. He had telephoned once but fortunately Owen had answered and made a pretence of a faulty line and not being able to hear.

Owen had been fielding letters from Ryan, opening them, replying with casual reassurances, telling him his parents were well and back on the farm. He said as little as possible apart from telling him there was no need to come home, reminding him how both Rachel and Tommy hated a lot of fuss. He didn't mention Harry Sutton being there or Daphne running the household. When they eventually came home he'd only need a few quiet lies to settle the matter. Misunderstandings happen in the closest of families and the Treweathers could hardly be described as close, when they were going to ignore his contribution and family connections and leave him a useless piece of land.

Seven

Having learned of Elsie's problem, Sophie didn't know what to do. If she repeated it did that make her a gossip? When did genuine concern for Ed Connors become nosy interference? She finally decided to talk to Daphne, who knew Betty well and might have been told something about the truth of the 'trapped nerve'.

'Are you sure that's what this nurse, Brenda Morris, meant?' Daphne asked.

'I mentioned her problem, meaning the trapped nerve, and she presumed I knew more and she said, "The saddest thing is that it will get progressively worse." How could I have misunderstood that?'

Daphne pondered for a moment then said, 'Will you mind if *I* mention it to Betty? Living at the Ship I can more easily mention it casually, perhaps as though repeating words said in jest, hinting that Elsie is the type to leave more and more work to Ed once they are married.'

'That's fine by me. Ed probably knows, but Betty can have a word with the nurse or the doctor if he doesn't. He's entitled to know the truth.'

Betty was upset, convinced that her brother knew nothing about Elsie's illness. 'We don't talk like we used to, him spending so much time at Elsie's B&B, but I'm sure he would have told me something as important as that. What can I do?' Like Sophie, she was afraid of being accused of gossiping or of trying to cause trouble between the couple. Eventually she decided to mention it as though it was common knowledge and note his reaction.

'Pity poor Elsie's hands are so bad, but I expect the doctors will do what they can as time goes by.'

'What d'you mean? A trapped nerve isn't serious and she'll be fine once she's rested it for a week or so longer. I do what I can to save her lifting and carrying. Between us we'll soon have her back to normal.'

'Oh, I see.'

'What d'you see? What are you talking about?'

'I thought it was more serious, something long term. I understood that it wouldn't get better, but in fact might get worse. I was wrong, was I? I misunderstood?'

'Of course you misunderstood! This is a terrible place for gossip. I'm happy and Elsie's happy and that's enough for people to want to spoil it. You as well, although I did expect better from my own sister!'

'This is a place where people care, and I care. I couldn't ignore this and let you walk into a marriage without knowing what you're facing!'

The words became more heated and Eddie eventually stormed out, leaving Betty to deal with the delivery he had promised to help with as Daphne was at the farm.

She was left wishing Daphne had said nothing. She couldn't change anything so wouldn't she have been happier not knowing? Then she admitted that being warned meant she was better armed for when things became difficult. Ed hadn't been very supportive of her since he and Elsie had become close but she would be there for him as she had always been.

Sophie knew that Bertie was excited to be at the farm, even though he was aware that Owen disliked him. Her intention that day was to deal with the kitchen and the cooking while Daphne dealt with the work among the animals and she made sure she said nothing to Bertie to make him hesitate to help wherever he wanted. Her aversions to farming were her own and she had no right to force them on Bertie.

She went to find Owen to ask whether sandwiches and cake would be acceptable for midday, and vegetable soup with fresh bread and some fruit for the evening, and in her haste she accidentally let some young piglets out of the barn.

She expected Bertie to run around in great excitement panicking the little creatures, but to her surprise he followed

Owen's calm approach, and, with the dogs helping, peace was quickly restored.

There was worse to follow, however. The plates she had chosen to use were the best ones, and Owen told her Rachel only brought them out on 'high days and holidays'. 'Heaven help you if you break one,' he warned. Being extra nervous, she did. A plate and a gravy boat, which Owen rather gleefully told her were irreplaceable.

As often happens in a moment of stark drama, she and Daphne couldn't stop laughing and the pieces of china broke into smaller pieces as they tried to fit them together to decide whether they could be repaired. The shattered remnants were put in a drawer until Rachel returned and they would be able to confess.

To her surprise Owen behaved pleasantly towards Bertie, and after the routine work was dealt with walked with him around the fields and explained what was going on. When Bertie came in for lunch, red faced and excited, she could see that the visit was a great success. He ate an enormous meal of sandwiches and cakes, then looked hopefully towards Owen, hoping for an invitation to follow him again. In case he was going to be disappointed, she said, 'Bertie, when we've dealt with the dishes would you like to stay with me? Perhaps we can help Daphne feed the chickens?'

'Oh, miss,' he said in a world-weary tone, 'they was – were – fed ages ago.'

'I'll take him to check on the sheep,' Owen said, cuffing the boy's head and smiling. He shared an amused glance with Daphne and added, 'I think I might need his help counting them.'

The phone rang when they were finishing their meal, and Owen jumped up quickly and pushed away from the table to answer it, but Daphne was there first. Sophie noticed his irritability as he snapped his fingers, demanding to take it from her. Daphne listened, then said, 'It's your Ryan, asking what's the matter, wondering why his mother hasn't written.' She was frowning, turning away and hugging the phone as Owen tried to take it from her.

'Give it to me,' he said, but she held it tightly and listened.

131

Then she said, 'But you must have been told they're both in hospital.' Another frown, then, 'Both hurt in an accident, yes . . . Hardly trivial! Your mother has broken an arm and . . . Yes, a broken leg . . . Yes, of course. I'll hand you over.'

At last Owen was able to take the phone.

'I was . . . No *you* listen, Ryan! I was thinking of you. We thought you'd worry and come home and there's no need, everything is running perfectly smoothly here.' He listened for a while, then, glaring at Daphne as though his secrecy was her fault, replaced the receiver on its hook and walked out.

Bertie watched him go and said, 'He forgot me, didn't he?'

'He's worried, Bertie. Maybe he'll come back later.'

Half an hour later the telephone rang again and Ryan told Daphne he was coming home at the weekend. Sophie felt a tense excitement when she was told, then reminded herself that he hadn't written and it was his parents he was coming to see. When Owen was informed, he went straight to the hospital for the afternoon visit.

'Uncle Tommy,' he announced, 'I've spoken to the doctor and arranged for you and Auntie Rachel to go to Tenby for a week. Convalescence, right? You're leaving at the weekend, it's all arranged.' He told them that Ryan was coming home but didn't tell them when, and felt sickened by the delight they both showed. All right, he wasn't their son, but he had shown them more loyalty, had worked many times harder and received far less reward than Ryan. He could have gone away, seen something of the world, found a job that was both easier and better paid, but he'd stayed because they had needed him. But when would they realize how much they depended on him? Never!

He sold a few lambs and chickens at the market that week and the money, paid in cash, went into the new account. The fourth deposit in as many weeks. With luck he had until the annual audit; by then he'd have made his move.

Although he'd never felt close to the family whose name he shared, and had few friends, he had moments of unease as he contemplated moving right away from everyone and everything he knew. If only he and Sarah could sort out their differences and she could be persuaded to go with him; sharing with someone would make the whole thing so much better. Trying to make friends with her son was a beginning. If he could win him over Sarah might reconsider. She was on her own too.

Sophie made an excuse not to go to the farm at the weekend when Ryan would be there. It was obvious he hadn't wanted to retain her friendship, and her appearance might embarrass him, so she told Daphne she was needed by Bob, who was pricking out another bed of seedlings. Bob was delighted when she offered to help, especially as Bertie was likely to be with her.

She joined Daphne at the farm on Friday and cooked a large pot of vegetable soup, baked cakes and filled the bread crock with several loaves. Then, making sure everything was in order and the pieces of broken china had been placed where Rachel would see them with a note of apology nearby, she said her goodbyes and went around with Bertie for a last look at the chickens, including the eight-week-olds being bred for Christmas, and the delightful piglets, whose fate she dared not imagine, and walked back towards Badgers Brook up the field and through the wood. She and Bertie wandered slowly at the edge of the trees, stopping to look around them, identifying birds in the trees, admiring the colourful display of wild flowers amid the grasses, hesitant to leave sight of the farm, as though something was pulling them back, a tugging regret at leaving the place.

'It's been fun, hasn't it?' she said.

'I like the chickens best, they shine with so many colours, don't they? Like rainbow feathers. And I like their beady little eyes. But I don't think I'll enjoy eating one, ever again,' he replied. Sophie said nothing. She didn't want to influence him and guessed that hunger would change his mind long before Christmas, which was the only time he was likely to find chicken on his plate.

Ryan reread the brief note he had received from Owen, staring at the words, wondering how someone suffering broken bones could be described as 'only slightly hurt'. Owen had lied; but why didn't he want him home? His

133

father and mother would need extra help for a while. Even when they were out of hospital they wouldn't magically return to how they were before. Their disappointment at his leaving wouldn't have prevented them expecting his help in an emergency.

He had telephoned the farm several times and been reassured by Owen, who'd said there was nothing to worry about, that Tommy and Rachel were out, or busy, but he'd give them the message. *Don't come home, your father would be disappointed if he interrupted your education for something so trivial*, Owen had written in another letter. So what was going on?

He sat on the train and tried to read a book but the words didn't penetrate his mind, thoughts of the farm, his parents, Owen and Sophie, hovered over the page. He had written to Sophie but hadn't posted the letter, even though he had made at least four attempts before he was satisfied with the contents. Their growing friendliness and warmth, then the sudden backing away from the lightest of kisses or even a touch, the offer of a hand to hold, puzzled him. They had seemed to be getting on well and he'd had visions of returning and carrying on where they had left off, their growing friendship being held in place by letters. But her apparent indifference at their parting had given him doubts – hence the hesitation in writing to her. She allowed him close but only within her limits.

Yet he knew she liked him. So what was holding her back from relaxing into an affectionate friendship? He wondered vaguely if she might be estranged from a fiancé or had recently lost someone she had loved. She was holding back for some reason, and it must be something important to her. He wondered if he would ever find out what it was.

On Cardiff Central station he sat and waited for his connection to steam noisily and importantly in. It came to a hissing, shuddering stop at the platform, the size and the din alarming. Doors opened and, half hidden by steam, people flooded out and rushed towards the exit. Most were carrying suitcases, and many were being met by friends and loved ones. Hugs wherever he looked. He felt a stab of loneliness until he saw a hand waving in greeting and saw Colin Jones waving to him. They found a seat together, Colin explaining he was on his way home after his shift.

'Come to visit your parents at last, have you?' Colin asked. 'We wondered why you hadn't been before. Had some college work to finish, did you?'

'I had no idea they were so badly hurt,' Ryan replied, grimly. 'Owen chose not to tell me they were in hospital with broken bones.'

Ryan showed Colin the letters written by Owen. 'Seems he didn't want me to come home, but I've no idea why. You'd think he'd be glad of the help with Dad out of action, and how are they managing without Mam?'

'Why didn't Sophie write to you?' Colin wondered. 'Helping up there she's been, her and that friend of hers, Daphne Boyd.' He glanced at Ryan and added, 'I thought you and she were friends?'

'My fault. I promised to write but I didn't. I wasn't sure whether she wanted me to or was just being polite. She's such a private person.'

'Her interest seemed more than polite, Ryan.'

'I'll see when we get home. I've gathered from Daphne that Sophie and the boy belonging to Owen's wife have been helping.'

'Strange that, how Owen could cut Sarah and the boy out of his life so finally.'

'Owen isn't an easy person to understand, but she didn't give him much of a chance, did she?'

Ryan received a further shock when he reached home to find that Rachel and Tommy were out of hospital but away from the farm for a week.

'Why couldn't they have waited?' Ryan demanded. 'They knew I was coming.'

'It had all been arranged before you got in touch,' Owen excused.

'Where are they? Tenby? That isn't far, I'll go down there tomorrow,' Ryan said, glaring at his cousin as though daring him to disagree.

'You can, if you think it's wise, but the doctors said they

135

need complete rest. Shock,' he explained. 'And they are getting on a bit.'

'Rubbish! What d'you think I'm going to do to them?' Ryan went out into the yard and examined the vehicles. The van was empty of petrol and had bald tyres, one of which was flat. The ancient car didn't look as if it would make the journey. 'I'm going, if I have to go in the tractor!' he said firmly. He spent the rest of the day checking and cleaning the car and getting ready for the trip to Tenby, about forty miles away.

At seven, a meal was ready for them, cooked by Daphne, and after they'd eaten Ryan telephoned the hotel to tell his parents he would see them on the following day. Only then did he set off to see Sophie.

Badgers Brook seemed filled to overflowing. Before he had knocked on the door the buzz of chatter and laughter reached him; he hesitated and was about to walk away when a face appeared in the kitchen window and a small fist knocked against the glass. Bertie had seen him. The door opened and a smiling Sophie invited him inside.

Stella and Colin were there, and Kitty and Bob, the men still in the clothes they wore for gardening, their boots left on newspaper on the kitchen floor. Betty Connors stood near the window, wearing a coat, a handbag on her arm, obviously just about to leave.

'Hiya, Ryan. Home to see Rachel and Tommy at last?' Betty called.

'I'd have come sooner if I'd been told,' Ryan said, glancing towards Sophie. 'No one told me how badly they were hurt.'

'You didn't know?' Stella queried. 'Didn't Owen tell you?'

'No, he didn't.' He glanced again at Sophie, making the words a criticism. 'Someone should have let me know.'

Sophie came towards him. 'I presumed you knew. Daphne and I were told that Owen had written several times. Isn't that true?'

He shook his head, then, smiling at the room in general, he asked, 'What's going on here then? Some sort of party?'

'My brother is marrying Elsie Clements next week and we're trying to organize a party,' Betty explained. 'I'll hold it in the pub, of course, but these kind friends are helping with the food.' She glanced at Sophie and then added, 'If you're still home, Ryan, why don't you come?'

'Thanks, I'd like that. Is there anything I can bring?' A discussion ensued about who would provide what and gradually the friends dispersed, leaving Ryan and Sophie alone.

'You didn't write,' she said softly.

'I didn't think you really wanted me to. So I left the decision to you.' He stared at her, trying to gauge her feelings but avoided making eye contact.

'There's some cider left if you'd like it. I think I'll have a cup of tea,' she said, turning away, gathering the last of the dishes from the table, putting the kettle on to boil.

He picked up the half-empty bottle and stretched across to reach a clean glass. 'What's going on at the farm?' he asked.

'I don't know. I suppose Owen has taken charge with you gone, and perhaps he didn't want you coming back and . . . taking over.'

'My father owns the farm and he's in charge, not Owen.'

'All right, Ryan, don't get angry with me. I don't even work there.' She smiled then and added, 'And I don't think I'll be asked to again, either.' She told him about the piglets and the broken china.

'I wish I could get in touch with Gareth,' he said. 'He sends an occasional card and phones the farm, according to Owen, but there's no way of us reaching him. I thought he'd be on his way home having heard about Mam and Dad, but perhaps Owen didn't bother to tell him, either. Sophie, will you keep an eye on what's happening and let me know if there's something going on I should know about? I'd love to hear from you anyway, to know how you are and what you're doing,' he added.

They carried their drinks into the living room, where a dying fire glowed. Through the open door came the late-evening sounds of birds settling and the faint scent of bonfire smoke, and the low rays of sun were casting shadows on to the lawn like fingers creeping out and grasping the last of the light. It was so peaceful they didn't speak for a long time, just sipped their drinks and enjoyed the perfect hour.

'I did write,' he said as the sun finally set. She stared at him curiously before he added, 'but I didn't post it.'

'I was disappointed not to hear from you,' she said.

'Well, here I am, but I don't expect to see you as much as I'd like to. I want to find out what's happening at the farm.'

'Harry Sutton is helping and happy to be doing so. He hated working at the kennels and is glad to be back with what he knows. Daphne is running the house. Even young Bertie has helped, and surprisingly your cousin had been kind to him.'

'I'm going to Tenby to see Mam and Dad tomorrow, will you come?' he asked.

'D'you think we might take Bertie, too? I don't think he gets many outings and he'd love to see the sea. He and I could play on the beach if you prefer not to take him to see your parents.'

She sensed she was being stared at, but when she turned to look at him he was smiling. 'Yes, of course he can come with us. Perhaps we could take a picnic, make a day of it.'

'Bertie loves picnics! I'll check with Sarah but I'm sure she'll agree to him coming.'

He looked at her with a hint of amusement and smiled.

They arranged to meet at eleven. Ryan was dressed in casual slacks and an open-necked shirt. Bertie looked startlingly clean in crisp new trousers and shirt, still with the creases in. His face shone with scrubbing and his eyes were as bright as diamonds. He carried some greaseproof-paper-wrapped sandwiches. Slightly embarrassed, he said, 'Mam bought this stuff for my birthday. It's a bit "new" isn't it?'

'Bertie, you look smart and not a bit "new", just well dressed. I'm very impressed,' said Sophie.

He made a deprecating grunt and thrust the sandwiches at her. 'They're only jam, but I like jam,' he added defiantly.

'So do I. I'll swap one of your jam for one of my home-made cheese and salad rolls if you like.'

'Home-made cheese? You can't make cheese!'

'I can when I'm given stale milk. I'll show you how one day, if you like.'

Ryan stood listening to their conversation with amusement, sharing a smile with Sophie. Bertie's package went into the boot with the wicker basket Daphne had packed.

The journey was uneventful but for Bertie it was exciting.

138

He asked endless questions and insisted on Ryan stopping when he saw something of interest that he wanted fully explained. Sophie and Ryan were caught up in his excitement, admiring the beautiful scenery and the spotless white-painted cottages along the route. They felt like day trippers as they parked the car and wandered with the rest of the visitors along the narrow streets of the charming and ancient town.

It was early for visiting the hotel – lunch would hardly have finished – and they willingly gave in to Bertie's request to go down on to the beach. Ryan bought him a brightly painted tin bucket and spade and the three of them found a place to unload their belongings. At once Ryan began to show the boy all he remembered about building castles with turrets and moats, while Sophie slipped off her shoes and wandered along the rippling tide's edge.

They ate their picnic leaning against the sea wall, Bertie with an anxious eye on the tide creeping ever closer, to Sophie and Ryan's amusement. Then, carrying the basket between them, Bertie following with obvious reluctance, they made their way to the hotel where Rachel and Tommy were staying.

To Sophie their greeting was less than welcoming. She was clearly a disappointing addition to their son's visit. Almost ignoring Sophie, Rachel gave much more than the usual attention to Bertie, who chatted away excitedly as he described all they had seen on the journey.

'Shall we go and look at the sea again, Bertie?' Sophie suggested after about ten minutes had passed. 'I think Ryan wants to talk to his mam and dad.' Ryan smiled his thanks.

He said nothing to defend himself when Rachel and Tommy accused him of indifference, but when Rachel went to join Sophie and Bertie outside to view the sea from the veranda, Ryan handed Tommy the letters he'd received from Owen.

'But these can't be all he wrote? He must have told you more about the accident.'

'You have them all. I was given to understand you and Mam were shaken but not seriously hurt.'

'What's he playing at? Could he have been thinking of you, not wanting to disrupt your first term?'

In reply Ryan raised an eyebrow. 'Doesn't he want to remind us – prove to us – how reliable and indispensable he is?'

'He does the accounts and manages some areas of the running of the farm, but your mother and I – and you and Gareth, of course – we're in overall charge, we make all the decisions.'

'If Gareth and I stay away more or less permanently, he'd be in a good position to take over when you and Mam want to retire, wouldn't he?'

'Rubbish. Owen isn't like that. He isn't that devious. Not Owen.'

'Watch him, Dad. Just watch him.'

'Besides, I'm not ready to sit back and watch someone else run things, and won't be for a long time. And then I hope it'll be you, not Owen.'

'Don't, Dad. Don't hope for that. Neither of us wants to take over. By the way, is Gareth on his way home?'

'Ask Owen.'

'Or hasn't Owen told him about the accident, either?' Ryan said slowly.

He left his parents with the promise to visit again before heading back to college. Tommy was frowning as he waved them off, Rachel giving Bertie a final hug and a sixpence for sweets.

'Thank you, Mrs Treweather,' he said politely, 'but can I buy chips instead? I'm starving hungry.'

Ryan was relieved to see laughter wipe the worried frown from Tommy's face, but Sophie wondered how they felt, seeing the boy who could have been a part of their life. Did they feel regret? There was certainly no sign of animosity, thank goodness, and Bertie had enjoyed a memorable day. He fell asleep soon after they started the drive back to Cwm Derw and Sophie and Ryan were able to talk.

'Owen was brought up on the farm and I suppose he's bound to feel some entitlement,' Ryan said. 'His father, Dad's brother, was killed in America and Owen came to us when he was very young. But he isn't heir to the land my father owns and never could be. He must realize that.'

'He's had a very unsuccessful life in many ways, hasn't

140

he? Perhaps he's resentful and would be better leaving and starting again somewhere.'

'I don't think he'll do that. But I know what you mean. His marriage to Sarah, that hurt him dreadfully. And never being included in business meetings apart from him giving a statement of accounts.'

'If he doesn't feel a part of anything it must be hard.' Sophie's voice was soft, and Ryan immediately picked up on the slight wistfulness.

'Is it like that for you? Not belonging anywhere? You never talk about your family, yet you must have one. Can you talk about it? Why you left? Why you cut yourself off from everyone and settled among strangers?'

'I don't have a family. There's no one.' From her voice it was clear she didn't intend to discuss it further. He glanced at her, her face turned as she stared out of the window at the hedges, and could only guess at the pain she must have suffered before arriving at Cwm Derw and finding a home in Badgers Brook.

'I'll have some work to do in the morning – for one thing I need to examine the books, make sure everything is on a sound footing – then perhaps we could go out again. With Bertie, if you need a chaperone,' he added in a hoarse whisper. 'But preferably just the two of us.'

She turned then, and smiled at him. 'Just the two of us will be fine.'

A sleepy voice from the back seat said, 'I don't want to be a chaperone, anyway, and I've promised to go with Mr Jones to help him build a bonfire on his allotment.'

'What's a chaperone, Bertie?' Sophie teased.

'Don't know but I don't want to be one. Right?'

The conversation was easy and relaxed for the rest of the journey, but Ryan knew he had to find out what it was in Sophie's past that so distressed her – although if she wouldn't talk about it, where else could he enquire?'

He began with Daphne.

'We served together in the WAAF's, and I know she'll hate me for telling you this, but she was about to be married, and he let her down. At the very last minute.'

141

'You mean she was jilted?'

'Afraid so, but please don't tell her I've told you. I'm sure she'll tell you herself one day.'

'Then what happened?'

'All her family were killed by a bomb. I'd been transferred by then, and I lost touch with her. It was remembering that this was an area she knew that made me come here on a cycling holiday. It was sheer luck that enabled me to find her. You cannot imagine how many times I asked about her.'

'But surely they weren't all killed?'

'She never went back and she won't tell me what happened. Not a word. If I even hint at being curious she shuts up like the proverbial clam. So, because I don't want her to lose touch again, I never mention anything that happened before she arrived in Cwm Derw. I have the feeling that when she does feel able to talk she'll be glad of a friend.'

Thinking of Sophie and of his cousin's unwillingness to tell him about his parents' accident, Ryan said, 'I seem to be surrounded by mysteries.' But he didn't explain.

There was a further mystery when he went to the desk and tried to find the accounts books. He went out into the shed to find Owen.

'They're with the accountants,' Owen explained. 'I was puzzled over something, a few hundred pounds that went out with no explanation of when and why, so I took the books in for him to check. Next time you're home, eh?' He took his cousin's arm and pulled him into the back of the shed. 'Look up there but don't make too much noise.' He pointed to where the chimney breast of a long-disused fireplace made a wide shelf.

Standing watching them was the pale shape of a barn owl. 'Marvellous, eh? He's been there since last winter. Lost a previous home maybe. Lots of older barns are being replaced as money becomes available. Your father wanted to take this one down and put the new one he plans to build in its place, but I knew about the owl and persuaded him to leave it.'

'He wouldn't have needed much persuading.' He glanced at Owen's face. 'Unless that's something else you didn't tell them.' He saw that he was right. 'Mam and Dad get great

142

pleasure from observing the wildlife around them. Why didn't you tell us about it? This lovely sight is something to share, surely?'

'Oh, I don't know. Keeping it to myself added to the magic, I suppose.'

Like problems with the farm accounts, Ryan thought curiously, but he said nothing more.

The phone rang as he went back inside and by good luck it was Gareth. He was shocked when Ryan told him about their parents' accident and said he would come home immediately. Ryan promised to be there when he arrived, and Tommy and Rachel ended their holiday early to be there too.

Sophie saw him first, as he was walking from the bus with a small rucksack on his shoulders. This time he didn't bother teasing her that he was Ryan.

'Why didn't Owen tell me about the accident?' he demanded when she greeted him. 'I was told about Elsie and Ed Connors's wedding but not that my parents suffered broken bones.'

'You'd better ask Owen,' Sophie said.

Less sharply, he said,' I understand from Ryan that you and Daphne have been angels.'

'Hardly! Besides, Daphne has done far more than me,' she replied. 'She's cooking a meal to welcome you home this very minute.'

The two brothers walked around the farm discussing all they had learned. Daphne had a sizeable lunch ready for them when they returned in silence to the house. She had managed to make some pasties with pastry made with suet scrounged from the butcher, and filled them with potatoes, onions and the smallest scraps of minced meat. She had also made a game pie for supper, with pigeon, rabbit, pheasant and a couple of leaves of sage and thyme and a few of Sophie's dried mushrooms.

They held a family meeting afterwards, excluding Owen, much to his chagrin, but before Ryan could discuss Owen's secretive behaviour Gareth said, 'I'm never coming back and, unless Ryan intends to, I think you should sell up. Why don't you get a small bungalow and enjoy a retirement, do all the things you've never had time to, relish the freedom while you

143

still have good health?' His words were hardly heard as both Rachel and Tommy shouted him down. When Ryan had calmed things he admitted agreeing with his brother. The row went on for a long time, with the boys trying to explain the reasons for their decisions.

Outside Owen listened and muttered aloud, 'And when will they tell me, I wonder? As the auctioneers arrive to begin the sale?'

It was clear to Ryan that for the present everything was running smoothly, and he was able to return to his studies. But it was with some doubts that he left after three more days, and he made sure his parents were aware of his promise to post a letter every Wednesday and phone the farm on Saturdays at twelve. 'We don't want any more . . . misunderstandings, do we?' he added, giving Owen a steely stare. 'And I'll telephone the accountant on Monday morning so he can explain the problem.'

'No need,' Owen assured him. 'I have an appointment for first thing Monday and I'll be able to tell you myself.'

A last evening with Sophie was successful. Mainly, Ryan guessed, because he didn't attempt to question her about her life before Badgers Brook. They found a public house where they served sandwiches, filled surprisingly and probably illegally with rather fat pork, which Sophie declined, and they both settled for salad with scrambled dried egg.

Later, they walked through the wood and sat until late, watching the sun sink down, leaving a beautiful afterglow. Then they waited, Ryan sharing his coat with Sophie as an excuse to put his arm around her shoulders, to see the badgers emerge. He had chosen their spot with care, making sure the light breeze blew towards them so the creatures were unlikely to pick up on the scent.

There were three adults and two young ones, running, playing chase, safe in the belief they were alone. Ryan watched Sophie's face as she marvelled at the wonderful sight, before the little group trotted off to forage for their supper.

'They're beautiful,' she gasped as they stood to leave.

'And so are you,' he said, taking her hand firmly as they walked back to the house.

Although she didn't pull her hand away from his, he didn't try to kiss her. Sophie, he decided with growing affection, was more nervous than the badgers.

Before he left after the usual late-night cup of cocoa, they discussed the wedding of Elsie Clements and Ed Connors. She told him of her suspicions about Elsie's illness.

'You did right to mention it, but let's hope it was nothing more than a misunderstanding.'

'You will come, won't you?'

He promised he'd be there to escort her to the church.

Owen was at the accountants before the office opened, waiting impatiently, determined to speak to the man who dealt with their business before Ryan could. He insisted that he was the only person he would speak to. 'I'll wait as long as I have to but I'm not going until I've seen him,' he said, aggression raising his voice to a threatening snarl. The assistant went into the office and told David Carter that Mr Treweather was demanding to see him and looked like trouble.

David Carter, who had dealt with Tommy Treweather's accounts for many years, put aside the work he was doing and invited Owen in.

'Is there a problem?' he asked, after sending the office girl to make tea.

'I wish to take my account elsewhere,' Owen said.

David Carter looked startled and asked why.

'I don't intend to go into it. I just want to take my papers and pay any outstanding monies.'

'I'm sorry, Mr Treweather, but your uncle is my client and I can't do this.'

'My uncle is ill and I am carrying out his instructions.'

'But have there been any discrepancies? I'm sure any queries can be easily explained. There has never been a problem all the time we have been dealing with your uncle's affairs.'

'All I know is that I need to ask for the papers.' He waved away the girl, who had returned with a tray of tea, and held out his hand.

'This is most irregular. It will take some time for me to get everything together to my satisfaction.'

Owen sat for the first time. 'I'll wait.'

'No need for that.' Mr Carter looked offended. 'I'll bring everything over at lunch time.'

'And any calls you receive regarding the defunct account will be referred to me.'

Owen went out, leaving a bewildered and concerned Mr Carter staring at the door in disbelief. He phoned the farm at once in the hope of talking to Tommy but the phone rang unanswered as everyone was out.

Sophie saw Owen leaving the accountants, and, when he spotted her, darting behind a lorry and then running into a nearby lane at the side of a shoe shop. It was obvious that he did not want to be seen. Pretending to be unaware of him, she walked on, looking into a shop window, watching in the reflection as he left the lane and ran to where the dirty old van was parked. He stood there for a moment, presumably looking for her, and then went into the bank.

He was behaving so suspiciously that she waited until he had come out of the bank and driven off, and then she went into the accountants. 'Is Mr Owen Treweather here?' she asked innocently. 'Only he left behind a notebook that he intended to bring and I've brought it in case it's important.'

David Carter came out and rather abruptly said that Treweather business was no longer his concern. Not knowing what to say, certain her questions would remain unanswered, she thanked him and went into the post office for a letter card; then she wrote to Ryan explaining what she had seen.

In the B&B, the bride-to-be was trying on her simple outfit, even though the time to leave for the church was an hour away. She'd had to deal with breakfast for five guests on her own that morning, and had dropped Ed's favourite cup. She had cleared the last of the dishes and told the two people who were staying that night that there wouldn't be any food that evening, but they were welcome to bring back fish and chips or make themselves some toast.

Many believe that every town, large and small, is a collection of villages. That was also true of Cwm Derw. The area around the main street, with the post office, Elsie's guesthouse, some large, once-imposing private houses, a garage and a park, and a path that led to the allotments and fields beyond, was an area where everyone knew everyone else. A side street led to Steeple Street, where Geoff and Connie's ironmongers and paint store and Nerys's dress shop were located. Most of the locals had lived there all their lives.

In the other direction there were a few more small shops, including Peter and Hope Bevan's fruit and vegetable shop, a dairy and Mrs Hayward's grocery, where most people bought their weekly food rations. Whenever anything important happened, everyone was involved. And Elsie and Ed's wedding was important.

Everyone who could get there planned to attend the wedding. There had been no need for invitations. Ed was well known, working in his sister's public house for so many years, and all his friends would be there to wish him well.

Although Saturday was one of Geoff's busiest days, he and Connie were leaving the place in the hands of his seventeen-year-old niece, Joyce, with a couple of lads to help with anything heavy.

Rachel and Tommy arrived with Gareth, and Sophie walked into the church with Ryan, who had come home again after just one day away, especially for the occasion. Daphne stayed at the farm with Owen, having promised to be at the evening celebration, which would take place at the Ship and Compass.

Ryan hadn't received Sophie's card, so she explained exactly what she had seen. He said nothing to his father – he needed to talk to David Carter first.

Stella couldn't close the post office until lunchtime but knew that the evening celebration would be the best part, so she didn't mind missing the ceremony. She'd hear all about it soon enough. Kitty and Bob Jennings, Peter and Hope Bevan, and many who Elsie and Ed would have been hard put to name, filled the pews. Outside, those who knew neither the bride nor the groom but simply liked weddings stood in the churchyard on graves and walls, and wherever they could get a view of the arrivals.

It was while they were waiting for the bridal car to bring Elsie the few yards from her home that Sophie overheard something that confirmed her doubts about Elsie's honesty.

Brenda Morris, still in her uniform, having stolen a few minutes to attend the wedding of one of her patients, was sitting beside Hope Bevan. 'I saw her this morning and she seemed fine,' Brenda said in answer to Hope's question. Once again misunderstanding what was a casual enquiry, Brenda added, 'She's coping very well with it, but it will get harder for her.'

'What d'you mean?' Hope asked. 'Is Elsie ill?'

At once Brenda changed the subject. 'Oh, no, not Elsie. I'm sorry, I thought you were talking about someone else.'

But a glance at Brenda's face convinced Sophie that there had been no error. So what *was* wrong with the bride-to-be, and did Ed know about it? She felt the terror of past mistakes milling around her head, warning her to say nothing. It was far too late and the safest thing was to remain silent.

Elsie arrived and was joined in matrimony to a proud Ed Connors. Instead of the formal wedding breakfast, they went with a few friends to a restaurant where a simple buffet was prepared. Sophie noticed that the bride firmly refused a drink of any kind. The crowd dispersed, cameras stopped clicking, chatter faded and people went back to their routine, promising to meet later on at the Ship.

Ryan took Sophie back to the farm with his parents. They walked around the fields, checking fences, looking at the animals and the newly ploughed fields, and stopped at the edge of the wood, looking down at the now derelict cottage where Sophie had once made a home.

'You just appeared one day, and settled, made it a home, and you'd probably still be there if it hadn't been for the storm,' Ryan said. 'Tell me, where did you come from? What brought you to my door?' he asked, wanting to hear it from Sophie herself.

'Oh, nowhere in particular. I just wandered after leaving the forces.' Abruptly, avoiding further questions, she turned away.

'I have to go back. I've made a cake for this evening's do, and I want to make sure it's edible.'

'Will you promise that you'll tell me one day? Not now, or even in the near future, but one day?'

She hesitated, staring at him, at his encouraging smile, the affection glowing in his eyes. 'Yes, one day. Now come on, Ryan. I've promised to deliver the cake to Betty before six.'

Ryan and Gareth made excuses about leaving for the Ship until Sophie and Daphne had gone, then Ryan faced Owen about the change of accountant. They all looked at him for an explanation.

'I'll explain more fully when I have the figures set out to show you. Briefly, he's become unreliable. There was a mistake in the tax we paid, we underpaid and you know what difficulties that can cause, receiving income and omitting to enter it. I get nervous trying to explain to Uncle Tommy when I've overstepped my responsibilities, but I think I was justified. Give me a couple of days to make out a report and I'll explain.' He knew the story sounded weak, given David Carter's integrity, but it would give him valuable time to hide the transfers from any but the closest investigation.

The potato cake Sophie had made looked strange: crisp on the outside but very un-cake-like inside. It was made with mashed potatoes, a little flour, a small amount of sugar and fruit, with nutmeg for flavouring. The fat content was lard, which Sophie hated, it being an animal fat. She had made the cake but wouldn't – couldn't – eat any. With the cake and a sponge carefully wrapped, she made her way to the pub.

Although the vague plan was for people to arrive around eight, they started coming before six o'clock with offerings of food to swell the feast, and then stayed and gathered around like shoppers queuing at a winter sale. When the doors opened to the rest, the place was stormed and the party began.

It was Ed's party, but it was clear he was needed on the other side of the bar, and he served drinks alongside his sister. When Daphne arrived with Tommy and Rachel she at once

149

volunteered to help. 'I can pull a pint, can't I?' she announced, and after a few frothy disasters she spent the evening helping Betty, allowing Ed to sit beside his bride.

When Ed was persuaded to give a speech, Elsie reached out to move his drink, and it slipped from her hand. Sophie watched as she grasped one hand with the other, as though sharing the strength. Ed laughed. 'She's lovely, my wife – Mrs Ed Connors,' he said to a ripple of laughter, 'but heck, is she clumsy!' Elsie joined in the laughter, which Sophie could see was forced, the woman's eyes filled with sadness.

The evening consisted of sing-songs and joke-telling and a lot of teasing, but Sophie and Ryan seemed set apart from it all. They sat in a corner near the fire and talked. Or, rather, Ryan did. He explained about wanting to teach, and not staying on the farm, and how he was torn by feelings of guilt that he wasn't there where his parents wanted him to be.

'You have to do what's best for you, don't you?' Sophie said.

'You mean I should stay at college and insist my parents realize that I'll never want to run the farm?'

'No, no, I didn't mean that!' Sophie looked alarmed. A sudden and painful reminder overwhelmed her of how her insistence that she knew best had resulted in the deaths of those she loved. 'I can't tell you what to do, you must make up your own mind! I must never persuade anyone to chose. It has to be your choice.'

A little puzzled by the emphatic response, he said softly, 'Not ever, Sophie, love? Not even when the decision affects you too?'

'I won't advise anyone, then I won't have to live with my mistake.'

'Some decisions have to be shared, especially if they affect the lives of two people. Sophie, you know I'm more than a little fond of you. Why does that frighten you so much?'

'It's a responsibility, loving someone and telling them what they should do.'

'Sharing isn't telling,' he corrected.

She tapped her empty glass on the table, a tattoo demonstrating her agitation.

150

'Look,' he said, 'guard my chair while I go and get us another drink. I think it's time we talked this through.'

When he returned, pushing his way through the lively crowd, Geoff and Connie were sitting at the table. Sophie had gone.

He had to find her, make her talk about what troubled her so much. Was she afraid of being let down again? Did she believe he was capable of leaving her at the church to wait in vain? How could he reassure her when he wasn't supposed to know about the man who had jilted her? Was it his family's occupation? His mother had shown disapproval of her, but that was owing to her unsuitability as a farmer's wife, something he had no intention of making her. He had to see her. Grabbing his coat, offering the drinks to his father and mother, he hurried out. He would go to Badgers Brook and wait for her.

Eight

Sophie was fighting an urge to run and run, leave Cwm Derw and find another place to live secretly and alone, as she had so many times in the past. It was hopeless to try to return to normality, make friends, find work, fall in love and settle into the life most women expect.

Thoughts tumbled around in her head like knives, hurting her: the faces of people she had harmed – Mam and Dad, her brother Frank and sister Carrie, her grandparents; all of them shadowed by the memory of the man she had once dreamed of marrying: Geoffrey, pushed away by her bulldozing her way through his doubts and hesitations, convinced she knew best.

Geoffrey had seen her for what she was: a pushy, over-confident young woman. He had been able to walk away, but not so her family. They were all gone for ever, and had lost their lives because they had followed her emphatic advice. By stopping her grandparents going back to their own home and taking her brother and sister with them, she had condemned them all to death. The dramatic words hit her like hammers, beating her shame into her brain, but the pain was not lessening by repetition.

She wandered in the dark, rain-threatened evening, unaware of where her feet were taking her, and found herself in the wood close to Treweather Farm. The horizon, lit by the last rays of a setting sun, seemed to tempt her, encourage her to set off and search again for a place where she might find peace. Suddenly she knew she needed to get back to Badgers Brook. This wasn't the time for running away, especially in the middle of a gloomy, late-summer evening. She'd be better to try to sleep, then, in the light of a new dawn, make her decision.

She wore soft-soled shoes, light sandals chosen for the wedding, and was little more than a pale, silent shadow as she passed between the trees and headed for the lane. She didn't make a sound as she walked up the path, and was able to see someone standing near the back door before being heard. She knew at once that it was Ryan and slid backwards using the shadows to hide. When she reached the lane she moved across the grass verge and into the trees. Leaning against the knobbly trunk of a birch she stood and waited for him to leave.

Ryan slid down the wall on which he was leaning and sat on his heels. No matter how long it took, he wouldn't leave until Sophie came home. After half an hour he became uncomfortable and wondered if she was already inside and just refusing to answer his knock. He stretched his cramped muscles and began to move around the house, intending to look through the windows of the living room and dining room.

Sophie had been allowing her concentration to drift, and when she screwed up her eyes and stared at the doorway she saw that he was gone. She waited a moment then crossed the road and walked up the path again, in time to bump into Ryan, who had walked around the house. She turned to run but he grabbed her, held her arms and pulled her round to face him.

'Sophie, talk to me. Just talk to me. If you don't want me to bother you again, at least tell me why. I can take rejection, but I would like to understand why.'

'I can't talk to you. I can't talk to anyone, so will you please go. I'm tired and I want to go to bed. Please, Ryan,' she pleaded, as he refused to release her arms.

He dropped his arms and lowered his head, defeated. 'I was beginning to think we might have a future together. I thought, once you learned to trust me, believe me when I promise I'd never hurt you, you'd feel the same.'

'It isn't you, it's me,' she almost shouted. 'Why don't you listen? I can't share my life with you, I'd make you miserable. It's what I always do!' She pushed him aside and ran into the house. Ryan heard the sound of the key being turned and the bolt being thrust home and the harsh sounds were like blows.

Hurt and bewildered, he crossed the lane and walked through the wood here and there without purpose. After an hour, when he was reasonably sure his parents and Owen would be in bed, he went back to the farm, but the house wasn't at rest. He found Owen in the office working on some forms, which he put aside when he heard his cousin come in.

'Hello, Ryan. I didn't hear the car.'

'No, I left it near the post office. I'll collect it in the morning.'

'Too much to drink?'

'No. Not enough.' Without another word he went to bed.

Owen waited a few minutes to make sure Ryan wasn't coming back down, then returned to the forms he was filling in with his careful, neat writing. Before he, too, retired, he slid them into a briefcase, which he put in the back of his wardrobe hidden under a couple of ancient jackets. Tomorrow he would meet the new solicitor and his new life would begin.

In the morning, although she had slept very little, the house had performed its magic and Sophie was calmer. She wouldn't run away; she had a house where she was comfortable and, although she hadn't enough money to live with ease, she would stay and maybe build a new life. New beginnings were always hard even without the memories and pain she was dragging along with her, but this time she would hold firm.

Throughout the summer she had been busy filling jars with her preserves. Instead of offering everything she had made to Peter and Hope to sell in their shop, she decided to take as much as she could carry to Maes Hir market. She knew that hiding away was the wrong thing to do, and she needed to be among people. Besides, money was getting low and with luck she'd earn enough to pay a couple of weeks' rent to Geoff and Connie, and maybe find a few bargains – perhaps a pair of shoes suitable for wearing at school.

She required very little money for food, taking what she needed from the garden and buying little more than the small ration allowance at Hayward's grocery shop. Like many others she bartered what she didn't want for other things and in exchange for her meat ration she gratefully accepted sugar and sometimes cheese.

She saw Sarah waiting for the bus, talking to Connie Tanner and Betty Connors. She felt the panic that accompanied the thought of having to sit and talk to someone on the half-hour journey. She wished she hadn't come. It was foolish to expect people to be friendly sometimes then allow her privacy at others. When would she relax and enjoy living among these lovely people?

She stepped back and allowed the small queue to find their seats before struggling with her laden baskets and finding a seat where she could have the baskets beside her. She waved towards the people she knew but turned quickly away, signalling her disinclination to talk. Taking out a notebook, she began to browse through the almost empty pages.

When they reached the market, Connie and Betty were among her first customers, buying mint sauce and, for Connie, the unusual carrot jam and another made with tomatoes.

'Any time you have pickles to sell let me know,' Betty said, refusing the jams suspiciously. 'I do a few sandwiches in the bar and I'd be glad to buy some that are a bit different. And Geoff loves your parsnip wine, doesn't he, Connie? Although I shouldn't be encouraging you to take my customers,' she added with a smile.

'The parsnip wine is only for gifts, not to sell,' Sophie said. She was looking anxious, wishing they'd go away; she knew from experience that after a few casual remarks, the questions would begin. She was raw from Ryan's persuasions and felt vulnerable and inexplicably afraid. Then she saw Sarah approaching with a reluctant Bertie in tow.

'Where did you learn about this preserving, Sophie? Sarah asked. 'From your mam, was it?'

'I just became interested.' Sophie looked to the side, where a newcomer was trying to attract her attention, holding up her only pot of wild raspberry preserve. She served the woman and the others thankfully moved on. With an eye on the market inspector, who usually pretended not to notice her, she was busy for the next hour and soon her baskets were empty.

She stood for a while, enjoying at second hand the bustle

and chatter of the customers wandering around the stalls. An outsider with an ache, a longing to be a part of it but invisibly manacled to past errors.

A crowd was picking over the pile of second-hand shoes that had been unceremoniously tipped out on to the ground. She saw there were none suitable for her. The lively bargain hunters were trying them on, searching for a match, debating colour and style. Besides hoping for a good buy, they were treating the search as an excuse for entertainment; laughing at the height of some of the heels, the poor quality and the impractical designs. A visit to Maes Hir and its popular market was an enjoyable day out. The faces of the customers and sellers alike told her that.

She stood watching the scene for a while, but when Sarah called and asked if she would join them at the snack bar for a cup of tea and a scone she declined and ran to catch the early bus. She felt a deep disappointment. She would have liked to stay a while, watching the crowd and perhaps picking up a bargain or two when the stalls were packing up, but the thought of travelling back with Sarah and the others was more than she could cope with. 'Idiot that I am!' she said aloud.

Betty Connors was on the bus. She didn't sit next to Sophie, but behind her, so the girl could talk or not, as she wished.

'I have to get back early to open for lunchtime. Banging on the door they'll be, like prisoners in reverse, demanding to be let in. And there they'll stay until I close the doors. Sad isn't it, how little some people have in their lives.'

Sophie agreed but she sensed the questions about to begin and took out her notebook and wrote a few words. Betty leaned forwards and patted her shoulder in silence, as though understanding her reticence.

Sophie wondered if she should repeat her concerns about Elsie, and cautiously she asked, 'How are Elsie and Ed today, after all yesterday's excitement?'

'I haven't seen them today. I might go and see them later, although whenever we meet these days we end up arguing,' Betty said sadly. 'It's hard to believe how he's changed. He's on the defensive all the time, treating me like the enemy instead of his friend.'

156

'Give them time. It can't be easy to adjust to sharing when you're used to making all your own decisions,' Sophie comforted.

'What about you and Ryan? You seem to get on well.'

Obliquely changing the subject, Sophie laughed and said, 'I don't think his mother approves of our friendship. A vegetarian and a farmer? A stranger as well? Impossible!' She turned back to the imaginary importance of her notebook.

Ryan telephoned the farm every day and soon after the wedding managed to speak to Daphne, who was still helping each morning, although Rachel was gradually taking over again. After general questions he asked about Bertie and, as though as an afterthought, about Sophie.

'She's changed so much,' said Daphne with a sigh. 'When we were in the WAAFs she was such a lively character. Outgoing, full of mischief, always ready for a laugh. If there was ever a hint of trouble she was usually in the middle of it. But she seems to blame herself for her family's deaths, and she refuses to tell me why. That's all I can tell you, Ryan.'

'Thank you,' he said. 'Sorry, I have to go, there's someone waiting to use the phone. I'll talk to you tomorrow. Oh, you don't happen to have the address of her previous home, do you?'

'Maybe. If I can decipher the scribbled-out words in my tattered address book. I'll let you know.'

'Thanks.'

'Who was that? As if I can't guess,' Owen said as he walked into the room. 'My cousin, who leaves me to run the place then checks up on me daily as though I'm not to be trusted.'

'Don't worry about him,' Daphne said. 'He knows you're running everything as efficiently as he could. He keeps phoning and asking questions simply to cover his guilt at not being here.'

'Well I wish he wouldn't. He should either be here or leave me alone to run things as I see fit. He can't have it both ways, can he?'

'Lunch will be ready in half an hour,' she said, avoiding a reply.

'Where are my aunt and uncle?'

'They went to order winter fodder. Harry drove them.'

'I have to go out. Will you stay until they get back?'

'Of course, but they'll be back for lunch, they never stay in town.'

'I'll wait and eat with them,' he said. 'There are one or two things I need to discuss. The new barns will need financing, and the road desperately needs to be resurfaced. I can sign cheques but I want authority for a larger outlay.' He left the room, still seeming disgruntled, and Daphne went into the kitchen to check that the food was progressing satisfactorily. She enjoyed pleasing the particular and fussy Rachel.

She liked Owen and thought he was treated with a lack of respect for what he was doing, but she avoided becoming involved in his complaints. Better to stay out of family arguments, wherever her sympathies lay. Working in the farmhouse and dealing with some of the lighter farm work, she was aware of a growing contentment, and joining one side of a disagreement, however casually, might see her time here ended.

Perhaps, she mused, if Owen hadn't been married she might have allowed herself to become more than fond of him and the life he offered. But he had never bothered to sue for divorce and she often wondered why, after all the years he and Sarah had been apart, he still didn't break the legal ties.

Leaving a note for Rachel and Tommy to tell them where she would be found, in case she failed to hear the van return, she went into the barn and began pulling down the bales of hay needed to clean out the chicken coops. She'd deal with the job once lunch was over. The work was gradually extending from the small tasks she had managed at first, and its attraction was expanding too.

Killing time, half listening for the sound of the van driving up the bumpy road, she began to brush up the loose hay, laughing at the dog's attempts at catching the mice she disturbed. Yes, she could be happy doing this for the rest of her life. If only Owen were free.

Sophie had a visitor one afternoon towards the end of the school holiday. Betty came after closing the Ship after lunch and brought a basket filled with assorted empty jars. 'I asked over the bar if anyone had any they didn't want and here they are,' she announced, plonking them on the kitchen table.

'Don't thank me,' she said as Sophie began to speak. 'Selfish I am. I want some of the pickles you make. In fact, have you any to spare now? I thought I'd go and see that brother of mine, take him a gift as an excuse. Crazy needing an excuse to visit my brother, eh? The truth is, I hardly see him since he and Elsie got married. She keeps him busy and he does a lot more for her than he did for me. The power of love, eh?'

Sophie thanked her, found a couple of jars of piccalilli and put the kettle on for tea.

She could see that Betty had something on her mind. She had settled into an armchair in the living room, sipped the tea and nibbled at the home-made biscuits, making the usual polite comments about the simply furnished room with its view of the garden. And Sophie stayed quiet, just making a few comments, waiting to learn the reason for Betty's visit.

'How are things at the Ship?' she asked after a particularly long silence, while she refilled their cups.

'Oh, I'm coping. Sarah does a good job of cleaning each morning, and Daphne is becoming very useful in the bar when I'm busy. She's such a hard worker that one. It's Ed that's the problem.'

'You miss him?'

'Yes, of course, but it isn't that. Sophie, have you heard any news about Elsie's condition?'

'Only rumours and they're best ignored, don't you think?'

Betty smiled at her. 'You're very good at that, aren't you? Answering a question by not answering it at all.'

'Sorry.'

'It's all right, but I don't know what – if anything – I should do.'

'She'll have spoken about it to Ed – perhaps you could ask him again.'

'I have and he says it's nonsense.'

'But you don't believe him?'

'I believe he thinks it's nonsense, but I also believe Elsie

159

has been lying to him as well as to the rest of us. Sarah suggested – thinking I knew – that Elsie married my brother because she's ill and will need someone to take care of her, and isn't he a wonderfully kind man.'

'If Ed doesn't want to talk about it you can't force him to.'

'But what if Sarah's right and he doesn't know? He should be warned at least.'

'And if Sarah's wrong? You'd upset your brother for nothing.'

'You think I should do nothing?'

'I don't know,' Sophie said at once, alarm widening her eyes. 'I don't have an opinion either way. You must decide what to do. Ed is your brother and you know best.'

That night she couldn't sleep, worried about having influenced Betty. However long she considered, whatever she did, her conclusions were always wrong. She was a danger to everyone she knew and cared for.

She was woken at eight o'clock by the sound of a robin singing in the tree outside her bedroom window. It was as though he was trying to cheer her, put her in a happier mood.

She had to admit to herself that avoiding involvement was impossible. If she were to stay here and become a part of the community, becoming involved with people was a part of the deal. One day she would be able to talk about her own tragedies, but this morning she would call on Betty and try to help her by listening. That was what most people needed, anyway, not someone forcing their opinion on them.

A long letter came from Ryan with news of his progress, and saying that when he next came home he wanted to take her out for a meal in a village some way away, where they could discuss their plans for the future. A future he hoped they might share. He promised there would be no pressure and he signed it with love. She read and reread it but didn't reply.

Sophie wasn't the only one in turmoil about a growing love. Sarah was beginning to warm towards Owen. He had begun meeting her from the shop and offering her a lift home. He brought gifts for her and for Bertie, and her response varied from anger and irritation to being amused and feeling flattered.

Swearing her to secrecy he repeated that he might be going away. 'I'd like you to come with me, you and Bertie.'

'Where to? I haven't got much but all I have is here. I can't go anywhere, I don't have the train fare as far as Cardiff. What *are* you talking about, Owen?'

'If things go to plan I'll have enough for all of us.'

'Doing the football pools are you?' she asked sarcastically. 'Are you sure you'll be one of the big winners?'

'Not the pools. This is a certainty. It's mine, it's what I'm owed and it will be enough for us to buy a place, you, me and young Bertie.'

She became intrigued and asked questions but didn't learn very much, just that it had to be a secret until he told her different. She left him convinced the whole thing must be a joke, an attempt on his part to persuade her to take seriously his efforts to befriend them. 'Treating me like a child being promised a treat,' she told Sophie when she called to collect Bertie. 'As if I'd believe a story like that!'

Sophie was in the post office on Wednesday morning when Ryan walked in. She smiled, a tremor starting in the corner of her mouth as she wondered how he would behave towards her. When she had bought the stamps she needed, and accepted an invitation from Stella to call on her at the country cottage later that day, she went out. Should she wait for Ryan to be served, or walk away?

She stood outside staring at her notebook as though checking a shopping list when he came out and joined her.

'Have you time for a coffee?' he asked rather formally.

'I'd like that. Thank you.'

They walked to the café, crowded with shoppers having a rest between errands, and found a place at a table, which they had to share with two others.

'How are the studies progressing?' she asked.

'Fine. I'm lucky to have this chance to prepare. I've visited schools and colleges, attended lectures, talked to ex-pupils and teachers, as well as doing a lot of reading. I couldn't have done any of it staying at home. I'm enjoying the prospect of college and feel more and more certain that teaching is what I want to do.'

'I was training to be a teacher but I gave it up and joined the WAAFs,' she reminded him.

'Why didn't you go back?'

'Everything had changed. I no longer felt certain about what I wanted to do.'

'D'you regret it?'

'I couldn't go back, too much had happened.'

'Such as?' he asked. She glanced at him and at the two women sharing their table, who were listening with great interest.

'I was no longer the same person. You can't go through an experience like that and stay the same.'

'An experience like what?' he insisted.

Cornered, unable to get up and walk away, hemmed in by the two women, she said, 'Death, destruction, and more death and destruction. It made what I wanted to do seem trivial and unimportant.'

'Daphne told me about losing your family,' he said softly. 'Can you tell me what happened?'

She looked at the women sipping their tea, implacably blocking her escape. She felt like screaming, shouting at them to get out of her way. She was filled with panic and finding it difficult to breath. Sensing her distress, Ryan's hands covered hers, and he whispered softly so the other women couldn't hear. 'All right, love. You don't have to talk now, but one day you will and I promise you the pain will be eased. I hope I'm there when that day comes. I want to be the one you tell.'

He stood up and politely asked the women to move, and, holding Sophie's hand firmly so she couldn't run away, he led her out of the café to where the farm van was parked outside the post office.

Stella was at the door, taking in the advertising boards. 'Don't forget to come and see us this afternoon, Sophie. You too, Ryan, plenty of cakes I've made. Only saccharine sweeteners, mind. I've run right out of sugar and she's got the fault – swapped me for some bacon for Colin's breakfast she did.'

Ryan went back to the farm for lunch, made by his mother, who was managing heroically with her injured arm. Daphne had gone and he sat with Owen and his parents, listening while Owen and Tommy discussed the finances for the new barn – the reason for his midweek visit.

He tried to take an interest in what was being said, costs, loans and percentages, but his mind refused to concentrate. He kept seeing those sad hazel eyes in that beautiful face with its frame of flyaway hair. Somehow he had to persuade her to talk to him.

Leaving Owen and Tommy still arguing over the position of the new barn, which Owen wanted to site away from the old brick-built one to avoid frightening the barn owl, he went to meet Sophie. He left the car in the lane and they walked together to Stella and Colin's allotment.

Scamp ran up to say hello as they approached the country cottage, then went back into his blanket-lined cardboard box.

'Kettle's on,' Stella called. 'Why don't you go and admire Colin's vegetables, while I pour? And wait till you see the chrysanthemums. Growing a treat they are, thanks to Peter's horse's generous contributions. Delighted he is to be growing a few flowers again.'

Colin was on the afternoon shift, but they duly admired the neat rows of vegetables and weed-free areas, dug and dusted with lime ready for next year's crops.

'It's all looking wonderful,' Sophie said, and Ryan agreed that Colin was a first-class gardener. As reward for their admiration they were given tea and cakes.

Rachel had promised to lend Sophie some old recipe books and Ryan used them as an excuse to invite her back. 'I'll drop you back at Badgers Brook as I leave,' he promised. 'I have to get back tonight.'

There was no sign of Rachel or Tommy when they got to the farm. Owen was nowhere to be seen and the chickens were hovering around the coops ready to tuck themselves up for the night.

'Where is everyone?' Ryan said with a frown. He went

upstairs to see if anyone was there and came down with the frown even deeper. 'There's no sign of them.'

'Phone the pub, Daphne might know,' Sophie suggested.

When he replaced the receiver a flash of anger crossed his face. 'Mam and Dad have gone to Tenby again. Owen decided to book the few days as a treat for them. He's driven them there. Why didn't he tell me?'

'A surprise?'

'I don't like secrets and Owen is keeping too many lately. I still haven't been told exactly why we have to change our accountant.'

'Might he be taking things into his own hands to make sure he's indispensable? Rumours about your selling must concern him a little.'

'He's taking advantage of my parents. They're so unhappy about Gareth and me refusing to take on the farm and he's playing on their vulnerability.'

'He's been trying to persuade Sarah they might have a future together. She treats it as a joke but he's told her he's moving away.'

'What's going on? What's he up to? Is there something I don't know? He didn't tell me how badly they'd been hurt in the accident, now he's shuffling them off on holidays without a word. Is there something else I'm not being told?'

'I don't think your parents are ill, if that's what you're thinking, just, as you say, unhappy. Perhaps Owen's aware of how hard they work and wants to give them a few days holiday before it gets colder. They enjoyed the last visit so much.'

'I'm their son, so why wasn't I in on the surprise?'

She shrugged. 'Do you want me to stay until Owen comes back?'

'I should stay, have it out with him, remind him of his position here and the need to keep me informed. But if I miss another day I'll be working all weekend and every evening to catch up.'

'Then go. I'll wait here, and as soon as Owen gets back I'll tell him to phone you, however late.'

'I don't want to leave you. Besides, I want to get to the bottom of it.'

'Shouldn't we shut up the chickens and check the barn doors?'

'I'll do that,' he said, reaching for a torch. 'Will you build up the fire? You might be in for a long wait.'

As he put on his coat and waited for a taxi to arrive to take him to the station he looked at her, and she stood and walked over to him. His arms came round her and he pressed her close. This time she didn't resist when he kissed her, and he left her wide eyed and a little anxious, her heart pounding as though it would burst, wanting to run after the taxi, call him back.

Ryan sat on the late-night train, his mind clear, but he couldn't look at the papers he had brought, and he thought only of Sophie. He hoped she hadn't been frightened away by his kiss. A kiss he had longed for ever since they had met. He wanted to look after her, not just now but always.

Owen came in at eleven and was surprised to see Sophie sitting beside the fire dozing in the cosy warmth.

'Sophie? What are you doing here?'

'Hello, Owen. Will you phone Ryan? He should be back by now. He said it didn't matter how late.'

'At this time of night? No, I won't!'

'It's important.'

He went into the hall and she heard his voice, low, but clearly angry, followed by the sound of the phone being returned to its rest. He came back into the room and said, sharply, 'Come on, I have to get you home. I have an early start, remember.'

It sounded like a reprimand, but she said nothing, just collected her bag and coat and followed him to the van. He hardly said a word on the short journey and when she stepped out at the gate of Badgers Brook he drove off without even saying goodnight, hardly giving her time to get out so he had to lean over to close the passenger door as he was moving off. He was angry and she wondered what had been said.

The following morning, Owen rose earlier than usual, and before Harry Sutton arrived most of the routine chores had been done. 'I have to go into town,' he announced as Harry reached for the overall he habitually wore. 'If I'm not back at dinner time, go in and make yourself a cup of tea.'

'Anything special you want me to do?'

'You know what needs doing, don't you?' Owen snapped.

The solicitor was with a client and Owen drummed a tattoo with nervous fingers on the table as he waited to be seen. The solicitor was new and enthusiastic and he listened carefully to Owen's instructions. When he left the smart new office, which still smelled of paint and varnish, Owen was smiling, all tension gone. The papers he held in his hand promised him a safe future. Ryan and Gareth could go and stuff themselves.

To his annoyance he saw Sophie and the dratted Bertie in the field and called to them, waving an arm impatiently.

'I want you to keep out of these fields,' he shouted as they drew near. 'This isn't a public highway!'

'We were gathering mushrooms to make some soup,' Sophie protested. 'No one will object to that, surely?'

'*I* object! Now get off this land.'

'I hate you!' Bertie shouted as they went into the wood.

'Hush, Bertie, he's only a bad-tempered man.'

'He keeps coming to talk to Mam, and he isn't bad-tempered then,' the boy grumbled.

Jekyll and Hyde, Sophie thought. Smiles for Sarah and a scowl for everyone else. If he was really interested in winning Sarah back, upsetting Bertie wasn't a good idea.

The surveyors came later that day and again on the following morning. If Harry was curious he didn't ask, he just got on with the work while the small group wandered across the fields and disappeared into the various outbuilding, but he watched them and wondered why Daphne hadn't come, and why it was being done while Tommy and Rachel were out of the way.

He didn't go into the farmhouse at midday to eat his lunch. Instead he drove down to the Ship and Compass on the tractor, where Daphne was behind the bar.

'So this is what you're doing. Skiving, eh?'

'Yes, and enjoying it,' Daphne said, pulling his pint. 'Owen said he could manage without me today, so I'm helping Betty. Nice to be popular, Harry.'

'Something to do with them surveyors no doubt.'

'Oh?' she looked thoughtful then added, 'Tommy did say something about getting a new barn, it's probably that. Pity they had to come when Tommy and Rachel aren't there.'

'They're doing a lot of measuring for one Dutch barn,' he muttered, before taking a first loud sip.

When Harry went for a drink on the way home that evening, he was surprised to see Daphne there, and on her own. 'Taken over, have you?' he asked, putting down a shilling. 'Blimey, girl, wherever I go *you* turn up. I'll have you know I'm spoken for,' he teased.

'Betty went to see her brother but she'd delayed so I opened up. She's sure to be back soon.'

He moved closer and asked, 'Do you know anything about the Treweathers selling up? The survey covered most of the land and all of the buildings.'

'Not a thing, I'd never been on a farm until I came here.'

Daphne was kept busy that night, but Harry helped, collecting and washing glasses and bringing up bottles from the cellar.

'I used to help Ed now and then, when Betty was out,' he explained. At closing time Betty still hadn't returned. She came in as Daphne was washing the last of the glasses.

'Sorry I am, I couldn't even let you know.'

'Is your brother all right?'

'Not really. Look, I'll make a cup of tea and I'll tell you what's been going on.'

'There's no need,' Daphne protested, but she found it difficult to hide her curiosity and hurriedly dealt with the till and locked the money away while Betty took off her coat and made a tray of tea.

'Today I made Elsie tell Ed the truth, and he's shocked beyond belief. The poor man is reeling. He had no idea. She's been running the guest-house, employing extra help and covering up her gradually worsening condition.'

'What will he do?'

'I don't know. I've revealed the problem but I can't offer a solution. I tried not to interfere but in the end I decided that

167

my loyalties were with my brother, not Elsie, and I made her tell him. Now I don't know whether I'm feeling guilty or relieved. Both I think.

'Look, I know it's an imposition, but could you manage here for a few evenings, while we discuss what's to be done?'

'Of course. Once Rachel and Tommy are back they won't need me any more, so I'd love to help.'

'Thank you. You, Daphne Boyd, are amazing.'

The next time Owen was waiting for Sarah outside the shop she marched up and demanded to know why he had sent her son off his land. 'He wasn't doing any harm. Even a nine-year-old can't do much damage to grass!' she shouted.

'I know and I'm sorry. It wasn't Bertie, it's Sophie I'm trying to discourage.'

'Why? What can *she* do to grass? Anyway, Harry Sutton told us your aunt and uncle have no objections to us being there.'

'Harry Sutton should mind his own business."

'So should you, Owen Treweather. So should you!' She pushed against the side of the van as though trying to push it over. 'And get this filthy old van out of my way, it lowers the tone of the street!' She was hiding her laughter as she hurried away.

Two days later, Rachel and Tommy returned to find Harry Sutton had been sacked and Owen had employed two part-timers. He made up some story about Harry's poor time-keeping, telling them he had done most of the chores before he arrived, without explaining that he had risen two hours earlier to make sure it happened. 'He also went to the pub at dinner and was twenty minutes late, explaining that he'd been helping Daphne while Betty was out. We pay his wages, not Betty.' It sounded reasonable.

The real reason he didn't want Harry around was in case he said too much about the surveyors' visit. The mortgage he had arranged was not intended to be used for a Dutch barn or resurfacing the approach road. Owen had a far better plan for the money, which had been transferred into a new account with himself as one of the signatures required for withdrawals and payments. He wouldn't have difficulties faking a signature for Rachel or Tommy.

He'd been treated as nothing more than a labourer and now he was going to take what he was owed.

Daphne protested about the sacking of Harry. 'He did much more than he needed while he was there and the twenty minutes was once only on the day the surveyors were there and that was my fault anyway.'

To her utter surprise he told her she was sacked and needn't come again, and her wages would be sent to her.

Shocked and puzzled, she told Sophie.

Ed and Elsie sat and stared at Betty; neither of them knew what to say. Betty had arrived that morning, was closely followed by the doctor and Brenda Morris, the nurse. The prognosis of Elsie's illness was discussed but Elsie herself said nothing.

'Deterioration is never constant. Sometimes there is little change for a while, then it begins to move again,' the doctor explained. Glassy eyed, Elsie still remained silent.

When the doctor had left and Elsie had gone to her room to rest, Betty asked her brother whether he thought he and Elsie still had a future together.

'I married her for better or worse and I'll stick with that. But I won't live with her. That would be too much of a farce.'

'You can't come back to the Ship, Eddie, you can't leave her alone.'

'I don't intend to do either. I'll run this place – I've been doing it for these weeks and I know the routine – and Elsie will go into a nursing home. The money this place makes and what she's got saved will pay for it.' That was his decision, he said, and it was final.

After walking around for a while, calling to see Stella and scrounging a cup of tea, Betty went back to the pub and asked Daphne if she'd like a permanent job there.

'I'd hoped that once Elsie and Ed had settled down, Ed would have come back to helping me. After all, Elsie ran her place alone for years and he wouldn't have been needed, but now the chance of that is well and truly gone.'

They talked about the tragedy Elsie faced and both admitted a sneaking sympathy for the dishonest way she had dealt with it. 'No one wants to be alone, and having an illness must make it even harder to face loneliness.' Betty said.

'Yet because of her you're losing the partnership of your brother after so many years.'

'I'll cope. Especially with you helping me.'

Daphne happily accepted the job then went to find Sophie to tell her the good news.

Nine

Ryan, unaware of the changes threatening his parents' farm, was in London. He had begged a lift from one of the lecturers and had found a cheap bed and breakfast for one night. He had a letter from Daphne in his wallet bearing Sophie's previous address and he went, without much hope, to the area where she had once lived.

Since the war had ended, many of the streets had been rebuilt, but the new walls and the clean lines of fences failed to conceal scars from that terrible time. In many of the streets there were gaps when houses had once stood, and in one the middle of what had once been a long terrace of beautifully built houses was now a park

He found the street without difficulty and saw, on the corner, a small grocery shop. A perfect place to begin his enquiries; everyone who used it would have a ration book and therefore would be a regular customer and well known to the proprietor. He tried the rather dusty door but to his disappointment it was closed. A Friday afternoon and it was closed? He looked around for a notice, hoping for a 'Back in five minutes' message, but there was nothing. He peered through the window and realized there was little likelihood of anyone returning within five minute or five weeks. It had clearly been closed for some time. Thinking of Stella Jones, and the gossip filter that was her post office, he asked a passer-by for directions to the nearest one.

The post office was a new building and the owners were also new. Another setback. He sighed to himself as he went to a café to decide what he should do next. He knew Sophie had lost her immediate family, but most people had other relatives: cousins, uncles, aunts, and friends and neighbours. There must be someone who knew her and could persuade her to talk, but where could he look?

He went back to the small grocery shop and tried three doors before he had a response. The door was slowly opened and the face of a very elderly lady peered short-sightedly at him. She was tiny, well under five feet tall. He felt tempted to sit back on his heels as when talking to a child. White hair waved around her face in an absentminded way, bright blue eyes stared at him, the mouth was screwed up like a rosebud. In reply to his question about the Daniels family, she said she couldn't tell him anything. 'The woman who ran the shop would know. I think they was related.'

'Wonderful! Where will I find her?'

'Gone she is, a long time ago.'

'You don't know where she went?'

'No, but you could try Mrs Harris in thirty-five,' she suggested, and he went there to be told Mrs Harris had died a month previously.

'So much for close neighbourhoods,' he said sadly to the new tenant. 'I'm looking for the family called Daniels who lived here until they were bombed in 1945.'

'I remember them, and what happened that night,' the woman said. 'Terrible. The whole family gone like that. I lost a brother the same night.'

'Then you'd know if there are any other members of the Daniels family left?' he asked hopefully. 'I'd very much like to find them.'

'There's her as used to keep the corner shop. She was related, of course, but she's moved into one of the new flats and I don't know her address.'

'Was her name Daniels?'

'No, she was on the mother's side. Now what was her name . . .?' She frowned deeply but there was no sign of her dredging up the name from the depths of her memory. 'I'm a bit forgetful these days, but it'll come, give me a day or so, it always comes in the end.'

'I only have today and tomorrow morning, then I have to get back,' he said, staring at her, willing her to remember. 'Would you mind if I called in the morning to see if the name has come back to you? Or I could give you my address so you could write to me? It's very important.' He took out a creased envelope and began to write.

'No, I ain't fond of writing. You come in the morning, young man, I might have got it by then.'

With that he had to be content. He knew how elusive memories could be. Even his mother, whom he considered to have a remarkable grasp of everything, could sometimes struggle to bring a half-remembered name to mind.

Before he left the following morning he called on the lady, whose name he learned was Brewster, but she still couldn't help. 'I promise to make a note of it if I do remember, in case you come back. I can jot down the name for you, even if I can't write letters,' she said.

He sat in a café to fill the remaining time, and as he was walking disconsolately back to the underground station, a face he remembered well stopped in front of him. The tiny old lady grabbed his coat and tugged. 'You that bloke who called asking about the corner shop?' Without waiting for a reply she pointed to a woman hurrying towards the bus stop, where the conductor was waving on the last of the queue of passengers. 'That's her! What used to run the shop. Hurry up or you'll miss her.'

Unable to believe such luck, he hesitated for a moment then thanked his elderly informant and ran. The bus was moving off and he called and waved, but the conductor called back that the bus was full and there'd be another one along in a minute.

'Told you to hurry, didn't I?' the old lady said, disgust pursing her lips even more tightly. He asked more questions, but there were no answers and she became irritated by his insistence and her own failure. If she had once known the name it was hidden deep among layers of other memories. Mrs Brewster was his only hope. He bought a note pad, envelopes and some stamps. He wrote his name and address on an envelope, stamped it and returned to Mrs Brewster.

'You don't need to write a letter, he explained. 'Just write the name and pop it into the envelope. Please? A young lady is very unhappy and you could help her if you remember the name of the lady in the shop. Will you try?'

'You hassling me don't 'elp.' She touched her head dramatically. 'I think it's gone for good.'

He gave her the packet of envelopes and the pad. 'Keep the rest in case you need them sometime. But please, write down the name for me, will you? Just the name.' On impulse he handed her the small fountain pen from his pocket. 'Take this too.' She was his only hope.

'Call again when you're passing, in case I lose the envelope,' she said, closing the door, damping his spirits even further.

He stopped one last time at the old shop. Looking through the window with a hand above his eyes to help him peer through the dusty glass he saw a notice that made him start with wild hope. Hand-written on a piece of cardboard, he read, 'Home Made Pickles and Preserves'.

The school term had begun and Sophie had agreed to look after Bertie after school until Sarah finished work at the dress shop. With the approach of autumn, Sophie was busy making the chutneys and pickles that would be in extra demand over the Christmas season. She was helped by a surprising number of people, who offered her their sugar allowance on the promise of a jar of their favourite preserve, or in exchange for her unwanted rations. She no longer went into Maes Hir market with her baskets, as Hope and Peter Bevan sold everything she managed to make. There was less profit, but it was much easier. Peter was able to charge more than she had done when she sold from her wicker baskets, and with the material cover added by Hope they looked as good as they tasted.

She usually walked Bertie back at half past five to the sad little room where he and Sarah lived and would wait for Sarah to arrive. Once she saw Sarah approaching she didn't stay unless there was news from school to impart. She would wave and walk straight back to Badgers Brook. But on one occasion in early September, Sarah called to her and invited her inside.

The room was still very overcrowded but there was an air of orderliness that hadn't been apparent before. The clutter had been greatly reduced and their possessions arranged in neat areas: books and toys on the window sill, food arranged under fly-proof nets. She showed Sophie that the few pans she possessed were hidden from sight in the oven of the old-fashioned cooker. Clothes were stacked in an attractive wooden box decorated with a woodland scene of trees and bluebells, which she was told had been painted by Hope Bevan.

Tea and biscuits were produced, Bertie helping to set out the small table near the fireplace, which boasted a rather large gas fire.

'Thanks to you,' Sarah began self-consciously, 'Bertie and I are hoping to move into something better before Christmas. I'm cleaning each morning and working in the shop in the afternoons, and my savings are already beginning to grow. Without your help we'd never have been able to move from here. Thank you.'

Embarrassed, Sophie hushed her and smiled. 'I'm not doing anything I don't enjoy,' she said. 'Bertie is my friend and we have a lovely time while he waits for you to come home to him, don't we, Bertie?'

'Yes, miss, and I help on the garden, don't I?'

'D'you know,' Sophie said conspiratorially to Sarah, 'your son is becoming quite knowledgeable in the garden. Bob Jennings says he's a natural.'

As Sophie was leaving, Sarah asked, 'Will you come with me when I look at places to rent? I know I sound feeble, but having lived here for so long I'm half afraid to try somewhere new in case I make a wrong decision.'

Again the fear of advising someone made Sophie hesitate. Finally she said, 'Of course I'll come, so you can use me as a sounding-board, but I'm sure you won't need any advice about where you and Bertie live. You'll know the moment you step in, like I did with Badgers Brook.'

'Oh, it wouldn't be as grand as that!' Sarah replied. 'A self-contained flat would be perfect,' she said dreamily. 'One day, perhaps, but for now just a couple of rooms and if we're lucky a bit of garden for Bertie to grow things. He's keen to show me what he can do with a patch of earth and a few seeds,' she added proudly.

*　　*　　*

175

Daphne was waiting for Sophie when she reached home, sitting on the step looking disconsolately at a pile of weeds she had pulled from the front border.

'I can't afford to pay you for gardening,' Sophie teased. 'People work in Badgers Brook for nothing, just for the pleasure of being here.'

'You're late. Is everything all right?'

'Fine. Sarah invited me to stay for a cup of tea. Seems she and Bertie will be looking for a better place to live soon. With two jobs and the determination to stop frittering her wages away she can afford to move. Good news, isn't it? I hope it's somewhere closer to the rest of us.'

'Good on 'em.' Daphne sighed.

Becoming aware of her friend's melancholy, Sophie asked what was wrong. 'Aren't you happy working with Betty at the pub?'

'Oh yes, I love it and Betty's so kind. But I'm so hurt at the abrupt way Owen dismissed me from Treweather Farm. I thought ... We seemed to be getting on so well ... I hoped ...' She turned to stare at Sophie, her eyes sad, her voice low. 'I was beginning to think we had a future, Owen and I. The farm was a place I wanted to be, I was even happier there than at the Ship and Compass with Betty. And with Harry leaving, Ryan and Gareth refusing to accept farming as their future and Tommy and Rachel no longer as fit as they were, I thought we'd be running it. He seemed to be hinting at that, discussing plans, gradually building up a picture of the two of us, side by side, him dealing with the farm and me running the house for them. But I must have been wrong.'

'He's still married to Sarah, remember, even though they've lived apart since before Bertie was born.'

'That's another thing. He went to the solicitor and started divorce proceedings. Why do that after all this time if he wasn't considering looking forward to a new beginning?'

'Perhaps he's afraid of risking another relationship. He was dreadfully hurt by Sarah and every time he sees young Bertie it's a cruel reminder of how his marriage ended.'

'I think it's something more than that. He was over Sarah

and I'd helped him to accept what had happened and he was thinking of a future with me, I know he was.'

'Doubts can be revived long after everything seems settled. Who knows what goes on under the surface of someone's mind? Words and expressions can conceal as well as display how someone feels. Look at Ryan and Gareth: their parents believed they were content, looking into a secure future, with no doubts about it being the correct one for them, while all the time they were both hating it and planning to leave.'

'I can't help wondering whether the change of heart was due to something I said. It was that sudden. One day he was talking about our future, then he told me I had to leave, that I was no longer needed.'

'D'you remember what you were discussing?'

'I mentioned seeing the surveyors walking around the house, yards, sheds and fields. Wondering why they needed such a thorough assessment and valuation simply to build a barn and resurface a road. He questioned me rather sharply about what I'd seen and heard. I mentioned looking at the maps and plans spread out on the kitchen table, and I told him I'd spoken to the surveyor's assistant. He didn't say much at first, just asked why I'd been there when he'd told me I wouldn't be needed that day.'

'And why were you there?'

'Oh, you know how it is, Sophie, when you're starting to feel an attraction for someone, you look for excuses to see them. I went to check the cupboards and make a shopping list, intending to buy a few necessities ready for when Rachel got back. Nothing really urgent, and I had to admit that when he asked. I thought he'd be pleased or at least thank me for helping, but he just told me to go, that I wasn't needed any longer.'

'It could still be his lack of confidence making him afraid of needing you too much. With a failed marriage behind him and the fact that he hasn't tried again since. Ten years is a long time.'

'Should we write to Ryan?'

'And tell him what? That your romance has failed to blossom?' She put out a hand to touch Daphne's arm. 'I don't mean to sound harsh. I'm really sorry you're upset, but I don't think Owen—' She was about to say that Owen wasn't the one for Daphne, but she stopped. How dare she say such a thing? She glanced at Daphne, who was staring at her, waiting for her to finish the sentence. 'I don't think Owen will let you go if he really loves you. Give it time. Let's do nothing and see what happens.'

'But how did I upset him?'

'Perhaps someone else did. He'll explain when things are settled.'

'He sacked Harry Sutton very unexpectedly, too, didn't he?' Daphne added doubtfully.

'I admit that was odd. Harry seems to be a good man. He often worked more than the hours he was paid for, yet Owen made a case for sacking him.'

'What if he's up to something? Shouldn't we at least mention it to Ryan or Gareth or Tommy? Let them decide?'

'Ryan and Gareth are both expected home at the weekend. Perhaps we can bring the conversation around to what's happening then.'

Gareth travelled from France on the boat train and arrived tired and weary having hitched lifts from Dover with Brian Powell. Gareth showed Brian into the spare room and went to his own, and they both collapsed into a deep sleep still fully clothed.

When Rachel and Tommy arrived they looked in at the two men and left them to sleep off their exhaustion. Rachel found Owen and immediately asked when Daphne would be calling.

'She won't be,' Owen said. 'She's been discussing our business at the pub and I suspect it was from her that the rumours about our selling up began. I told her to leave.'

'We'll have a family meeting this evening,' Tommy said. 'Ryan will be here by then and Gareth will surely have woken.' He looked hard at Owen. 'You'd better sit in on it too.'

'Thank you, Uncle Tommy.' Owen tried not to sound sarcastic. Why shouldn't he be involved? He did most of the work. But it was more important than ego now. He needed to be fully aware of their intentions so he could match his arrangements to theirs. Things were moving fast.

Ryan walked along the lane towards Badgers Brook carrying a small suitcase. His father's letter asking him to come home that weekend was inconvenient but he'd had to obey. He didn't want to be absent when the running of the farm was being discussed; there had been too many changes recently that he hadn't been involved in. He and Gareth had written to each other and neither of them was easy about what was happening in their absence. Owen appeared to be taking control and encouraging their father to leave more and more of the decision-making to him.

Sophie was out. The house was silent with that peaceable silence that many old properties have, and he was tempted to sit in the garden and wait. Better not. Gareth would be home and he needed to talk to him before the family meeting began. Picking up his case he wandered through the wood until he was looking down on the roofs of his home. Gulls gathered on one of the fields, shrieking at each other, arguing over what they found. It was a beautiful place and one he hated to leave, but he couldn't take it on as his father had done. And that decision was partly influenced by his feelings for Sophie, for whom the life of a farmer was inconceivable. The desire to see Sophie was strong and, leaving his case near the top of the field, he went back to Badgers Brook. Still no sign of her, so he walked along the lane to the main road and the Ship and Compass. If she wasn't with Daphne, her friend might know where she was to be found.

Betty opened the side door and invited him in. 'Sophie's here if that's who you're looking for,' she said. 'She and Daphne are trying to re-cover an armchair to give to Sarah, although from the giggles and shrieks I don't think they're making much progress.'

'It's all right, Betty,' Daphne said. 'We're off to ask Hope Bevan to finish it for us. We know when we're beaten.'

Sophie appeared behind her and stepped forward to greet Ryan. He took her hand. 'I've been looking for you,' he said.

179

'Well I'm off so Hope can do this before Sarah sees what a mess we've made of it,' Daphne said, edging past them.

'Don't go yet,' Ryan said. 'I wonder if you can tell me how things are at the farm?'

Sophie and Daphne shared a glance. Betty went to make the inevitable tea.

'Sophie and I don't go up there any more.'

'We've been told to stay away by Owen,' Sophie told him.

Ryan tightened his grip on her hand and looked questioningly at Daphne.

'It isn't for us to say, but we think there's something going on that you haven't been told about.'

They explained about the dismissal of both Harry Sutton and Daphne. The survey was mentioned and at once Ryan said, 'At least that's above board, we're having a new barn built and the architects need to know the best site, and the ground would be tested for drainage and things like that.'

'What I saw was a thorough survey of the farm, including the buildings and all the fields,' Daphne said. 'Even the woodland. I don't pretend to understand exactly what would be needed, but for one small barn there was an awful lot of investigation.'

Ryan was thoughtful as he drank the tea Betty had made, but said nothing more. He needed to talk to his brother.

He walked back with the two young women and, after collecting his case, went down the field to the farm.

Ryan was met at the door by a bleary-eyed brother and a man he didn't know. Both had wet hair and were dressed in scruffy trousers and shirts.

'Heavens, Gareth! Did you swim from France?'

They stepped towards each other, slapping shoulders affectionately, then Gareth turned and said, 'Brian, meet my brother.'

'God 'elp,' Brian gasped. 'If you hadn't just washed your hair I'd be lost to know which of you is Gareth!'

The twins sometimes forgot how alike they were, and meeting new people for the first time was often amusing, but today Ryan was too worried to enjoy the joke.

'Excuse us, Brian, but I need to speak to Gareth urgently.'

'Your mother is cooking us something, so don't be long, I'm too hungry to wait for you and you could be too late and find all the pots empty,' Brian warned, still looking from one to the other in amazement.

Briefly, Ryan told Gareth what he had heard from Sophie and Daphne.

'We need to discuss this without Owen being there,' Gareth said. 'I have to eat, so will you tell Dad he has to change his mind about allowing Owen to sit in? We can talk about the problems as we eat.'

'Supper will be late,' Rachel told Owen. 'Why don't you go for a pint and get back for ten o'clock?'

'Is this a polite way of telling me I'm not invited to the meeting after all?'

'Of course not,' Tommy said. 'We'll have the meeting in the morning, after milking. Gareth is still half asleep anyway.'

When Owen had left for the Ship and Compass, Tommy opened an accounts book and placed a notebook on the table.

'Before we start on anything else,' Gareth said, 'I want you all to know that Brian and I have decided to buy a farm in France. We've already started proceedings and whatever the outcome is of these discussions, nothing will change that. We hope you can all come and see what needs doing – your help will be invaluable, there's a lot to be done.' He took a deep breath, having gabbled the announcement. Then he smiled at his parents, trying to hide the tension he had been feeling since he arrived.

'Now, where should we begin?' he asked. 'With you, Ryan?'

'France? What are you talking about?' White faced, Tommy clutched Rachel's arm and stared at his son. 'This farm is yours and Ryan's. Your life is here. Why won't you accept that?'

'Leave it, Dad, there's something we need to discuss first,' Ryan said. 'There was a thorough survey of the farm done while we were all absent. You and Mam had been sent on one of Owen's little holidays, I was away and Gareth was in France. So what was it for and why weren't we informed about what was going on?'

'No mystery,' Tommy said, still looking at Gareth. 'We are

181

having a new barn. It was your idea, Gareth. You said the old ones all need replacing.'

'Daphne saw the maps and sketches spread across the table and the survey covered every yard of the land we own. Why would Owen have that work done for a new Dutch barn?'

'She wouldn't understand what she saw.'

'When Owen knew what she had seen and overheard, he told her to go, that she was no longer needed.'

'Coincidence.'

Ryan looked at his father. 'Sure about that, are you?'

'Of course. Stop trying to make a drama about every little thing!'

'But you won't mind me talking to someone at the surveyor's office, just to find out for sure?'

'I'll do that,' Tommy said. 'Now, Gareth, what's this nonsense about France?'

'Brian and his wife and I want to buy this place in Northern France, and we need money, so I want you to release a part of my share of this place. We'll have to sell it anyway, now both Ryan and I want to do other things. Better sooner than later, so you and Mam can enjoy your retirement.' He looked at Ryan. 'Do you have any objections to selling?'

'None, but I don't think Mam and Dad are ready to leave, just yet.'

'Can I have a loan – part payment of what I'll get when we do sell? The place we want is run down and needs a lot of capital before it will support Brian's family and mine – when I eventually marry.'

The discussions rumbled on until almost ten o'clock and outside Owen listened, growing chilled but unable to move until the meeting had broken up. He didn't want to miss a word.

When Owen called and came inside, Ryan was surprised at how cold he looked. 'You look as though you walked back but I heard the car. Drove with the windows open, did you?'

'I've been standing watching the badgers in the wood,' Owen said.

His immaculate, mud-free shoes were noted but Ryan said nothing. Like most farmers, Owen would have had wellingtons in the boot of the car.

Supper would have been a silent meal if it hadn't been for Brian, who entertained them with stories about his attempts to survive on a tiny plot of land and handouts from his loving family. 'I knew the size of plot would make it impossible to make a good living, but it's taught me that growing things and building up a herd of cattle is what I want to do.'

Owen sat in the big kitchen and listened to Brian and Gareth talking about their plans to Tommy and Rachel. There was an edginess about the group, and he felt that it was only the presence of the stranger that stopped them erupting into a row. He listened and waited for an opportunity to break into the discussion. When Brian mentioned the cost of resurrecting the abandoned farm he and Gareth wanted to buy, he said quietly, 'You aren't trying to persuade Uncle Tommy to sell, are you, Gareth? He's got many years of satisfaction ahead of him yet.'

'Don't talk rot.' Tommy shifted position and turned to glare at Rachel. 'Where's my cup of tea then? It's time we were all in bed.'

'You would let me know if you do plan to sell, won't you? I need notice if I'm to find a new place, remember. I'm not family, am I?'

'Of course you are,' Rachel said soothingly. 'And if we make any momentous decisions like that we'll tell you straight away.'

'Thank you, Auntie Rachel.' Again the sarcasm went unnoticed.

It was clear that things were coming to a head and he had to speed up his plans. It would be interesting to see what would be discussed at tomorrow's meeting when he would be allowed to attend. Nothing of great importance, he guessed.

Tommy went to see Daphne early the following morning. The side door of the Ship and Compass was open and there, to his embarrassment, was Owen's estranged wife, washing the floor. She had a scarf over curlers in her hair and a thick sacking apron covered her clothes.

'Morning, Sarah,' he said, stepping over the damp patch she had just wiped. 'Bertie all right?'

'Hello. Yes, he's fine,' was her automatic reply. 'As if you care,' she mouthed silently.

Daphne was in the cellar, counting bottles and making out an order for the wholesaler. Invited by Betty to go down, he descended the stone steps and walked over to where Daphne was crouched, trying to read labels on some old stock.

'D'you know, Betty, I think some of these might be valuable, shall I make enquiries?' She looked up and saw Tommy. 'Oh, sorry, Mr Treweather, I didn't expect to see you.'

'I want to know why you were told not to come to the farm again. Did Owen give a reason?'

'Not really. He just said I wouldn't be needed any more. Rachel – I mean, Mrs Treweather – is able to cope now, and it was only a temporary arrangement, wasn't it?'

'Yes, but the decisions are mine and Rachel's to make, not Owen's.'

'I thought that as he runs the farm and is a cousin he has as much say in what goes on as the rest of you.'

'Like arranging a survey, you mean?'

'I don't know about that, but I did think it a bit strange, such a thorough investigation, and done while you were all away. But it's none of my business and I've enough to do here with Betty.'

'Rachel and I would like you to come and meet Gareth's friend, Brian Powell. They are planning to farm in France. Daft idea if you ask me, and probably nothing more than a whim, but you might find it interesting. And we'd like to thank you for your help. Bring Sophie, too, if she'll come.'

'She was told not to go to the farm, too, but I imagine it's because of Bertie. I think it must be hard for Owen to see the boy.'

'Sophie too,' Tommy said firmly. 'Sunday do you?'

'The best day for us both.'

Sophie was walking through the wood later that morning, gathering small pieces of wood for kindling. She enjoyed the luxury of the fire in the evenings, even though the days were still warm. Badgers Brook was a house that attracted visitors and it was rare for an evening to pass without one or other

184

of her friends calling and being persuaded to stay for a cup of tea and a cake. With her basket almost full, and carrying a useful branch under her arm, she almost bumped into Gareth.

'Hello, Gareth, nice to see you. How long are you staying this time?'

Gareth grinned. 'Caught you! I'm Ryan,' he said.

She shook her head. 'You can't catch me.'

'Couldn't resist trying.'

'How are you?' she asked. 'Still enjoying your travels?'

'Not any more. I want to settle down and build a place of my own.'

'You're coming home? Your parents will be so pleased.'

'Not this home. I'm arranging to buy a place in France with a friend of mine.' Cupping his hands, he called, 'Brian, come and meet the girl of my dreams.'

She turned to smile a welcome. The stranger came along the path and approached them. Gareth put an arm on Sophie's shoulder and asked, 'Gareth not with you?'

'Oh, you're Ryan. Sorry, Gareth must have gone another way,' the man stuttered, staring into the face of his friend.

'Stop teasing the man,' Sophie said, laughing at the man's puzzled expression.

Introductions completed Sophie walked with the two friends, listening to their plans for the place they were about to buy. They gathered more logs as they strolled through the trees then went with her back to Badgers Brook to put them on the log pile.

'You'll hear all about our plans on Sunday,' Gareth said as they parted.

'Sunday?'

'You and Daphne are invited to tea.'

'Does Owen know?'

'What has it to do with him?'

'Nothing I suppose,' she said doubtfully.

As it was Saturday, Sophie was looking after Bertie, but, as he had been invited to stay with a friend from school the night before, it was almost twelve o'clock by the time she went to collect him. She had cooked some potatoes and they were slowly warming in the oven with a thin drizzle of oil over them. With a slice of cheese melted over leeks, it was a meal Bertie always enjoyed. She had made a golden syrup cake for pudding, another of his favourites.

He came running out of the house as soon as she touched the front gate. 'Starving I am, miss. Got anything nice for dinner?'

'Ground up coal and sour milk,' she said.

'Miss, I think I could even eat that, I'm so hungry.'

He walked beside her, chatting about the games he had played with his new friend. She was thankful that at last he was beginning to enjoy school and was making friends. His mother's increased interest in him was reaping wonderful harvests, she thought poetically. Owen drove past them in the muddy van but didn't acknowledge them. Bertie pulled an impressively ugly face.

Owen had been to see the solicitor. Progress was being made, he was told, and the money should be in his account within the month. Time was running out, but if he could stall Tommy and the others for just six or eight weeks before they began preparations to sell up, he would be in the clear and away from here. Whatever else happened, they mustn't try to sell the farm. Not yet.

Both Sophie and Daphne dressed with care to go to tea with the Treweathers. Sophie was dressing to please Ryan, and Daphne wanted to give Owen a chance to explain his hurtful dismissal of her. Well-chosen clothes would give them extra confidence; something they both needed.

As they approached, Ryan came to meet them.

'This is Mum's way of saying thank you to you both for your help when she needed it so badly. Today you are guests and here to be spoiled.'

Gareth and Brian both stood to greet them. Tommy nodded and looked away, staring out of the window at the yard and distant fields. There was no sign of Owen.

When Rachel came in with the large teapot, the teatime spread was complete and they all found their seats. Tommy forced his gaze away from his land and tried to be sociable.

'We're thinking of selling up,' Rachel said, glancing at Tommy. 'We have to face facts, and the truth is neither of the boys wants to continue. So we're seeing next year out and then we'll retire.'

Not quite knowing what to say, whether sympathy or congratulations were in order, Sophie said, 'I hope your last year here will be a very happy one for you all.'

They ate from the generously covered table but it was clear that no one was really enjoying the occasion.

'Tommy looks as though he's had a death sentence,' Sophie whispered to Daphne when they were alone.

'And Rachel is about to burst into tears. How soon can we make our escape, d'you think?'

'No sign of Owen, so we might as well go,' Sophie replied. 'Ryan and I are meeting later, so I don't mind if we leave early.' She looked at the leftover food and added, 'Pity young Bertie isn't here. He'd have cleared the rest of this, wouldn't he?'

Rachel re-entered the room, having taken out the dirty plates. 'Take something for Bertie if you wish. Boys of that age are constantly hungry. I'll pack him a bit of everything, shall I?'

'Thank you, he'll love it.'

Daphne and Sophie refused a lift and walked back through the field and the wood, carrying a selection of sandwiches and cake wrapped in a tea towel. 'Pity it's for Bertie,' Daphne said. 'I could eat the lot now we're out of that room. It was more like a house of mourning than a family gathering, wasn't it?'

'Tommy and Rachel *are* in mourning. Selling the farm is the death of a dream. They imagined growing old there and watching sons and grandsons following in their footsteps.'

'I was beginning to believe I'd be the one looking after them,' Daphne added. 'Owen and me. I wonder why they don't accept that Owen is their continuity? He seems more than willing and he is a Treweather, Tommy's brother's son, but they treat him like an unskilled labourer.'

'And he's clearly resenting it. Do you have the feeling that something is about to burst?'

187

Ten

Elsie looked around the house that had been her home for all the years of her marriage to George Clements and ten years of widowhood. Marrying Ed had been a desperate attempt to stay there for the rest of her life, but cheating hadn't been the way to achieve that goal. Ed was sitting opposite her as they waited for the matron of a nursing home to arrive. Today she was being assessed to decide on the level of care she would need, and then she would leave this place and never return.

'Would things have been different if I'd been honest with you?' she asked.

'I thought you really cared for me, that's the hurt. You used me, saw me for a mug and decided to flatter me, tell me a lot of lies and make me think you wanted to marry me and share my life.'

'The daftest thing is that I am fond of you. I think we're too old for passion, but I've never found another man I'd be prepared to open my house and heart to.'

'Rubbish.'

'I was wrong about not telling you, but I'm not lying about that.'

He looked at her and she stared him out, willing him to believe her. It was true in a way. Perhaps she wouldn't have allowed things to go this far if she hadn't been ill, hadn't needed him, but she was fond of him and they worked so well together that she was trying desperately to convince herself, and him, that they would have married anyway.

'There'll be many months, perhaps years, before I'm really helpless, Eddie. Can't we at least enjoy the best of the time together? We could employ someone to do most of the work, and we'll be here to feed our guests and enjoy the company. I've always enjoyed the company.'

'You hurt me, Elsie, and I can't forgive you. This is the only solution, me working to keep you in a place where you'll have the best attention.' How could he admit that he was unable to cope with her illness, face years of increasingly difficult care, watch her as her health deteriorated. He was a coward, afraid of taking on something he couldn't manage. How could he tell her that?

Elsie guessed that the shock had been devastating, that he had looked forward to a few more years running the guest-house then a happy retirement. She also knew that they would have needed some good years behind them before she could have expected him to take on the care of an increasingly help-less invalid, but she hadn't been given that time. If only they had married years ago, before the diagnosis had changed everything, then he'd have been a part of it, would have stayed, bound by love, and shared the grief.

Tommy waited until Owen came in for breakfast after the early morning chores. Ryan had stayed on and he and Gareth were sitting at the table as Rachel handed out the plates of food. Brian had eaten a slice of toast and gone for a walk, knowing the family had something private to discuss.

'Why were there men walking around my farm with maps and clipboards, Owen?' Tommy asked, almost conversation-ally.

'Oh, something to do with a national survey. They are doing a country-wide assessment of the acreage of woodland and arable land, and the quality of the farm buildings.' There had been some mention of such a thing and he found the lies coming easy.

'And when were you going to tell me?'

'At the meeting to which I wasn't invited. Remember? You sent me off to the pub.'

'When did you know about this? Before *you* sent *us* away to Tenby?'

'It slipped my mind, it wasn't important to us, just a general gathering of information.'

'You have some names? Phone numbers? Somewhere I can check to find out what's going on?'

'There's nothing going on, Uncle. They came and they went and we can forget it.'

He stood up, pushing aside the half-eaten omelette. 'I'd better get on, there's a delivery of feed tomorrow and I want to get the barn cleared and cleaned up. We'll have to get the rat catcher here again, too. There's an infestation of the damned things. Would you like me to phone him in the morning, Uncle Tommy?'

'Thank you, yes, if you will.'

'I'll deal with it first thing.'

'What d'you think?' Tommy asked his sons when Owen had gone. 'Is he hiding something, or just determined to keep certain things to himself, be indispensable?'

'I don't trust him,' Gareth said.

'I think you should make sure you see everything that comes by post and insist either you or Mam answers every phone call,' was Ryan's opinion. 'He's changed. He's full of resentment, which he tries to hide with a subservient smile.'

'This is nonsense,' Rachel said. 'Owen has lived here with us since he was five. I've brought the boy up, and he isn't the type to do anything devious. He's glad to have a home here and he'd be a fool to risk that, lose his job and his home. I think we're making a fuss about nothing.'

'Unless he thinks he's owed more than we give him,' Gareth said with a glance at his brother. 'I think I'll stay around for a while, just to see what's going on.'

'Your mother and I would be happy if you'd stay, and it wouldn't do any harm. Your friend Brian, too, if he'd like to.'

'He has to get back to his wife. Dad, is there any chance you and Mam can help me, financially, to buy the farm we want in France? I'd appreciate it if you'd come over, give the place the benefit of your experienced eye, tell us what we should be doing there, you know the sort of thing, and you know how easily a project like this can go dreadfully wrong. We'd really appreciate it. Why don't you both come for a week? We'll arrange accommodation, make it a working holiday.'

'I don't think I want to be away from here at present. But I'll go and talk to the accountant tomorrow,' Tommy said. 'The money is yours as soon as we sell. We plan to arrange for you and Ryan to have a lump sum. There's no point in keeping it for some time in the future when it's now you need it. Your mother and I agree about that.'

'Thanks, Dad, and you, Mam. Just so that you know, though, Owen told me there's some kind of problem with the accountant – he said he was going to prepare some figures to show us.'

The accountant was surprised and not very pleased to see Tommy on Monday morning. 'I don't know why you're here, Mr Treweather. Your nephew made it clear that you were dissatisfied and I sent all your papers back to him. Who is dealing with your affairs now I have no idea.'

'But I don't understand.'

'Neither do I. But your accounts are no longer in my hands.'

'But you must know who is dealing with them?'

'Sorry, but I can't help you.'

As he left, Tommy turned and said, 'David, what the hell's going on?'

The man shrugged and picked up a sheet of paper and became engrossed.

Owen was in the milking parlour, washing down and dis-infecting the implements they used.

'Sorry I'm late with this, Uncle, but one of the men I employed didn't turn up and I'm a bit behind.'

'Why have you changed accountants without my say-so?' Tommy demanded, marching in and shutting off the tap to the hosepipe.

Owen carefully removed his rubber boots and gestured towards the house. 'Go into the office and I'll explain.'

The paper he showed his uncle was a comparative list of charges, one headed Treweathers and two others bearing the names of other local farms. 'As you see, we're paying a lot more for roughly the same amount of work. I though we'd do better to change.'

191

'You don't do anything like this without telling me, d'you understand? I've known David Carter for years and I wouldn't have agreed to the change for a fiddling amount like this. What's got into you, Owen?'

'Nothing's got into me. I'm in charge of accounts and spending, and I decided we could save money by changing, so that's what I did.'

'Then you can change back as soon as you like. Right?'

'That would appear very unprofessional.'

'So what?'

'At least let it stay for a month or two, then I can make the excuse that we don't work well together.'

'Just get it sorted. Right?'

'Oh, and, Uncle, I don't think it's a good idea to take money out for a while. Can't we just wait until this barn and roadway are dealt with? Can't Gareth wait? I don't like the risk of overspending and we need to be sure we know exactly what it will cost.'

'Wait before helping Gareth? How do you know about that?'

Owen stared at him, before turning the tap on again. Accompanied by the hiss of water through the pipe and the sound of it hitting the floor, he said, 'I overheard. I listened. It's the only way I get to know what's going on.'

Ryan had booked a tutor to help him with maths revision. He had already missed several days of the three weeks he had arranged. He and a friend had also been given permission to observe at a junior school and he had been absent more than he liked there, too. With the problems at the farm and the search in London for Sophie's family, he had allowed his attendance to drop. He was fortunate having a friend who wrote his notes making a carbon copy for him, and he was also willing to share with him all that had been discussed. These sessions with his friend, plus a great deal of reading, assisted by a helpful librarian, enabled him to keep up with the rest of the group. So it was with some embarrassment that he asked his tutor if he might finish early on the following Friday. Given extra work to do over the weekend, which he hoped to do on the train journey, he set off again for London.

He hated appearing unappreciative or unreliable but he had no choice.

He went firstly to see whether Mrs Brewster had miraculously remembered the name of the lady in the corner shop. Why hadn't the proprietor used her own name above the door instead of calling the place Victory Stores? he thought with mild frustration.

Mrs Brewster shook her head and said 'sorry' several times, and he left with the vague promise that he would hear from her if she eventually called the name to mind. Without much hope, he knocked on the door of the elderly lady who'd pointed out the woman who had known the family. Perhaps she'd be able to help. Memory can sometimes be completely illogical, discarding useful information and clearly retaining unimportant details.

She opened the door wearing the same suspicious expression, mouth pursed, brow furrowed with a deep frown as though preparing to say no, whatever was asked.

'You might remember me, I called a couple of weeks ago asking about the lady who used to keep the shop?'

'I remember, but someone else was here asking the same question a week ago. Not you, someone else.'

Thinking she was confused, and he was the person she referred to, he ignored that and asked, 'You haven't remembered the name, or where the lady lives?'

'He asked the same, said his name was Geoffrey something or other. I told him the same as you. I can't help. But I see her sometimes.'

'On the same day? Does she come here to pick up her pension, perhaps?'

'How d'you expect me to know that? Eh? You're worse than 'im with yer questions. Look, go and talk to the old woman at the grocers near the post office. If she picks up her pension she'll get her rations from the shop next door more'n likely.'

He thanked her and went to find the grocery shop. It was closed for lunch.

At two fifteen he was waiting with a huddle of women as the bolt was pulled back on the inside and the door opened to reveal a young woman. He looked around hopefully for an older assistant but the girl was on her own. When the shop had emptied he asked his questions. An elderly woman came through at the young woman's request and told him that the woman he was looking for was Victoria Morgan.

'I see why it was called Victory Stores,' he acknowledged with a smile. Thanking the two women he went back to the main road. With a name, it should be easy to find her.

There was very little time, just three hours the following morning, as most offices closed at twelve on Saturdays. He began with the Citizen's Advice Bureau, and on to several council offices. By pleading, bluffing and telling a great many lies, at eleven fifty that Saturday morning he had managed to learn Victoria Morgan's address.

At the block of flats he checked the number on the paper he'd been given, even though he was certain he'd never forget it, and went up the steps. He paused at the door, preparing what he would say, settling his features into a smile, and knocked. True to form, there was no reply. She was out and he had very little time left.

An enquiry at the flat next door was both a relief and a disappointment. Yes, it was the lady who had once owned Victory Stores, but no, she wasn't there. 'Staying in Wales with friends, and won't be back for a week or more,' he was informed.

'Is there any chance of seeing her if I call next weekend?'

'No, she ain't coming back till after next weekend. I'm looking after her cat,' the lady added, as though that clinched the matter.

The name Geoffrey kept entering his mind. Who was he and why was he looking for Sophie, or, at least, one of her relations? Could he be a cousin? An ex-neighbour? Or a lost boyfriend? How could he ask her? He didn't want to explain that he was in London searching for her roots. Not yet. Perhaps Daphne would know.

Invited by Rachel and Tommy, Sophie and Daphne went to the farm the weekend after Ryan's visit, while he was in London. They helped Rachel with some work she still found

194

difficult and Sophie made bread and a few cakes. She enjoyed the luxury of baking with fresh eggs instead of dried with Rachel using the excuse of broken eggs to make this possible. She also made fluffy omelettes for lunch and was praised by Rachel for her skill.

'Omelettes with chopped chives was one of my mother's specialities,' she said.

'A good cook, was she? Is that where you learned your expertise?'

Sophie didn't reply. The words had slipped from her unguarded mouth, weakened by the praise. 'I have to go or I'll be late for Bertie, I'm collecting him from a friend's house. He's always hungry and I like to have something ready for when he gets home.'

'Take these,' Rachel said, handing her two fresh brown eggs. 'Not a word, mind, or we'll be in trouble with the ministry.'

'Thank you! He'll love these, lightly boiled with slices of brown bread.'

Rachel and Tommy asked about the boy, showing an interest in his school work as well as his aptitude for gardening. Sophie praised Sarah for the way she had changed her life and how much happier they both were. 'Once they get out of that miserable room they'll be fine,' she told them.

'That's what we think,' Rachel said, glancing at Tommy.

'She's looking at two rooms in Barker Street tomorrow.'

'That's not much better than where they are now, and it's a long way from the school, and you.' Tommy said.

'There isn't a great deal of choice,' Sophie reminded them.

The phone rang while Sophie and Daphne were getting their coats. Rachel handed Daphne the receiver, and Sophie went outside to wait in the already darkening evening.

It was Ryan, asking, 'D'you know a friend or relation of Sophie's called Geoffrey?'

'Yes, he was the fiancé that jilted her,' she said in a low voice. 'Why, do you know anything about him?'

'I haven't met him. His name cropped up, that's all. I'll explain when we meet. Not a word, though, it's too complicated at present. All right?'

Daphne handed the phone back to Rachel and joined Sophie, who was standing at the edge of the chicken coop, where the birds were searching the ground for food, their bright eyes alert for the smallest item. 'That was Betty,' she lied. 'She wants me to pick up another loaf on the way home.'

Tommy was worried about Bertie and his mother. 'A little money would help them a lot,' he said to Rachel, 'but we can't just hand her some.'

'There must be something we can do,' Rachel said. 'Neither of them deserves to live like they do. I can't believe we've done nothing all these years.'

'Supporting Owen meant trying to forget Sarah, and when Bertie was a baby we got into the habit of forgetting him, too.'

It was seeing the small cottage on Fern Street that decided him. He went to see the owner and complained about the state of the place, the need for some maintenance and anything else he could think of. Then he struck a bargain that the rent would be reduced if the new tenant would deal with the redecoration and general cleaning. It was dirty and neglected, and he thought that with help Sarah could make it into a pleasant home. Now he had to convince her.

A letter intercepted before it reached Owen confirmed the name of the accountant he was using, and Tommy and Rachel went to see him. An hour later, the money Gareth needed had been transferred and an arrangement made that everything had to be countersigned by either Tommy or his wife, and a sample of each signature was recorded.

Tommy didn't know whether Owen was being dishonest, and he preferred to think he was not. But it wouldn't do any harm to keep a closer eye on things. Perhaps he had been slipping. Best he pick up the reins again and prepare to sell. He must try and forget any hope of his sons following on the tradition of generations.

He took Rachel into a café for lunch and said sadly, 'Seems we need to start making plans for when we leave the farm, and the sooner the better.'

196

Rachel admitted to an interest in some bungalows being built not far from the main road. 'Handy for the shops when we can no longer drive,' she said with a twinkling eye, 'and we walk with the aid of sticks.'

'Damn me, girl, you'll have me old before my time!'

Thankful she had made him smile, she touched his arm affectionately. 'A bungalow with an enormous garden, so you aren't bored.'

'And a field for some sheep, and a couple of pigs.'

'And definitely a dozen or so chickens!'

Sophie was working in the garden. Bertie was with her and they were turning the soil, collecting the remaining vegetables for the compost heap and putting roots to dry ready for the bonfire. Bob was cleaning out the greenhouse, washing the windows with a hosepipe, until he offered the job to an excited Bertie.

Bob waved to someone at the gate, then beckoned. Ed Connors came round the side of the house and Sophie welcomed him before going in to make a tray of tea. It was close to lunchtime, but she didn't think a couple of cakes would spoil anyone's appetite after the hard morning's work.

Bob left an hour later, but Ed stayed for lunch. It was clear he needed to talk but was inhibited by Bertie being there. When it was time for Sophie to walk Bertie home Ed was asleep in a chair beside the fire, so she left him there and they tiptoed out like conspirators.

Ed slept through the rest of the afternoon, and it was the tempting smell of casserole cooking and home-made bread rolls warming that woke him. He began to apologize but Sophie waved his words aside. 'I'm glad to have company for my evening meal, so long as Elsie won't be worried.'

'I'd better go,' he said, looking embarrassed. 'I don't know when I slept so long – I slept like a baby.'

'It's this house, it calms people and gives them peaceful dreams,' she said, serving a dish of the vegetable casserole, offering the plate of bread. 'Sometimes it solves problems while you sleep, too.'

He ate automatically, his mind clearly on something else.

'I think it's sorted out something for me,' he said. 'A problem that was tormenting me now seems so clear.'

'I'm so glad.' From what she'd been told by Daphne and Betty, she guessed the reason for his dilemma. He had made a decision about his sick wife and it had been the wrong one. She didn't ask, but he told her anyway.

'I was going to work to keep Elsie in a home where she'd be properly cared for,' he said, talking almost to himself. 'But it's in her own home she should be. I'll run the guest-house and employ someone to look after her. That's best, isn't it?'

'Best for you both. You'll be lonely without her and she'd be unhappy away from you.'

'We laugh a lot. She makes me happy,' he said.

She walked with him back to the guest-house and watched him go inside, heard him call his wife's name, saw through the curtains of the lighted window the silhouette of them coming together.

Owen was becoming anxious. Now he no longer had a free rein to deal with money matters at the farm, it might be more difficult to do what he planned. He felt utterly lonely and in his melancholy he longed to talk to Sarah. After ten years apart that was stupid. Whatever they once had, it was gone for ever, yet when he saw her something pulled at his heart and he found it impossible to continue hating a small boy.

He was on his way to the bank to raise the money for the week's wages. The two part-timers had not been a success and, now Tommy knew his side of the story about the survey, there was no reason not to re-employ Harry Sutton. He had called and left a note in the small cottage where Harry lived with his wife and youngest son, and hoped for a favourable response.

On impulse he went into the café for one of their popular doughnuts and Sarah came in with Bertie and sat near him.

'There are angels in the place where we're going to live,' Bertie told him.

'Angels?' He looked at Sarah for an explanation.

'Angel fish,' Sarah explained. She was carefully made up, her hair worn in a sleek under-roll and her coat open to reveal

198

a smart skirt and V-necked jumper that hinted at the attractions beneath.

'Angel fish?' he asked, wanting to continue the conversation, something he usually avoided.

'We're looking at places we can afford to rent, and one we looked at yesterday had a large aquarium with angel fish and the name appealed to Bertie.'

'Where is it? This place you want to rent?'

'Barker Row. It's only two rooms but there are places for Bertie to play and grow things.'

'Not a very suitable place, is it? A long way from the school and the shops and a long walk for you to get to Nerys Bowen's shop, too.'

Irritated, Sarah said, 'We don't exactly have a choice, do we? It's what I can afford, not what I'd like.'

'Pity the old farmhouse is such a mess . . . We were happy there, weren't we?'

'Once! A very long time ago!' She pulled Bertie away from his chair and he grabbed the cake he had half eaten, spilling crumbs down his jacket, protesting as they left.

He saw her again later the following day, having managed to be near the dress shop as it closed. 'The van's around the corner if you want a life,' he offered.

'No thanks. I'd rather crawl on hands and knees.'

'Don't be like that. We've both been hurt, but it's worth at least trying to be civil, isn't ?'

'Why? After all these years, why?'

'Because I regret how I dealt with what happened. I have for a long time.'

'And it's taken you ten years to tell me this?'

'It was a mess, for both of us.'

'More for me and I had to deal with it alone.'

'I'm sorry.'

'What?'

'I really am sorry. I was a fool.'

They were walking towards the corner, where Geoff and Connie were closing for the evening, pulling down blinds, taking in the advertising board. Connie waved then ducked out of sight. 'Can you believe it, they're talking!' she whispered to Geoff.

Sarah was relieved to see the bus coming and, although she was some way from the bus stop, she waved a hand and the driver slowed for her to get on.

'Extra for a taxi service, mind,' the conductor said cheerfully, handing her the ticket.

She sat on the bus looking out at the gathering dusk and tried to settle her confused thoughts. Why would Owen decide they should be friends after all this time? Did she want to take the friendship he was offering and risk being hurt all over again when he let her down? He'd never accept Bertie and she would never let her son suffer a moment if she could avoid it.

Tommy went to see Sarah and told her about the cottage. 'It's a right mess, mind,' he warned. 'But I've spoken to the owner and she's agreed to drop the rent if you'll do the decorating and cleaning up. I'm sure you have friends who will help. At least come and see it.'

They went together, Tommy, Sarah and Bertie. She could see through the mess and muddle that there was a pleasant home there for the two of them, but she frowned at the rent.

'I'd have to stay where I am until it's cleaned and I couldn't afford two payments. I haven't saved enough yet. It's too soon,' she said sadly.

Tommy went to see the owner, and handed the woman a month's rent, insisting she mark it in the new rent book he had brought with him. Then he told Sarah she needn't pay rent for a month whether or not she moved in, and the deal was done.

It was by sheer luck that Geoffrey Francis, Sophie's ex-fiancé, found Daphne's mother. And extreme good luck that Mrs Boyd could tell him her daughter had found Sophie.

He had been looking up anyone he remembered from the days when he and Sophie had been planning to marry. At first he had searched for Sophie's family, but there had been little information to help him. Then he remembered Daphne and hoped that by some good fortune the two friends had kept in touch.

200

All he knew about Daphne was her name and the area where her family lived. The name was unusual and he found Mrs Doyle working in a cafe in Weston.

He asked if she could help him find Sophie Daniels. After he had fully explained his reasons, she gave him the address of the public house where her daughter worked.

Since being demobbed he had been very restless. Finding his previous job in the electricity company unsatisfying, he had moved to one that took him out of the office for four of the five days he worked. He represented a firm making leather goods, which he sold to gift shops throughout the southwest of England. The large area he covered meant he had a car.

He was due a holiday soon, and he decided that he'd use it to go to Cwm Derw and complete his search. It was a bit late to apologize, but he didn't think being jilted was something easily forgotten. Even after all this time he had to explain why he hadn't turned up for their wedding. He owed it to her to tell her why he had let her down then failed to get in touch.

Ed called to his sister as he opened the side door of the Ship. He stepped inside, still calling, feeling foolish asking permission to enter the place that had been his home. But the way he had left Betty without warning combined with his unfortunate marriage and its sad outcome had made him less confident of how people felt towards him. He knew he had been criticized for what he planned for Elsie, and even though his intentions had changed, the disapproval would remain for a while.

Betty came out of the bar, wearing her working overall over skirt and jumper, pulling off the sacking apron used for dirty work. She looked hot and a little tired, her face as red as her hands. 'Daphne has the day off and I've had to wash the floors,' she said by way of explanation

'Done the filling up yet?' he asked. 'I've got an hour if you want the shelves filled or a barrel tapped.'

'Thanks. There's dregs in the barrel so I'll need a fresh one for tonight. I was going to ask Harry Sutton, he doesn't mind giving a hand when I'm stuck.'

He went down and sorted out the stock, wiping the bottles

and putting the new behind the old, and set the new barrel in its cradle and checked the connections to the bar. He even polished the copper and washed the cellar floor. Then he went up to where his sister had a tray of tea ready. She was pouring the boiling water on the tea leaves as he came in.

'Thank you,' she said, offering the biscuit tin. 'You didn't have to do that, Ed, but I have to say I'm glad. I struggle to manage sometimes.'

She was lying. She and Daphne managed the work with ease.

'I've been selfish, haven't I? Letting you down like I did.'

'Of course not. Taking a chance of finding happiness and companionship? I don't call that selfish.' She thought Elsie had been the selfish one, marrying him without telling him she was ill, but she said nothing. 'Least said soonest mended' was a true saying.

'Every decision I've made has been the wrong one.'

'I don't agree with that, either. You married Elsie without knowing the facts.'

'I'm going to look after Elsie. She should stay in her own home for a long as it's possible. The truth is, I'm scared of illness, and the thought of having to look after someone really sick was terrifying. But now I wonder how I could ever have thought of sending her away. She's good company and I enjoy being with her. We're really happy together. This dreadful sickness won't change her; the real Elsie will still be there, won't she? It will just make it harder for her to do what she's always done.'

'We all say and do stupid things when we're upset and you were certainly upset.'

'Well I've thought it out now. I'll arrange help for the things we can't do and run the guest-house as it's always been run.' He reached for the teapot to replenish his cup. 'I'll be here any time you need me, too. For a couple of hours while Elsie rests, so I can do the jobs you find hard.'

'There's no need.'

'I need to. I want to put everything right. Between us we can manage, like we always have, ever since Mam and Dad died.'

He peered into the biscuit tin and shuffled the contents 'Is this the best you got?' he said, a smile assuring her everything was back to normal.

Daphne was surprised to find her work had been done and insisted on taking Betty shopping. 'Tea and a cream cake somewhere, and I need a big bunch of flowers to thank Hope for transforming that armchair. Because it's for Sarah she refuses to accept any money.'

'How will you deliver it?'

'Push it down the road, how else?' Daphne laughed. 'Want a ride?'

Owen arranged to open another account, called Land Development West, in Cardiff. The money was transferred from the bank account he had been using for money taken from the farm payments. He went there on a rare weekend off and paid in a large cheque and an address in the Somerset town of Portishead.

It was a risk to take so much soon after Tommy had written a large cheque for Gareth, but with Tommy's decision to sell within the year there was no time to waste if he was to get away before enquiries began.

In the farm van he drove along the A48 through Newport, past the turning for the route that would cut miles off his journey but where he might be remembered, to Chepstow, Lydney, Blakeney and on to Gloucester. He crossed the River Severn and turned on to the route for Bristol. After passing through Berkeley and Thornbury, as the river widened, dividing England and Wales, he travelled on to the small town beside the estuary where he was buying a property.

It wouldn't be his for a few more weeks but, like a child, he had to have another look, focus on the dream of his new life far away from the family he had served so well and who had treated him so badly.

The day was a pleasant one, an unexpected treat, as autumn had begun to grip, and he wished he had invited Sarah and Bertie along. Although it was too soon to share his secret. He smiled as he imagined telling Sarah and driving down with her beside him on their way to a new beginning.

It was as he turned into the narrow lane leading to the property he was buying that a car reversed out of a driveway and swung around without warning. The driver's side of the van collided with the driver's side of a smart new Vauxhall and the screech of metal mingled with Owen's shout of anger. This couldn't happen. It mustn't happen. He didn't want to explain what he was doing here.

He left the car by the passenger door and began to shout at the other driver, who held up his hands in defeat. 'My fault entirely,' he admitted. 'I drove out without looking and I admit full responsibility. It's such a quiet lane, you see.'

Taken aback, expecting argument, Owen said. 'I'd rather not involve the insurance company. So if we can deal with it between us?'

'Sorry, but it isn't my car, so I'll have to tell my employer.'

Taking a couple of large, white five-pound notes from his wallet, Owen said, 'Shall we say a drunken driver who didn't stop?'

'Suits me. Better than explaining my stupidity.'

The man thanked him and they went their separate ways.

'Look at this! I parked for just a few minutes while I bought some bread and some idiot bounced off the van and drove off,' Owen told Gareth when he returned to the farm. Gareth was unlikely to know what the mileage had been, but just in case, Owen drove it straight to a garage.

Sophie and Bertie were walking down the lane towards Badgers Brook at the same time as Owen was walking back from the garage. He stopped and offered Bertie a sixpence, ruffling the boy's hair before walking away. He was whistling cheerfully as he headed for the wood.

'A tanner, miss. A bag of chips, unless . . . If you've got something nice for dinner, I could save it for when we move.'

'Has your mum found anywhere yet?'

'The house with the angels is too far away but she was looking at somewhere today, when she finished at the shop.'

When Sarah arrived, she looked puzzled.

'It's Owen,' she explained. 'He said not to look for some- where else to live, he has something in mind that would be perfect.'

Sophie smiled. It probably meant nothing and she pretended to enjoy the mystery. Everything Owen said and did was suspect and added to the puzzle of what he was planning. Better she tell Rachel and Tommy, though, in case what was making him so apparently happy would affect them. Or, better still, she would write to Ryan. They corresponded a little, but she still felt she needed an excuse to contact him.

Sarah went again to look at the cottage Tommy had found for her. It would need an awful lot of cleaning and she wondered if she dare ask Sophie and perhaps Daphne to help her.

When news got around she was overwhelmed with offers. Beside, Sophie and Daphne, Betty, Kitty and Bob, Stella and Colin and several others volunteered. The chair was delivered to Badgers Brook to wait until the place was ready for her.

'So many friends,' she said tearfully. 'Nothing Owen Treweather came up with could be as good as this.'

Eleven

Writing to Ryan was always difficult. An attraction for him vied with a fear of misunderstanding his feelings for her, making her afraid of looking foolish. She realized that through this lack of confidence she could lose him, but she couldn't relax and feel easy about their growing fondness.

After several attempts at a casual letter that each time tangled into a muddle of over-cautious politenesses, she went to the shop and bought a couple of postcards showing local views. A sentence saying only that Owen had promised Sarah a solution to her housing problem seemed so ridiculous that she tore it up and threw it away. Whatever she and Daphne suspected, the bald facts would tell him nothing.

Later that day she again scribbled the brief facts on a postcard and pushed it into the post box before she could change her mind.

Sarah and Bertie's move went easily. With so many helping the decorating was swiftly done. Geoff had contributed some tins of paint, and had even found some suitable wallpaper amid his old stock. With Connie's help he painted and put up wallpaper. Bob and Colin dealt with the garden. Owen didn't appear. 'So much for his "revived affection" and his promise to care,' Sarah said to Sophie.

'Just as well, there wouldn't be room here for any more helpers, would there?'

Everyone worked well together and in ten days the place was clean and the garden under control, with Colin and Bob conferring with Bertie about where his vegetable garden would go and the position of his swing.

They didn't have many possessions and most of them

arrived on Tommy's farm van. As usual when friends were involved there was a party mood from the moment Sarah gave Bertie the key to open their door. Tea was immediately made for the inevitable breaks, but it was still only midday by the time everything was in place.

The last item to arrive was the newly covered armchair, pushed amid great hilarity by Bertie and some of his school friends, guided by a patient Bob Jennings. The oddments of furniture looked lost in the rooms. Floors had been varnished, and on the front doorstep red tiles shone like new. Sarah felt a mild panic at the thought of sitting in the orderly but soulless place. Somehow it reminded her how alone she was. Friends were wonderful but she feared the silence that would inevitably descend when the door closed for the last time and Bertie was asleep in his own bedroom.

She thought of Owen and his revived attentions and wondered whether life with him would be better than loneliness, but shook her head with irritation. She wasn't that desperate: she wasn't yet thirty, hardly an old woman! There was plenty of time to think about remarrying. She made up her mind to urge Owen to make haste with the divorce. This was a time for new beginnings.

Sophie often went to the old farmhouse, beside which the ruins of her one-time cottage home still remained. The months since she had left had added to the look of decay, the rotten wood with the crumbly consistency of biscuits providing homes for myriad insects, the old stones weathered into various shades of green, grey and yellow by lichen: miniature fields over which snails grazed.

She had explored the farmhouse, which was now seldom locked, and had sheltered there sometimes when rain tempted her into its protection. The place was still sound, with the exception of one window, now boarded. The cupboards were empty, their bare wooden shelves ridged with years of scrubbing. She wondered idly whether anyone would live there again.

Outside, nature had taken everything back with the exception of the fruit bushes and the neat herb garden that she had nurtured. Rosemary and sage bushes, fennel, lovage, chives and the three different kinds of mint that had to be controlled from taking over the rest. She looked after them and used them in all in her cooking.

To her surprise she heard someone coming, singing an old but still popular song, 'Sing a song of sunbeams, let the notes fall where they may . . .'

She stepped away from the farmhouse and waited until Sarah came into view, then sang along with her.

'Oh! Hello, Sophie, I didn't expect to see anyone out here.'

'I've come to collect a few herbs,' Sophie said, showing her the bunch she had picked.

'I don't know why I'm here. I just set off for a walk after a bit of gardening. Bertie's with Kitty and Bob. I found myself on the muddy track and became curious to see the place where Owen and I once lived. Having a house of my own after all this time, I suppose.'

'Fred Yates's cottage has gone. It fell about my ears! But the farmhouse is still sound,' Sophie told her and together they wandered through its echoing rooms.

'I've been thinking a lot about Owen in the past few days, and perhaps I wanted a gentle wander down memory lane. We lived here when Rachel and Tommy moved to the new house, and we were happy here, for a while.'

'Pity everything has to change.'

'It didn't just change, I caused it all to fall apart.' Sarah didn't sound angry, just sad.

'Is there no hope of mending it?'

'Owen is more civil these days, and he made that half promise to help us find a new home, but he'd never accept Bertie even if we did think of giving it a try.'

'He enjoys his company more these days, I think. He's taken him for a walk around the fields once or twice. Answering Bertie's endless questions, pointing out things of interest. He must know none of this is Bertie's fault.'

'Maybe, but there's no logic in anger, is there?'

There were a few odd cups on a shelf, covered with dust. They had been discarded by Sophie when she left the cottage. She washed them under the outside tap and offered Sarah a drink of water. They sat silently looking round them at the residue of generations of living and loving. Hollow rooms and a garden left to disappear under layers of summer growth. There had been paths but they were gone, choked by rampant grasses and wild flowers. Without thought, Sarah began to pull at some of the larger plants until the paving stones beneath were revealed.

Sophie helped and after an hour they smiled in delight at what they had achieved. The area between two line posts was cleared.

'At least the ghosts can now hang out their washing,' Sarah said, as they washed the worst of the dirt from their hands.

Sophie saw Sarah turn to look sadly back at the place that held the ghosts of her marriage. 'Why haven't you and Owen divorced?' she dared to ask.

Sarah frowned. 'I don't really know. It's never been discussed until recently, and then Owen didn't follow it through. Neither of us has met anyone else, I suppose.'

'You still love him, after all this time?'

'I don't think what I feel for him is love. I let him down, hurt him dreadfully. Anyway, I've asked him to sort it out, arrange a divorce. He seems unwilling.' she frowned. 'Strange how the marriage vows are such a strong tie, isn't it?'

'And Owen, has he ever . . .?' she left the sentence unfinished.

'I thought for a while that he and Daphne might care for each other. In fact, I thought meeting her was what led him to see a solicitor, discuss divorce. But nothing seems to have come of it. I don't know what's happening, but he hints about leaving the farm. He wants me to go with him and start again somewhere else. Do you know if it's true, that the Treweathers are selling and he's going away?'

'There are so many rumours, but I can't imagine Rachel and Tommy sending him away. It's his home as well as his job. He's one of the family.'

'He isn't always treated as though he is, mind. I've never understood why.'

They walked back up the field and through the wood, Sarah reminiscing about her childhood, and the time she and Owen had lived at the farmhouse. Sophie listened, adding an occasional word to encourage further memories, and occasionally thinking about the life she herself had once led, a happy family life that had been so cruelly ended.

'Haven't you ever met anyone you wanted to marry?' Sarah asked as they left the wood opposite Badgers Brook.

'Once, but he changed his mind and I waited at the church in vain.'

'You mean he jilted you?' Sarah was shocked. 'But why?'

Sophie smiled sadly. 'That's one of the many things in my past that I can't understand. If I knew why, I might one day feel free of it.'

'What an unlucky pair we are.'

'Unlucky? In your case, yes. In mine, my disasters have been because I thought I knew best. Lacking confidence can bring unhappiness but having too much can be far worse.' She didn't explain, and Sarah knew better than to ask.

Ryan called to see Sophie, leaving his parents and Owen and a newly re-employed Harry Sutton to run the farm. She accepted his kiss with more ease but still moved away from him when he sat on the couch, and sat on a chair near the window. They discussed the note she had written and Ryan teased her. 'When I read it out to Gareth he said it was like a newspaper report and remarked that you aren't too generous with love and kisses. Why is that, Sophie? I had hoped you were beginning to feel the way I do.'

'There are problems I have to resolve.'

'You know I'm here for you, if you want me to help. I want to always be here for you.'

She walked across and touched his cheek with her lips and went into the kitchen to find them a drink of wine. Handing it to him, she said, 'Let's talk about Owen and his mysterious plans, shall we?'

'Gareth and I are both worried but we're afraid to discuss the problems in front of our parents. Gareth feels that Owen is planning something we won't like. We've discussed ways of dealing with Owen, but not knowing what – if anything – he was planning, we decided that Gareth would stay on the farm and report anything of importance to me, while I go back to complete my studies.'

'Daphne and I will visit when we can. I don't think your mother objects to me like she did at first, so we can just call without waiting for an invitation.'

'I've only a few more days to do at the school where I'm observing, but I don't want Owen to know exactly where I am, or how long I'll be away. Just watch him, please, Sophie.'

'I will,' she promised.

'And think about us, too.'

Seeing her frown, he said, 'Whatever it is, don't worry, just think about us and our future. There's nothing we can't sort out. Love conquers all, doesn't it?'

The kiss as he left her was gentle, but they stayed in each other's arms for a long time. As she watched him leave she felt the stirrings of hope, a promise of better things.

Geoffrey Francis was not far from Cwm Derw. He had finished his calls for the day and was idly walking about one of the small towns nearby, doing a little shopping, buying a gift for his wife's birthday and something for their baby daughter. Without much hope he asked at a few of the shops for someone called Sophie Daniels. No one he asked could help. He knew that it was likely she was married and her name would have changed. It seemed hopeless, but something made him keep trying.

He wasn't far from the seaside, and although the day was glowering, with clouds low and filled with rain, he drove towards Barry, a few miles away, thinking that a walk on the sea front might be pleasant. He stopped in Cwm Derw, on the main road, and went into the newsagents to buy a magazine to read later.

'Geoffrey?'

'Daphne? I don't believe it. What luck!'

'What are you doing so far from London?'

'Enjoying a change. And you?'

They talked briefly, then Geoffrey asked, 'I don't suppose you know where Sophie went, do you? I know her family used to live near here and I've asked in several places without any luck.'

'Why are you looking for her?'

'I don't expect a loving reunion, that's for certain. I just wanted to explain. I feel so guilty about what happened. I'm married now and very content, but what happened on that day still haunts me.'

'Sophie too, I imagine.'

'Exactly, which is why I'm trying to find her. Can you tell me where she is?'

'No. But if you tell me where you're staying, I'll tell her where *you* are. Right?'

'Perhaps we could meet this evening? The three of us?'

He wrote on a piece of paper the address of the guest-house and Daphne nodded. 'Elsie Clements's – er – Connors's place. Yes, we'll meet you there at seven. All right?'

'Thank you.' He walked back to the car, the walk along the beach forgotten. He needed to prepare what he would say to Sophie in a few hours' time.

Sophie was at the farm, having arranged with Rachel to measure and list the furniture as a preliminary to deciding what they would need for the small bungalow she and Tommy intended to buy.

'I have to remember that both Gareth and Ryan will want to keep some, so it's probably only the very large items we'll have to sell, 'Rachel said, touching the huge wardrobe that stood on the landing. 'We were lucky to fit these things in here, but if we buy one of the new bungalows they don't stand a chance.'

'I went to look at the old farm yesterday and I met Sarah there,' Sophie told her. 'It's still sound apart from one boarded-up window.'

'Silly, I know, but I sometimes wish we were back there. I don't mean move there when we leave here, that wouldn't be sensible – too far away from everything and too much work – but everything seemed so simple when we lived in that old place, and I wish those days could return.'

'I dream of going back in time, too. But in actual fact there's nothing to go back for, not even a building. I lost everyone I loved.'

212

'Have you ever gone back, to see where they're resting? Talk to old friends?'

'There aren't any. What would be the point of going back? They all disappeared on that terrible day.'

'But to walk along the roads, see the places they knew, wouldn't it help?'

'I didn't even attend their funerals. I didn't know until it was all over. So no, it wouldn't help.'

'Would you like some of these chairs?' Rachel, surprised at the revelation, changed the subject to avoid distressing Sophie further. A dozen bentwood chairs were tucked away in one of the spare rooms. 'In my mother's day we had huge farm suppers to celebrate success at the sales and shows, or the retirement of one of the men or women who had worked here all their lives, or the birth of a child, and, of course, there were the annual suppers to celebrate harvest home. A great long table groaning with food and home-brewed beer. Laughter, good friendships, we were all a part of a wonderful team. We needed all these chairs then and still didn't have enough. And now it will all end with Gareth and Ryan turning away from all that has been.'

'What about Owen, doesn't he plan to stay, follow on the traditions of the Treweathers?'

'That's never been the plan and he's known that all his life. We gave him a home and a good living, but it's always been made clear that the inheritance wasn't his and never would be.'

'He doesn't resent that?'

'Why should he? He's been very lucky.'

There was a tightness about Rachel's lips that forbade further questions. They went on listing and measuring in companionable silence. They decided to offer the chairs to the local community hall, and started on the linen.

Rachel gave Sophie a lift home, and when she walked up the path she saw she had a visitor. The gas light was glowing in the kitchen, and as she approached she smelled the tempting aroma of onions cooking.

'Daphne? What's happening?'

'I'm making us some cheese and onion patties. Betty gave

me some stale cheese and I found some onions and potatoes in your larder.'

'Lovely, but why?'

'We have to go out at a quarter to seven.'

'Pictures? Lovely! Shall we invite Sarah and Bertie?'

'No.' She turned the heat low under the frying pan and held Sophie's arms. 'Look, I don't want you to flip, but we're meeting someone from your past.'

At once Sophie began to back away, shaking her head. 'No, Daphne, you know how I hate surprises.'

'Not a surprise, more a shock. It's Geoffrey. He's been searching for you – not to rekindle a romance,' she added quickly. 'In fact, he's happily married. He wants to see you and explain.' She released her hold on Sophie's arms, and added, 'I know you don't owe him a thing, but I do think you need to listen to what he has to say. Lay one of your demons to rest, eh?'

It took a long time but she eventually persuaded her friend to go with her and meet the man who had hurt her so badly and contributed to her feelings of guilt.

Walking into Elsie's lounge was like walking in treacle, her feet seemed so reluctant to take her forward to face the man who had hurt her. She had fleeting visions of herself waiting in a borrowed bridal gown and veil outside the church and she felt again the chill of that moment when she knew he wasn't going to appear. She saw again the faces filled with both sympathy and embarrassment, and felt unable to breathe.

Sensing her anguish, Daphne said, 'Remember this is to make *him* feel better. You've long ago risen above it all.'

Head held high, a false smile on her lips, she stepped into the room as Geoffrey leaped out of a chair and stood to face her.

Geoffrey hadn't changed much, except that it was strange to see him in civvies, having imagined him in RAF uniform whenever she thought of him. She took in the worried frown, the slight tremor in his voice as he greeted her, then relaxed. Daphne was right, for her it was over.

Geoffrey spoke in jerky sentences as he admitted to losing

his nerve, feeling pressured, wanting to cancel the wedding. 'I was a coward, I admit that, but when I tried to tell you I wanted to wait I couldn't. Then as I was about to leave for the church that morning I was called back to camp. I couldn't get through on the phone and I left a message with the local police, begging them to contact you and explain, but I learned later that they failed to deliver it.

'I was superstitious, I suppose, so many of my friends had been killed. I thought that marrying and making plans for when it was over would seal my fate and I'd join my friends and be nothing more than a name on a memorial.'

'I pressured you.'

'No, absolutely not! I pushed things too fast and I lost my nerve. You did nothing to deserve what happened. Nothing.'

Listening to him, taking in the halting words, Sophie felt the weight of the memory eased away. They didn't stay long, just enough time to admire photographs of Geoffrey's wife and baby daughter, and for Geoffrey to say, 'I was so sorry to hear about your parents, and your brother and sister. I was fond of them.'

'All my family being wiped out in a moment is still hard to accept.'

He was about to argue that it wasn't the entire family, but presumed she had been referring to the immediate family and said nothing, not wanting to dwell on her sad memories.

Feeling some relief, comforted by Geoffrey's kind words, Sophie walked back to Badgers Brook in the darkness of the September evening. As always the house wrapped itself around her, welcoming her. She stirred the fire and added fuel, and sat beside it trying to think more positively about her role in the hastily planned and sadly aborted marriage. Despite Geoffrey's words, she knew that she had rushed him, but allowed herself to accept that he had wanted it too.

Everything had been frantic during those years; people grasped at happiness afraid that the morrow would see it disappear, like a rainbow, perfect and wonderful one moment, the next fading and vanishing for ever. She felt more cheerful than she had for a long time. The guilt over rushing the marriage arrangements and the humiliating outcome were drifting away. She knew the one thing left to do was visit the graves of her family, face up to that guilt, too. Then perhaps she would be free.

Surprisingly, the dream of the air raid returned that night. Meeting Geoffrey had revived more than memories of her disastrous wedding day. Although some of the guilt had been chipped away there was still the thought that if she hadn't persuaded her family that the dangers were over and they would be better staying together, at least her brother and sister and grandparents might have survived.

She woke at about three a.m., tearful and choking with regrets, and got up to make a hot drink. She opened the back door and from the wood across the lane came the eerie sound of an owl. Apart from the lone hunter wandering the sky, and occasional rustlings of small creature on their own search for food, everything was quiet, and the peace of the early hour calmed her. But, afraid of a return to the dream, she sat up and read beside the still warm ashes of the fire for an hour before returning to bed.

Gareth left his friends to deal with the purchase of the farm, knowing that in a year he'd have his share of the money from the sale of Treweather Farm, which they would spend on rebuilding and stocking the place. Until then, Gareth, Brian and his wife would find work, live in the farmhouse, in truly primitive conditions, and wait. Before finding work he needed to find out what was happening at home; the occasional letters and phone calls created more queries than the solved.

'I'll stay a while,' Gareth told his brother on the phone that evening, 'and bemoan the fact that I'm desperate for money and Brian Powell is pestering me for my fifty per cent investment. If Owen is being secretive it has to be about money, so I'll sympathize, complain about Dad's meanness, even ask him to suggest a way of getting money out of him.'

'I'll stay here and pretend everything is smooth.'

'No, Ryan. Let him hear us rowing, then storm off as though you don't intend to come back.'

They discussed this for a while and made their plans.

When Ryan telephoned to tell his parents he would be home at the weekend, Rachel had answered. She explained with forced cheerfulness that she and Sophie were sorting out the house contents to decide what she would take to the new bungalow. 'I'm glad you're coming,' she said. 'While you're here you can choose what you want from the list of unwanted pieces. We can always put them in store if you aren't ready to take them'

'Have you given Owen the chance to pick what he wants?'

'Oh yes, your father asked him but he said, rather huffily, that he doesn't need a thing.'

Ryan's expression was grim when he replaced the phone. With his cousin's constant reminders of how attached he was to the family and its traditions, it didn't make sense that he didn't want a few mementoes.

Gareth and Ryan found it easy to create arguments every time Owen was near, and on Sunday morning Ryan built up a row that resulted in him leaving the farm before lunch, to which Daphne and Sophie had been invited.

It began with Gareth asking him for a loan. Making sure Owen was able to hear, Gareth pleaded at first, then accused his brother of selfishness, greed and a determination to ruin his chances.

'I can't expect Brian to wait for ever. Dad refuses to help me and you're my last hope. I need the cash before next year if I'm to stop Brian taking another partner. He's had several offers from people could can put the money up immediately. Men with supportive families. Not like mine, who resent my not wanting to stay and are making me suffer for it.'

The row went on and finally Ryan shouted, 'I'm going back. I don't have to listen to this. The farm in France is your choice and you should be dealing with the finances, not pestering the rest of us.'

'But you're my brother and I'm asking for your help.'

'I'm leaving. If you wait a year you'll have the money as Dad promised, but no, you have to have everything now, this minute! Well I'm not putting up with your miserable complaints any longer.' He stomped up the stairs and slammed the bedroom door behind him. Then he stood, all pretence at anger gone, hoping that Owen had heard enough.

Then he stormed out of the house and drove off in a car he had borrowed. He was sorry not to see Sophie at their Sunday lunch, but he had another visit planned, one that wouldn't wait. He stopped at Badgers Brook and explained what he and Gareth were planning, thanked her again for her help, kissed her lightly and left.

When he had found a place to stay the night he went straight to the flats and knocked on Victoria Morgan's door. There was a heart-stopping silence and it wasn't until he'd knocked three times that the door opened a crack and a carefully made-up lady with a smart hairstyle and carrying a cat under her arm peered out.

'You don't know me,' he began, but she had obviously been informed.

'You're enquiring about Sophie, I understand? You'd better come in.'

For no particular reason, he had been expecting a frail old lady like the two he'd recently met in the area, but this lady was attractive and beautifully dressed. There was no sign of a stoop, in fact she stood upright and seemed to challenge him with her bright, intelligent eyes. Her grey hair, with its hint of the fairness it might once have had, fell about her ears in soft waves in defiance of the combs with which she tried to control it. She had an air of authority as she demanded. 'You'd better tell me why you've been trying to find me.'

'Are you connected in any way to Sophie Daniels?'

The hazel eyes, so like Sophie's, widened, but she said calmly, 'Why do you want to know?'

'She told me every single member of her family was killed when a V2 rocket landed on the street where they lived. She was in the WAAFs and didn't know about it until the funerals had taken place. She blames herself, having persuaded them all to stay together as the war was almost over, and, well, she's never been back. She can't face that row of graves for which she feels responsible.'

'She never came back to see me, and I've wondered why. Now I know. She thought I was dead like all the others.'

'You're a relative? She believes they all died that night.'

'Young man, I am her grandmother.'

'But I don't understand. I – she – though you all died. Why wasn't she told?'

'She didn't come back or she'd have found me. I was in hospital for a while, then in a temporary room while the shop was repaired. When the shop was reopened, I didn't want to stay there. I waited long enough to realize she wasn't coming back and then I closed it, leaving my name there in case she did come looking for me. More than two years I waited, then I took this place, still hoping she'd walk in one day.'

'But how did it happen? You surviving, the others all gone?'

'Stupid really. I'd gone with a neighbour to get us some fish and chips. The shop was closed and we went further afield, caught a bus to the next one and, well, we didn't get our fish and chips that night, but we survived.

'I dodged the wardens and went into the ruin of the house, hoping to find them, and I was hurt when part of a wall that was teetering fell on me.'

He listened, staring at her in amazement, allowing her to talk about the night she had lost almost everyone she cared about. Then he said, 'How do I tell Sophie?'

They discussed the best way of breaking the news, both aware that Sophie would blame herself once again, this time for not going back to find out what had happened. Being unable to face the sight of that row of graves had deprived her of her grandmother for more than four precious years. When Ryan left he felt sadness at leaving her all alone, her sad memories revived by his visit – but at least he had given her hope.

'I'll see you very soon,' he promised. 'With your granddaughter.'

Gareth waited anxiously for an opportunity to speak to Owen – he had no wish for his parents to give away the fact that there was no real rift in the family. He found Owen in the hay barn tidying up the bales and said, 'If there's a way of getting money out of this place before next year, I'd take it.'

He saw a tremor cross Owen's face and knew he'd touched a nerve. 'Like I suspect you have,' he added, grabbing Owen's arm.

'Don't talk rubbish! What could I do? I'll be leaving this place with nothing more than the few hundred pounds I've managed to save.'

'Don't take me for a fool. You changed accountants, and solicitors, d'you expect me to believe there wasn't a reason for that? Since when have you taken decisions like that?'

'I saw a way to save a few pounds, that's all. I do the accounts and always look for ways of saving your father's money. It's my job.'

And although Gareth continued to press him, he still didn't manage to get anything out of him.

The next morning a letter came and Gareth picked it up as Rachel made the postman a cup of coffee. It looked official and bore the name of a firm of insurers. As the postmark was not a local one, he read it then handed it to Tommy and made his father promise to keep the contents to himself.

He was smiling when he found Owen in one of the top fields. There were stone-built pens up there, which they used during the annual sheep-shearing and lambing, and he was sitting against a wall, eating his sandwiches.

'How much d'you hope to get away with?' Gareth asked conversationally.

'What are you talking about now?'

'Enough to buy a place in Somerset?'

This time Owen failed to hide his alarm.

'Unfortunate, you having an accident with the van, wasn't it?'

'Somerset? I've never been there. When do I go as far from home as Somerset? A visit to Barry Island feels like a safari! I never go anywhere. When did I last have a holiday? Answer me that?' Owen replied, panicking, as he realized that the man must have reported the accident after all.

'Your honeymoon, I suppose. Dad's tried to persuade you to get away, offered to pay for a week somewhere of your choice, but you've never wanted to go. You preferred to stay around playing the part of the poor relation in some Victorian melodrama! Making yourself indispensable, hoping for a share of this place.'

He handed him the letter with the insurance claim and saw from Owen's drooping shoulders that he was ready to admit it.

'All right, I did go, but it was to see a woman,' he said. 'I met her in the Ship and Compass, one of those tourists on bicycles, like Daphne. But she didn't want to know, so I won't be going there again. Now, satisfied?'

'No, I'm not. Look, Owen, whatever you're planning, you can count me in. I'm desperate too.'

Gareth spoke quietly and after a few more threats, as he exaggerated what he actually knew, Owen said, 'All right, I've taken out a small mortgage that your father doesn't know about. You can have half of it. I'm entitled to something after all these years, aren't I? I need something put away from my old age.'

'How did you plan to cover it up?'

'I deal with the accounts, don't I? It would have been easy, once the farm is sold. The price they get won't be what they'd hoped for and I'll be long gone.'

'To Somerset?'

'No! Not Somerset. Why are you obsessed with Somerset? I want something on a larger scale. Yorkshire probably. North never south.'

Gareth was convinced that Somerset was the place. He wrote to the insurance company, as the owner of the van, and asked for the exact details of the accident. If he knew where it happened, he might be able to learn something by going there.

Owen felt he needed someone to share his worries. He had always been a self-sufficient man, well able to cope with difficulties as they arose without the need to discuss every small problem, but this was different. He needed a family. Not for ever, just until he had settled into his new life.

He knocked on Sarah's door and smiled as it was opened by Bertie, who returned his smile with a frown.

'Is your mum there?'

'No, she's at work, and I've just come back from work too.'

'Work?' Owen questioned.

'I work with Mr Jennings, and Mr Jones, too, sometimes. Gardener,' he added impatiently. He was given confidence by having Sophie there, unseen by Owen.

'Oh, I see. Well done. Tell your mum I called, will you?'

'If I remember,' Bertie said, closing the door.

Owen went to the ladies' dress shop and asked to speak to Sarah. 'I called at the little terraced place,' he said disparagingly, 'and found your son there alone.'

'Sophie's with him. She walked him home early as she's helping him to cook a meal for me,' she explained. 'My son isn't neglected.'

'Oh, I didn't see her. I'm sorry. Can we meet when the shop closes? There's something I want to discuss with you, in private.'

They arranged to meet at five thirty and he would drive her home. He parked the van outside the house and switched off the engine.

'I can't stay long, mind, I don't want to spoil Bertie's meal.'

'I want you to come with me when I move.'

She turned to stare at him. 'What?'

'We haven't divorced, we're still man and wife, and we could try living under the same roof, with your son, see if we could make it work.'

'We can't! I know that without trying!'

'There's something else.' He brought out some papers and tapped them. 'I'm increasing the payment I make for you and your – and Bertie. I agree to pay the larger amount until he's twenty-one.'

'What's the catch?'

'There isn't one. I want to do something more for you, make you think more kindly of me as well, if you think that's a catch. All you have to do is sign here.'

He opened the pages and she glanced at the legalese and nodded. 'However we feel about each other, I won't deprive Bertie of extra money. Where do I sign?'

He folded the pages, keeping some of them out of sight, and handed her a fountain pen. She innocently signed the agreement to buy the farm near Portishead in the name of Sarah Grange.

Through the window Bertie watched as his mother and Owen Treweather talked. He was impatient; the pie, which was golden brown with potatoes mashed and then patiently ridged with a large fork, was just perfect, so why didn't she come in? Sophie had gone, leaving him to proudly present the meal, although she had warned him not to take it out of the oven.

He knocked on the window but inside the van he could see them still talking, unaware of his anxiety. Opening the door he walked down the path, shielded by overgrown privet.

Owen had tried again to persuade Sarah to leave with him, and the first thing Bertie heard was his mother shouting, 'But it's ridiculous, Owen. I can't just walk away from everything here. Bertie has to be considered. I know you pretend, but you can't really accept him, and I won't go without him.'

'Just think about it, and keep it to yourself,' Owen said as she stepped out of the dirty old van. 'He'd be all right – there are plenty of people to look after him while we get settled. Sophie loves him and he'll be happy with her. I need you more than he does.'

Bertie ran in and closed the door. He was sobbing as he grabbed a thick padded cloth, lifted the beautiful vegetable pie from the hot oven and threw it to the floor. As Sarah came through the door he pushed past her shouting, 'I hate you!' and ran, unseeing, towards Badgers Brook.

Twelve

Sophie was surprised to see Sarah running up the path, and she opened the door expecting to hear praise for Bertie's culinary efforts. Instead, Sarah called, 'Is Bertie there?' When Sophie shook her head, she went on, 'I think he's very upset, and I don't know where he's gone.'

Between sobs she told her friend what she suspected. 'Owen came to talk to me and he tried to persuade me to leave with him. When I said I wouldn't and that I knew he would never accept Bertie, he more or less admitted it and went on about my leaving Bertie and going with him. I refused, of course. I'd never do anything to hurt Bertie, and I would certainly never leave him, but I think Bertie was listening and got it all wrong.'

'What made you think he'd overheard?'

Sarah hastily explained what had happened.

'We have to find him,' Sophie said. 'I'll go to the places he went to with me and you go to Betty and ask if she can spare Daphne for an hour. Don't worry – an hour will see him safely back home.'

'Owen said to tell no one he's leaving.'

'It's no secret, the farm is to be sold in a year's time.'

'Sooner than that! He wanted me packed and ready by tomorrow night!'

Although Bertie was the priority that moment, Sophie took some coins with her and stopped at the phone box on the lane and managed to speak to Ryan, explaining about Owen's plan to leave and about Bertie.

'Finding Bertie is the most important but if you see Owen say nothing, and if Gareth phones, tell him to hurry home,' Ryan responded.

'I think Gareth's gone away,' she said.

'No, he went to check on the area where Owen had his car accident, he'll be back tonight.' Before she rang off, he said, 'Sarah would never go back to Owen, surely?'

'Of course not. And she'd never leave her son.'

'You're sure Owen is planning to leave tomorrow?'

'That's what he told Sarah. Owen is cheating you in some way, but why is he leaving so soon?'

'Thanks to you, my darling girl, we're going to find out.'

'See you soon,' she whispered. She was shaking as she replaced the receiver. Was she his darling girl? Something inside her began to push away her doubts and she fervently hoped that she was. Most of her anxieties had been resolved, and she was beginning to feel capable of love again. Now she had to forget everything else and find Bertie.

As she spent so much time with the boy, she thought she would know all his likely hiding places: the favourite spots in which he played, the many special places they had explored together. She crossed the stream using a stepping-stone bridge that she and Bertie had made and headed towards the old farmhouse.

On the way she searched each hidey-hole and picnic place that she remembered, calling, becoming more anxious as there was no sign of him. The weather was closing in and darkness was approaching fast. She was afraid he'd be out all night unless she could find him soon and persuade him to go back home.

The wind was rising, and black clouds warned of rain. He had to be inside somewhere. If he wasn't, where could he be? The house looked uninviting and things began to move around the yard as the wind increased. Trees creaked, branch rubbing against branch; somewhere pieces of metal screamed a protest as they were pushed one against the other, the sudden gusts lashed against the stout walls of the old house.

The door was tugged out of her hand as she pulled it open it and went inside, tugging it closed, relieved at the reduction in the noise of the storm. She stood for a moment and called his name. The silence was ominous. Her footsteps were an intrusion, tapping on the stone floors, and the stairs creaked disapproval as she climbed up to check the bedrooms; she had to force herself to continue up to the gloomy landing.

She looked inside each room, but there was no sign of anyone being there. The door to one room, the small one at the back, didn't give under her push, and she saw with surprise that the door was firmly padlocked. She pushed and called, half afraid Bertie had been locked inside, no matter how silly it seemed, but there was no reply even though she listened with care, and no sound except from the weird wailing of the wind whistling under the door.

Sarah and Daphne knocked at the doors of all the people Bertie called his friends. Stella and Colin offered immediately, and Kitty and Bob were already searching, having heard from Daphne of his disappearance. Several of his school friends offered suggestions of places to look. Even Peter and Hope went to the woods and fields, calling the boy's name.

Tearfully Sarah wished she had taken more interest in her son before she had decided to leave the factory. All the years she had ignored his chatter, which would have been useful now, giving a clue to where he might be. Ashamed and frightened, she ran once again towards Badgers Brook, his favourite place, and widened her search.

Sophie walked back through the wood, despair wrapping her in its cloudy heaviness. Trying the farm, she met Tommy and he went with her. The wind was wild and several large branches had fallen. An old tree had given up the fight and had fallen, its saucer of roots like a huge wheel on the ground. Tommy increased his speed. 'If Bertie is among the trees he might have been injured,' he warned.

Caught up in the urgency, the storm with its wailing seeming to join in their concern, they walked through the agitated branches and falling twigs and leaves. Tommy seemed to be following a definite route and Sophie followed without question. They found him crying, squashed inside the hollow tree.

Knowing the facts, she said at once, 'Bertie, your mother loves you and would never ever leave you.' She took him in her arms, and, helped by Tommy, he struggled out of the tree. 'Furthermore, she would never, ever do anything you didn't

226

want her to do, like going away with Owen. She puts you first every time.'

'What d'you mean? Tommy asked curiously. 'Where's Owen off to?'

'Oh, nowhere, Mr Treweather. It was a misunderstanding. Bertie heard his mother talking and got the wrong impression, that's all.'

Tommy lifted the boy and carried him a little way, holding him close, revealing his own fears for the child. Then he put him down, chatting to him about the storm that was still building to its crescendo, warning him there was worse to come, and led him back to the farm.

The telephone rang and Tommy picked it up. Frowning, he handed the receiver to Sophie. 'It's Ryan, asking me to ask you to call him. He seems pleased that you're here.'

'Thank goodness,' Ryan said. 'Look, I have an idea. D'you think you could ask Sarah to convince Owen she's changed her mind and will go with him? The police can't act on suspicion alone and we need to force him to make a move and at the same time know what he's doing.'

'She won't risk upsetting Bertie.'

'She mustn't go with him, just convince him that she has reconsidered her decision, gain his confidence.'

They talked for a while, and Tommy walked up and down, glancing at her, still wearing the frown. When she put the phone down, he said, 'What's going on, Sophie? Don't say "nothing". My sons are up to something and I want to know what it is.'

'Sorry, Mr Treweather, but it's something private, between Ryan and me.' She hated lying but knew that both Ryan and Gareth wanted to deal with Owen without involving their father, just in case they were wrong and Owen was doing nothing more than make plans for when the farm was sold.

In a lane some distance away from them, Sarah and Owen were arguing. Unaware that Bertie had been found, she said, 'If you care as you say you do, Owen, help me find him.'

'I can't. He wouldn't come to me. If he heard me calling him, he'd run in the opposite direction. I'd be a hindrance not a help.'

227

'Stop making excuses and help me, please. It's getting dark, the storm's getting worse and he's out there alone and frightened.'

'No point,' he said emphatically. 'He'd hardly think I'm a friend, would he? Thanks to you.' He touched her shoulders and pulled her to face him. 'But that could change. We could become a real family if you'll come with me. I have a place just waiting for us to move into – you'll love it and so will Bertie.'

'Go away, Owen. It would never work. Any hint of disagreement and you'd remind me how lucky I am to have been forgiven. To you, Bertie would always be a weapon, not an adorable, bright, intelligent child.'

They heard someone calling and around the corner came Tommy and Sophie and, between them, Bertie. Bertie walked towards them, refusing to let go of Sophie's hand, but as Sarah turned to him arms outstretched, sobbing in relief, Owen held her back. 'Not a word about my plans, mind. You must keep it to yourself. We'll talk soon – I have to have your answer today.'

'There's my answer!' She pointed at Bertie now standing hesitantly near them. 'My son is more important to me than you could ever be.' Pulling herself free from his grip she hugged Bertie and offered her tearful thanks to Sophie and Tommy. With a brief nod for his uncle, Owen turned away.

Sarah and a rather subdued Bertie went with Sophie to Badgers Brook. At Sophie's suggestion they left Bertie with Kitty and Bob to tell them of his adventure.

'He'll be all right with Kitty and Bob,' she assured Sarah. 'It's very important that I talk to you.' She explained Ryan's suggestion and at first Sarah refused.

'Owen wouldn't believe me anyway. I was quite emphatic. And what if Bertie got it wrong again? I can't risk upsetting him any more. He's only a boy, Sophie, and he's been through so much.'

Eventually, after assuring her that Bertie could be with Sophie when she and Owen were presumably leaving, Sarah agreed. 'Any doubts, mind, and I'll call everything off,' she warned. 'Bertie's more to me than all of the Treweathers.'

It wasn't difficult for Sarah to talk to Owen. She took Bertie to stay with Sophie until it was time for school and went to the farm. Tommy told her Owen was in one of the sheds and she found him and smiled her sweetest smile.

'I've been awake all night,' she said.

'Oh? What was the matter?'

'You, Owen, that's what kept me awake. You and your offer for us to make a new start. Were you serious about caring for Bertie?'

'I'll treat him like my own, as I should have done ten years ago.'

'I'm not managing on my own, and after ten years it's a sad admission. I thought with this new home and a bit of help from friends I might have coped better than in the past, but I can't do what I want to for my son.'

'Sarah, I believe we can make a success of a fresh start but not if your only reason is Bertie.'

'I can understand your doubts after my insistence that I'd never come back to you, but I didn't think you'd ever want me, and my anger was a cover for my real feelings.'

'You haven't given me much hope. So what has changed you if it isn't a better life for Bertie?'

'The fact that in more than ten years I've never found anyone else must tell you that I still love you. Crazy, I know, but last night I did some honest thinking.' She saw the expression on his face soften and a smile begin. 'Please, Owen, can't we try?'

'I'll do my best for you and Bertie, but you realize that we have to leave without any delay? I've made arrangements to take over a place and I can't be casual about it. It's now or never.'

She stepped closer and touched his face with her hands, slowly drawing him towards her until their lips were close. 'It can't be too soon for me. I regret every moment I've been away from you.'

'This change of mind is very sudden,' he said. 'Can I believe you?' He wanted to, he had her name on the deeds and everything would be easier if she were with him.

'Let me show you.' To kiss him wasn't a hardship, after

all, he was the only man she had loved, even though that love was gone for ever, and they came out of the shed with shining eyes and promise in the closeness of their bodies as they walked.

'I'll give you a lift back to the shop. From the way you're dressed that was where you were going.'

She said thanks and glanced at him, her eyes detecting a few remaining doubts. She even had a few of her own, wondering if she was doing the right thing trying to catch him out in his thieving, but shrugged away her hesitation and said, 'Owen, I've dreamed of this ever since we parted, but I didn't believe it would happen. Last night, while I considered the future, I was filled with doubts about whether you really meant it. Then, towards dawn, I knew I had to believe you.'

After phoning to tell his parents and particularly Owen that he wouldn't be back for a few days, Ryan left for the drive home. He had borrowed a car and broke the speed limit on many occasions as he dashed back to Cwm Derw. He stopped at Badgers Brook and he and Sophie shared all they knew.

After telling her what he and Gareth were planning, he kissed her lightly, then he held her closer and said, 'Be careful. Stay at Sarah's place. This isn't a night to be outside. Any sign of trouble and I want you and Bertie and Sarah to stay well clear, promise me.'

'I'll be helping Sarah to look after Bertie, keeping him well out of the way.'

'Don't take any risks. You're too precious. I'd rather Owen take everything than you even get frightened.'

She relaxed in his arms and when their lips touched the moment engulfed them both completely. Owen and his plans were forgotten, and they were aware of nothing but themselves and the promise given with the kiss.

Leaving her with great reluctance, leaving the car in the lane, Ryan walked through the wood and cautiously approached the farm. He managed to get inside the house without being seen and the first thing he did was change from his smart clothes into some belonging to Gareth. Baggy corduroys, a lumberjack shirt, an Arran jumper, frayed at elbows and cuffs, and well-worn wellingtons.

Although Owen obviously knew them well enough to distinguish between them, as children he and Gareth had often played games, dressing in each other's clothes and confusing him. They had always had differing tastes, Ryan choosing good-quality suits, well-cut sports jackets and greys, while Gareth rarely dressed well and treated whatever he was given with indifference. Ryan trusted that Owen, presuming he was in London visiting a friend, wouldn't look at him closely enough to notice and would only see what he expected to see.

A weary Gareth arrived in the early evening after a journey spent contemplating all he had learned. He said nothing to explain his absence during the day and neither Rachel nor Tommy asked. They were so keen to describe the search for Bertie and its happy outcome that no one gave a thought to what he had been doing. He went to his room and waited for Ryan to appear.

A few minutes after Ryan had left her, ignoring his plea for her take no chances, Sophie had followed him. There was something she wanted to do, to help if she could, both for Ryan's sake and for Sarah's. She didn't go to the farm, but walked down the steep field to the old farm buildings. There was no one about and the place looked unwelcoming.

Although the storm had subsided, rain was still falling, darkening the already stained grey stone walls, adding its quiet hissing sound to the last gusts of the wind and more gentle rattle of objects moving around the yard. Uninviting as the lonely house appeared, she went inside.

She forced herself to go up and try the back bedroom door again but the padlock was still firmly in place. She was disappointed but knew there was a ladder in one of the sheds and if she could raise it to the window she might be able to look inside the locked room. She knew she ought not to take such a risk. Alone, no one knowing where she was and far away from any help, it was decidedly foolish. Nevertheless, she decided, as she tugged uselessly at the padlock, that she would try to look into the room to find out what was important enough to justify such protection.

The rain wasn't a deterrent as she was soaked through already, and the window was in a spot that was sheltered from the last sighs of the wind. And, she reminded herself soberly, it was out of sight – a place where no one was likely to find her if she fell.

She found manhandling the ladder into place extremely difficult. It was heavy and she only managed it by lifting it a few inches then resting it against the uneven stone wall, then raising it some more. Even in the lee of the building the occasional gusts almost pulled it from her hands, but she eventually had it propped against the wall below the window and she stood and leaned on it for a moment or two to recover her breath. Making the foot as secure as she could with some bricks and stones she climbed up. It was getting dark but she had come prepared with a torch.

It took a moment or two for her eyes to adjust to the darkness within, but eventually she saw several boxes securely tied with string and an oak chest with its drawers piled beside it, each filled with newspaper-wrapped items. There were also four of the bentwood chairs she had helped Rachel to put into the barn, and a small table. Having helped with the sorting, she recognized the things as having been taken from the items put aside to sell. What could they be doing here?

She was in danger of slipping, as the ladder rungs were wet and her shoes were unsuitable for such activity. Cautiously she slowly made her way to the ground, where a voice startled her.

'What the hell are you doing?' Owen, very wet and very angry, stood beside her.

'Owen! Oh, you did give me a fright!' She was shouting above the steady hissing of the continuing downpour. 'Can we go inside? It's impossible to talk with all this noise and I'm soaked through.' When he had followed her into the house, she explained. 'I came here the other day and found that one of the rooms has been padlocked. I wanted to see what was inside. Did you know there was some stuff from your uncle's farm in there?'

'Of course I knew! I've been watching the place hoping to catch whoever has been stealing from us. Now you've ruined it.'

'Sorry.'

'We might as well take the stuff back. You can give me a hand putting it into the van.'

She helped him bring the furniture and boxes down and into the van, then Owen told her gruffly to get in. 'Filthy old thing, but it will get you home quicker,' he said, attempting to brush some mud from the passenger seat.

She took her time getting in, deciding to take off her sodden coat. At the last moment, struggling to free her arms from its clinging wetness, he slammed the door and shouted, 'Sorry, I can't wait any longer for you,' and drove away.

She called out, running after him and slithering on the muddy surface, but he was soon out of sight, the red rear light vanishing around a bend in the lane. Her attempt to delay him had failed and she was a long way from the farm. She knew that the sensible thing would be to go the same way, but it was a couple of miles along the road and she wanted to know what was happening at the farm and warn Ryan about the van apparently packed ready for departure. She couldn't see the top of the field nor the wood beyond it, but, knowing it would save time, she began to walk up the steep field, her feet, in their unsuitable shoes, slipping on the wet grasses.

She made it into the wood, and although the day was already dark she knew her way and began to hurry through the narrow paths towards the brook. Her mistake was deciding that as her shoes were probably ruined it wouldn't matter if she tried to jump across the stream and landed in the mud. The stepping stones were further up stream but she was in a hurry and every moment counted.

She jumped, but slipped as she took off and landed with a foot across a dead branch and fell awkwardly, her weight on her ankle.

Gareth watched as Owen returned, noting that he parked the van well away from the house, just inside the gate, and, surprisingly, locked it. He stood in the shadows as his cousin then went about the usual evening tasks of shutting the chickens in and checking the sheds. Ryan stayed out of sight. Then they changes places.

'Everything in order?' Ryan asked Owen.

'Of course, Gareth. Don't fuss so. As I've told you, we'll find the money waiting in a new bank account and we can share it out and get away from this place for good. You to France and me to wherever the fancy takes me.'

'Thank goodness! My partner is pushing me for my share of the cash and I don't want to lose this chance.'

'It's all arranged. I'll leave early tomorrow as soon as the morning tasks are done. Then, while the fuss about my disappearance confuses everything, you leave the day after. I'll ring you at the phone box outside the post office at ten a.m. Just make sure you're there.'

'What are you going to do with your share?' Ryan asked. 'You've never said.'

Owen shrugged. 'I don't know. Not a farm, that's for sure, I've had enough of farming. I'll get a job and give myself time to consider. I'll be free as I've never been free before. And,' he added, with a cold look, 'with no need to be grateful to anyone. That's real freedom.'

Sophie's ankle was painful yet he knew she had to move. Staying there cold and soaked through was asking for pneumonia – or worse. Moving was extremely painful and she guessed the ankle was severely strained or even broken. Feeling around the muddy ground, using the torch to help her search, she managed to reach a suitable branch, and after breaking off some of the side branches with hands that were unwilling to perform she was eventually satisfied that it was the best she could do. She tied it with the belt of her coat and her soggy cardigan. It made a reasonable splint. It took a while before she had the nerve to try but she slowly and painfully began dragging herself backwards, pulling with her hands, sliding on her bottom. She didn't call. There would be no one to hear and the sound of her own voice, meagre in the empty wood, reminding her of the danger she was in, would have made her feel worse.

234

She knew her hands were bleeding, the cuts and bruises were hurting even though partially numbed by the cold, but there was nothing she could do about it. No gloves, and no alternative to struggling on. Restricting the movement of the damaged limb had made it less painful, but the journey to the farm meant going uphill and then down. Cold, wet and exhausted as she was, it was going to be a very long way.

For both Owen and Ryan, supper would be an anxious affair, with Owen worrying that something might stop him at the very last moment, and Ryan afraid his parents would call him by his name and remark on him wearing such unusual clothes, persuading Owen to look at him closely and realize his mistake. He said he wasn't hungry, made the excuse of being tired and went to Gareth's room, although even then his anxiety didn't leave him.

He walked up and down, knowing it would only take a careless word to make Owen suspicious, but from the low murmur of voices he gathered that nothing untoward had happened. He released pent-up breath as he heard Owen leave the room and go outside, saying he was going for a drink.

'I'll tell Gareth and he'll probably join you later,' Tommy called. Ryan gave a sigh of relief. Those few words could have ruined everything.

Ryan darted through the gate up the field and dashed through the wood, unaware of Sophie struggling not far away from where he crashed through the trees, and hurried to join Sarah.

Heart racing, but smiling, Owen drove through the lanes. In a small suitcase under the passenger seat he had all the necessary deeds and bank statements and accounts, including the farm statements that would show the money taken from the account. The bank would provide copies once Tommy asked, but at least it would allow him a little more time. He tucked the latest bills, for which he had accepted payment in cash and not put through the books, into his jacket pocket. He didn't want to leave anything incriminating behind him to speed up Tommy's reaction. Still wearing a satisfied smile, he drove back to the old farmhouse.

No sign of the tiresome, interfering Sophie, he thought, as he cleaned the van thoroughly. The long spell of rain had helped and it was soon its original green, with chrome shining in the light of the lantern he had brought. He looked at it in satisfaction; it was unrecognizable for the filthy thing it usually was, unless someone remembered the registration number, and who bothered with that, apart from the police? Especially on a night like this. He'd drive with care, making sure not to do anything to make the police look at the van with any interest. But perhaps he would avoid the Aust ferry just in case. Being with people even for a short time might result in him being remembered. Best if he stayed on the roads.

When he called on Sarah she was alone; there was no sign of Bertie. She looked upset. 'He's run off again,' she said at once

'Sarah, we have to leave now.'

'I can't, Owen. I have to find him.'

'We can come back for him. He'll be safe, there are plenty willing to look after him.'

He was standing at the door, the engine running outside the gate.

'What is the matter with you? He's only ten years old! I don't know where he is! How can I leave not knowing what's happened to him, without even telling him I'm going or explaining what's happening?'

He grabbed her arm and began pulling her out of the door. 'Come on, you stupid woman. I have to leave and you have to come with me. Hurry or it'll be too late. Don't you understand? There's no time for this nonsense!'

'Trouble?' Ryan said, stepping through the gate.

'Oh, it's you, Gareth. I'm just explaining to Sarah that we have to leave now. Trouble is, the boy's disappeared again.'

'He can follow on with me. You two go. I'll be joining you in less than twenty-four hours, won't I, Owen?'

'That's right. Just twenty-four hours,' he said coaxingly to Sarah, 'and Bertie will be with us.'

'No. I won't leave without him.'

'All right, you go, Owen, and I'll bring them both tomorrow.' As Owen hesitated, Ryan asked, 'What route are you taking, Gloucester or the Aust ferry?'

'What d'you mean?' He looked very agitated. 'Oh, you mean the place where we can wait till the money comes through? It'll be somewhere in Hertfordshire. I can't tell you where. I'll need to find a place to stay, so, as arranged, I'll phone the box outside the post office at ten o'clock tomorrow morning. I've got the number written down – not that I'll forget it. I'll have all the details then, so be there.'

'Off you go, Owen. We'll be meeting very soon.'

'Yes. Cheerio, Gareth.'

'I'm not Gareth, Owen, I'm Ryan.'

Owen stared at him, and his face seemed to shrivel as realization dawned. Then he pushed him, making him stagger, and dived into the van.

As he drove off at speed Ryan turned to Sarah. 'Well done! You and Sophie make a wonderful team. Thank you. Now I'll phone the police and tell Mam and Dad what's been going on, then we can all go to the Ship and Compass to celebrate.' He looked towards the stairs, where Bertie was sitting. 'You, too, young man. I'm sure Betty will let you stay in her back room.' He leaned on the banister and called, 'Sophie? Come on down, love. It's over.'

'She isn't here,' Sarah said with a frown. 'I thought plans had changed and she must have stayed at the farm.'

'No. We'd agreed that you two would stay together in case of trouble and I'd be outside.'

'Bertie?' she called, 'D'you know where Sophie is?'

'Badgers Brook?' he suggested, as though the question was a stupid one. 'It's where she lives, isn't it?'

'But we arranged for her to be here with you. Where can she be?'

'My guess is the farm,' Sarah said. 'Come on, it's time we told your parents all that's been happening.'

Collecting the borrowed car from outside Badgers Brook, they checked to make sure she wasn't there, but the house was in darkness. Ryan drove them to the farm and at once asked whether Sophie was there.

'We haven't seen her. What's happening? Gareth has been coming and going like will o' the wisp, today. And where's Owen? I thought he was meeting Gareth at the Ship? And

237

you were supposed to be in London! Come on, Ryan, tell us what's going on? I know you're up to something.'

Gareth came in at that moment and nodded to his twin. 'The police have been informed,' he said.

Tommy looked from one to the other, then at Sarah. 'Will somebody tell me what's going on?'

'Mam, Dad, we have something to tell you. Owen has been stealing money from the business and he's just driven off to a farm he's bought in Somerset. He thinks Gareth is in on it but thought I didn't know, until half an hour ago. But Gareth has been there and the place is in the name of Sarah Grange.'

Tommy glared at the young woman, who calmly stared back.

'How he managed to get her to sign the papers I've no idea,' Gareth said, 'but I do know she's helped us trap him.'

'He told me it was a more generous allowance for Bertie,' she told them.

Before anything else could be said they heard knocking on the door and Rachel opened it to find Sophie, looking like death, soaked and obviously in pain, lying on the ground.

Rachel took charge and attended to her while Daphne phoned for a doctor. Ryan carried her upstairs and Rachel gently removed her wet clothes, rubbing her to get her warm and talking soothingly. Sophie wallowed in the care but wished it had been Ryan who was closest to her. Dressed in a nightgown belonging to Rachel and with hot water bottles around her she felt that wonderful relaxation that presages sleep, but woke when the doctor came and insisted she went for an X-ray to find out exactly what she had done to her ankle.

Meanwhile Ryan and Gareth were facing their father. Gareth took out a sheaf of papers and showed his father entries marked in red.

'This hasn't been properly checked but we think these withdrawals have no invoices to tally with them. We think the money went into a bank account belonging to Owen.'

'Where is Owen?'

'The police have been informed that he has gone to the farm that he bought in Somerset.'

'You're letting him walk into the arms of the police? We can't do that! We have to stop him.'

'But he's been robbing you, Dad,' Gareth said. 'We can't let him get away with that.'

Tommy reached for his coat. 'Why wasn't I told? I might be thinking of retiring but I'm not too stupid to be told what's going on! I'd have dealt with it, and I wouldn't have needed the police. Come on, give me the keys to that car you've borrowed, it's bound to be faster than the van.'

Gareth and Ryan stared at each other and nodded. 'We have to do what he says,' Ryan said. He ran upstairs to where the doctor was giving instructions for Sophie's care and said, 'Sophie, my love, I have to go out. Dad thinks we have to catch up with Owen, hear his story. Will you be all right?' She assured him she was feeling fine and with a kiss he left her, calling back instructions to his mother to give her the best care as he ran back down the stairs.

'Come on,' Tommy shouted. 'There isn't much time.'

'We don't think he'll risk the ferry,' Gareth told him, as they hurried out. 'But we will, and with luck and the fast car we'll be there before him.'

'I have to wait for his explanation before I make a judgement and the police talk to him,' Tommy said. 'It's my fault for not being kinder to him, I know that.'

Luck was against them and the Aust ferry wasn't operating.

'How much time did he have before we left?' Tommy demanded, and they did fast calculations and realized that if they weren't to break the speed limit and be stopped by the police, they were unlikely to see Owen before the police found him.

At Gloucester Gareth took over the driving. 'I know the way,' he explained, 'and I will save a little time by avoiding taking the wrong road, which is what I did yesterday.'

As they drove, Tommy began to talk about how he and Rachel had taken Owen, at the age of five, into their home. 'He practically landed on our doorstep as in some Victoria drama,' he said.

'I thought his mum and dad went to America and died there?' Gareth said.

'That was what I told Owen. It seemed the kindest thing to do at the time.'

'But the truth . . .?' Ryan coaxed.

'Your uncle brought him to us and said the child's mother had abandoned him, and as the child was his she said it was up to him to care for him.'

'But I don't understand, he was married, so where did Owen come from?'

Tommy appeared lost in his memories and when he spoke it was to himself, justifying his actions, facing his guilt. 'There's poor little Bertie, who's been treated even worse,' he muttered. 'And they say lightning doesn't strike twice. At least we gave Owen a decent home. Rachel and I weren't willing to take on another unwanted child, so we pretended Bertie was nothing to do with us. Which was true, but unkind.'

Near Avonmouth Owen had a puncture. He felt the sudden dragging sensation as the van lost direction and he pulled over to the side. 'What damned bad luck,' he muttered as he began to reach for the tools. The spare was fully inflated, something he had checked before leaving, and he thanked his foresight as he rolled it to where it was needed.

Tommy was lost in his reminiscences, explaining to his sons the reasons why he and Rachel had never accepted Owen as an equal member of the family. 'We always presumed the boy was my nephew, but his father died before he could answer any of our questions.'

They drove towards Avonmouth, and as Gareth began to look for the turning they were to take they passed Owen. The shining van was ignored by them, its appearance so different from the usual filthy old van, that it was a moment before Ryan said, 'That was the van!'

Gareth slowed down and managed to turn and make his way back to where Owen was just starting the engine, turning the starting handle and jumping in as the car slowed to a stop. Owen stared in disbelief at the faces of his uncle and Ryan and Gareth. How could they have found him so soon? How had they known where to come? He rejoined the road and accelerated fast. Foot down he urged the van to move as quickly as it would go.

Gareth had to wait before he could turn again and set off in pursuit of the shining green van.

Owen had reached the turning into the narrow lane that led to his new property and, seeing them closing in on him, he was desperately looking for an alternative to leading them straight there. Anything would do: a turning into another lane, a farm gate, anything to stop them finding his smallholding. If only he knew the area better.

Then, as he saw in the headlights a darkness that seemed like a narrow turning promising escape, a man appeared and raised a white-gloved hand to stop him. As the light showed him more clearly, he saw with utter despair that it was a policeman. Damn, he must have been speeding. He stopped, there was nothing else he could do, and his mind began to sort out what he could say to his uncle. Defence or attack? Probably a bit of both, but he had no excuse whatever he said.

As Gareth stopped behind the van the police were searching it, and as he walked towards Owen with Ryan and Tommy following he saw them take a box containing papers.

'It's all right,' Tommy said at once. 'It's all been a mistake.'

'Sorry, sir, but this is an ongoing investigation and we have to take him in for questioning.'

It was early the following morning before Ryan and Gareth set off back to the farm. They tried to persuade Tommy to go with them but he insisted on waiting until Owen had been released, which would not be for some time. 'I have to do what I can for him. Give him my full support. Only giving half measures is what's brought him to this,' he said sadly.

The twins slept in the car for a few hours, uncomfortable and impatient to be home, then found a café for breakfast. When they drove into the farmyard Rachel greeted them, and Ryan ran in to see Sophie in an armchair with a leg propped on a stool, Sarah and Bertie in the kitchen with food ready to serve.

After hugging Sophie and being assured that all was well and the damage was only a severe sprain, Ryan thought to himself that now, after an unforgivable delay, he would talk to Sophie about her grandmother. Perhaps this would be goodbye to the last of her demons.

Thirteen

Sophie was staying at the farmhouse being spoiled by Rachel and regularly visited by Daphne, Sarah and Bertie. Ryan was in London making arrangements for accommodation during his year's teacher training course, which threatened to be concentrated and very hard.

Gareth had stayed, having sent money to his partners in France, and had promised to help with the sale of animals and other stock. He and Daphne worked together and spent a lot of time discussing his new life in France. For Sophie the preparations to sell the animals for slaughter was upsetting and she pleaded to be allowed back home to Badgers Brook long before it all began.

There was little news about Owen, who was staying in Somerset, lodging in a guest-house alone, and filled with hatred towards the Treweather family. Having learned of his indifferent parentage had hardened him. Tommy had tried to stop the charges but fraud was a serious offence and it was impossible. He wrote letters to Owen promising him a home when everything was over, but although Owen read them he then tore them up. He didn't owe the Treweathers anything. He didn't know if he was even entitled to the same name.

Ryan was on his way home for a final visit before starting college. He knew this was his last chance to let Sophie know about her surviving grandmother. Telling Sophie that Grandmother Morgan had lived when the rest of her family had died the night of the rocket attack had not been as easy as he'd thought it would be and the longer he avoided it the worse it had become. He should have walked in that first time and said, 'Guess who I've found,' but she was so easily upset and the words hadn't come.

Weeks had passed since he had found Victoria Morgan and learned of her close relationship to Sophie, but he was still trying to decide on the best way of breaking the news. What a fool he'd been to wait so long. The weeks between hadn't made it any easier.

On the train journey down, he considered a dozen ways of breaking the remarkable news and discarded them all. His fear was that as well as the happiness at finding her grandmother, Sophie would once again be filled with remorse for not finding her earlier. She would be ashamed of her cowardice at not going back to see the ruined house and face the row of graves to say her last goodbyes.

Now, with Victoria Morgan having been very patient, accepting his plea for her to wait, he had no more time to dither. He'd taken too long and now she was threatening to come without warning and face the girl. He had to act.

When he went again to his parents' farm, Sophie greeted him with joy. Their reunion was wonderful, their love for each other no longer a secret. She was relaxed and happy, and he could see the outgoing girl Daphne had described, blossoming once again. So he was fearful of sending her back into guilt and unhappiness.

'I'd like you to come up to London with me this weekend, Friday till Sunday,' he suggested after they had eaten and the room was quiet. 'We can leave straight after school and you'll be back for Monday morning.'

'But won't you be busy? You still have some work to do before starting college,' she said. 'In fact, you ought not to have come home today.'

'There's a place I want to see and I want you to go with me.'

'Tell me.'

Instead, he said, 'It's odd how the war is still affecting people. I read in the paper a while ago that after all these years a man appeared after his family had been told he'd been killed. The poor wife had remarried, had a child, and I can only begin to imagine how she must have felt, having shared

243

her life with two men whom she loved. Strange things happened then, didn't they?'

'What has that to do with us going to London? There's nothing there for me, you know that.'

'I want you to visit the graves and talk to some of the neighbours, see what you can learn about what happened.' He held her close and went on, 'Darling girl, if you can get everything clear, go back and face it, then you'll stop blaming yourself. I want you to feel free of all that. I want us to have a future in which you'll be happy.'

'I'll never be free.'

'I suppose that's how that poor woman who married twice in all innocence felt, but she dealt with it.'

'But there's nothing there for me to "deal with". What's the point of talking to neighbours? Anyway, I doubt there'll be any who remember me after all this time.'

'What if there *is* someone there, someone who you can talk to and who'll help you?'

She pushed him away, stood up with her hands on her hips and demanded, 'Ryan, stop creeping around the edges of what you have to say and just say it!'

So after all his planning, his intention of turning the conversation gently around, the fine words he intended to use, he just said it. He stood up and held her tightly and said, 'Your grandmother Morgan is alive and I know where we can find her.'

He felt the shock of it hit her; she started to fall and would have collapsed on the floor if he hadn't held her.

'You must be wrong,' she murmured.

'I'm sorry, darling. I was so clumsy. I tried to break it to you gently but there wasn't anything I could say to make it less of a shock. She is longing to meet you. She believed you had died during those last fearful months too.'

He made her a hot drink and added plenty of sugar. His mother wouldn't mind such extravagance this once.

'What will she think of me not going back to find her?'

As he had feared she was immediately blaming herself.

'She understands you not going back. So far as you knew you'd lost them all that night. Why would you expect to find her alive? She's a wonderful lady and she's been so kind to wait, allowing me to tell you before I take you to see her.'

'Can we go tomorrow?'

'By the first train,' he promised. He held her for a long while but she didn't say any more and he allowed her the silence. He guessed that tomorrow the talk would be plentiful. As he helped her to her room that night she suddenly asked, 'How *did* she survive?'

'Believe it or not she went out to buy fish and chips.'

She laughed, then a moment later the giggles changed to tears and he held her until they stopped.

Victoria Morgan was on the telephone. It was an extravagance but she had been used to having the convenience of one when she owned the shop and had one installed in her new flat. When she picked it up that evening and heard Ryan telling her Sophie would be there the following day, she thought it was worth a thousand times more than it cost her. She longed to talk to her but agreed that they should see each other and break the long parting with hugs and kisses rather than through a mechanical voice on the phone.

She didn't sleep, imagining all they would say, and at seven the next morning went for a walk, cleaned the flat, then bought what food she could find, preparing for the most remarkable meeting of her life. Two people brought back from the permanence of death.

Ryan took Sophie straight from the station to the churchyard and led her to where well-tended graves bore the names of her brother and sister and her parents. Nearby were her grandfather, Auntie Maggie and Uncle Albert.

A smartly dressed woman approached.

'Nana!' Sophie sobbed. 'I didn't really believe it!' They stared at each other through tear-filled eyes before running to hold each other as though never to let go. Smiling, Ryan sat on an ancient grave and waited.

The talk went on and it was a long time before Ryan was included. He led them from the churchyard to a café, where they wasted food by allowing it to go cold while they talked and laughed. They walked round the shops seeing nothing but each other. Another café and still they talked, while he sat listening with happiness almost as great as theirs.

When Sophie explained that Ryan was the son of a farmer, Victoria looked surprised.

'I would never have imagined you living on a farm,' she said. 'You used to be too soft-hearted to cope with all that.'

'She still is,' Ryan said. 'Our life together won't include cows and sheep. A dog maybe? Or a cat?' He reached out and held Sophie's hand. 'In fact, now my parents are selling up, she needn't go there again.'

'But I'd like Nana to see the place, and she must come to Badgers Brook. In fact, I don't want to lose sight of her for a moment.'

Ryan finally led them to where Victoria now lived, and Sophie saw that the small bedroom contained an open, partly packed suitcase.

'I thought you would like to take Nana back with you tomorrow,' Ryan said. 'I have to search for accommodation. A friend has given me a few addresses. I'll come in the morning to take you to the station then I'll phone you at the farm later.'

Their parting was sorrow mixed with excitement. Her eyes were dark with love as she kissed him goodbye. 'Thank you for finding her for me.'

'She's a wonderful lady,' he said. 'Almost as wonderful as you.'

Tommy was prowling around the house and Rachel knew he was worried about Owen. 'When will he be coming home?' she asked.

'Never. He hates us for keeping the secret he was entitled to know, and for setting the police on him when he stole from us.'

'But we can hardly be blamed for that – he stole a lot of money. How does that make him angry at us?'

'We shouldn't have involved the police. I owed him something. Whatever his true status, he's been a part of the family since before he was five years old. If I'd been kinder to him, offered him a share of the farm, treated him like a son, he'd never have done it. So yes, he can blame me.'

They had both written and promised him a home, talked about the land on which he could build a house, but there were no replies. Rachel gave him news about Sarah, who, now he had been charged and the facts were known, was surprisingly sympathetic. Even Bertie made a drawing and asked that it be sent to him. Nothing produced a response.

Money had been deposited for a lawyer to defend him and they offered to give evidence of extenuating circumstances, but the solicitor wasn't hopeful. A crime had been committed and Owen would have to take the consequences.

Sarah was the only person Owen wrote to. It was very brief, just a thank you for her letter and Bertie's picture. He said he appreciated them both, as he felt very much alone. Sarah took it to show Rachel and Tommy. It added to their growing sense of shame.

'We took the boy in and gave him a home, but we shouldn't have done it. Doing something half hearted is not much better than not doing it at all,' Tommy said.

'I didn't look upon it like that. He wanted a home and a family and we gave them to him. We couldn't be expected to love him like our own.'

'He deserved better than we gave him.'

'We'll make it up to him. Come on, Tommy, stop beating yourself. When this is all over we'll make a new beginning.'

'If he'll let us.'

Victoria loved Badgers Brook. 'I hoped that you'd be living in a place you'd be happy to leave,' she said. 'I thought you'd come back with me, at least for a while, but how can you leave a beautiful home like this?'

'I have a job, too, Nana. I work in the local school.'

'Can I stay here for a while then? I hate the thought of going back to my flat so many miles away from you.'

'Please stay. Then I'll visit you at half term. We won't wait long between visits.'

'Ryan will be in London more or less permanently for a year, won't he?'

'I'll want to see him, too,' she admitted.

247

After introducing her grandmother to Kitty and Bob, then Stella, Colin and Betty, they booked a taxi and went to the farm.

Her leg was still painful, otherwise she would have walked her through the wood and shown her where the badgers lived. 'But next time we'll walk through the paths and animal tracks and you'll see why I love it here so much.'

As Sophie had phoned the farm earlier, Rachel was ready with the table filled with home-made food. Daphne was there helping Tommy and Gareth sort out items for the farm sale, and she greeted Nana with delight.

Sophie rested her aching ankle while her friends showed their visitor around.

'I'm so grateful to Ryan for finding her for me. I can't believe how stupid I've been by not going back.'

'Oh, we all do stupid things sometimes, dear. Like the way we were with poor Owen.'

'Ryan wishes he and Gareth had handled things differently. They were outraged at the way he was stealing from you and did what their anger told them was right. But Owen will be back. You're still his only family.'

School kept Sophie away from Badgers Brook most of each day, but Victoria filled her days happily by wandering around the area, getting to know Sophie's friends, most of whom were amazed at the unlikely reunion.

One day she was sitting outside the Ship and Compass, sheltered from the wind and enjoying some late sun, when Betty came out and invited her inside.

'Your granddaughter hasn't been here long, but we love her,' Betty said. 'I hope you aren't going to take her away from us?'

'I don't want to part with her for a moment more than I have to, but neither do I want to intrude on her life. I did think that, as Ryan will be in London for a year, she might like to stay with me. Then when they come back, perhaps I'll come back with them. D'you think I could make a life for myself here?'

'Cwm Derw is a friendly place. And we love newcomers bringing in a breath of fresh air. Yes, I'm sure you'd settle perfectly well.'

'As long as Sophie is happy about it. I won't come if there's a chance of spoiling anything.'

'What did you do before you retired?' Betty asked.

'I ran a small grocery shop. Victory Stores,' she added with a smile. 'I made a lot of jams and pickles.'

'So does your Sophie! Wouldn't it be perfect if she reopened the business. Any chance?'

'I think I've a few years of work left in me, but I can't see her wanting to. Her life is here.'

Ed came in and went straight to the biscuit barrel. 'This all you've got?' he asked with a grin after he was introduced to Victoria. 'My sister used to look after me, but now I've got Elsie she doesn't bother.'

'Ed's wife runs the bed and breakfast near the post office,' Betty explained. 'In fact, they run it together.'

'That must be interesting.'

'Hard work,' Ed replied, helping himself to a cup of tea.

Betty stood up and apologized. 'I have to get the bar ready to open up. The regulars will soon be banging the door down,' she explained.

'And I must get to the school. I'm taking Sophie and a young man called Bertie for lunch in the café.'

After Victoria had returned to London, Sophie felt a change in the house she had called home. It was when she returned from school on Monday. The fire refused to draw, the usual warmth gone from her favourite room overlooking the garden. Nowhere in the house could she feel its welcome. She was puzzled but said nothing to anyone; they would think her crazy to imagine that a house could have moods.

Geoff came to bring her a kitchen mat she had ordered and he stayed for a cup of tea. He looked around the living room, its view of the garden now hidden by the dark evening. It was comfortable as always but there was something missing and he couldn't define the difference.

'Is everything all right?' he asked. 'No problems with the house?'

She stared at him. 'Everything's fine, I think. But I don't feel—' she stopped. How could she say what she felt without appearing stupid?

'The house changes towards people sometimes,' Geoff said. 'It welcomes a new tenant, then, when it's time for that person to move on, it seems change its mood, to be telling them to go. As though it knows now is the right time to move on.'

'Perhaps that's what it's telling me.'

'Ryan and your Nana both being in London, perhaps?'

'I want to be there with them but I've just started working in the school.'

'And you can give them notice. You could leave at Christmas, perhaps?'

'It's what I've been thinking, Geoff.'

'Everything seems to be coming to an end,' she told Daphne that evening. 'Ryan leaving, Nana back in London, Owen beginning to talk to Sarah and softening towards Bertie. The Treweathers are leaving the farm and Gareth is settling down in France.'

'And you?'

'I want to go back to London, just while Ryan is there. Then I want to come back and persuade Nana to come here too.'

'You're going to London on Friday, discuss it with them both.'

'Tuesday, Wednesday, Thursday – four more days,' she sighed as she counted on her slender fingers. 'I can't bear it, it seems for ever.'

Daphne was helping Betty that evening and while she was there the phone rang. She was smiling as she replaced the receiver.

'Can you spare me for a moment to fetch Sophie?' she asked, and Betty willingly agreed.

'Why do I have to come to the Ship?' Sophie asked. 'I have to cut some cards for school tomorrow.'

'Stop asking questions and complaining,' Daphne said. She pushed her friend impatiently into Betty's back room and into the arms of Ryan. Behind him stood Nana, wearing a wide and happy smile.

'Please, come back with us, we can't cope on our own,' he said as she ran into waiting arms.

Newport 250 Library and Information Service

4/3/05

Central Library and
Information Service

Z433949